THE
CLEARING
A NOVEL

CASSANDRA J. KELLY

Boyle
&
Dalton

Book Design & Production:
Boyle & Dalton
www.BoyleandDalton.com

Cover artwork provided by Michael Miller
michaelmillerfineart.net

Hardback ISBN: 978-1-63337-777-6
Paperback ISBN: 978-1-63337-776-9
E-book ISBN: 978-1-63337-778-3

LCCN: 2024903312

Printed in the United States of America
1 3 5 7 9 10 8 6 4 2

To my mother,
for being my first
and best friend

1

I LIKED TO COUNT THE MILE MARKERS. It put me in a sort of trance and drowned out the rattling of our 1986 Ford Tempo. I glanced at my mom, struggling to hold the wheel, careful not to use her right hand, which was sore from too many pokes because the nurse couldn't find a vein. She looked pale, clammy, and exhausted, and I wished more than anything I was old enough to drive so she could relax. Then the car sputtered, jolted us forward, and began to slow.

"Oh no." Her voice dragged. She pulled the car off to the side of the road and plucked a stray cigarette from the bottom of her purse.

"What's going on?" I tried not to sound frantic, but my voice cracked.

We were surrounded by a muddy field, which had yet to be sown in corn or soy, the only two crops anyone ever grew around here. There were no other signs of life around.

"Looks like we're goners," she teased.

We didn't have a cell phone, and this was the only case in which anyone said we'd really need one. The common-sense phrase "Well, what if you get stuck on the side of the road?" rang in my ears.

"We passed mile marker fifty-four a while back," I said, trying to offer her some context, anything to get us out of this mess.

"I don't know anything about that." She looked down the road as if she could summon our rescue, and I believed she could. "But for goodness' sake, we've made this drive enough times. We've been going back and forth for ten years! How far do you think we are from that Marathon station?"

I shrugged. "Twenty miles?"

"Pahhh," she exhaled, releasing some smoke. "No way. It's gotta be like two miles tops."

She rubbed her sore hand and looked at her eyes in the rearview mirror. I could tell she was thinking about how to pull this off, if her body would allow her to pull this off. "Maybe we should just wait."

We got out of the car and started walking into the field. The thick mud swamped my sneakers and seeped into the small tears around the soles.

"Gotta get far enough away or we'll be a target. People will lose their focus and drive straight into you if you're not careful."

After what felt like forever, a maroon Mustang pulled up, and a scraggly older man popped his head out. He hollered out into the field. "Need some help?"

My mom left me in the field and approached him. "Yes, do you have a cell phone?"

"Nope." He sucked his teeth, revealing a wad of chewing tobacco. "Don't believe in 'em."

"Well, can you drive us to the Marathon up the road?"

"Sure." The man waved out to me, and I followed my mom into his car.

The back of the Mustang reeked of cigarettes. The leather was sweaty, and my shoes leaked muddy water into the interior.

"Think it's only a couple miles," my mom said as the man eased back onto the road. "We really appreciate it."

"No problem. Where ya comin' from?"

"Memorial. I have treatments once a month, but it feels like we live there."

"Oh, sorry to hear that." The man's eyes grew distant, making the face people often made when they learned about my mom's condition. "Why isn't this one in school?"

"Homeschooled." My mom didn't skip a beat. But that was a lie. The truth was I didn't make it an hour into class that day before one of the boys who sat behind me blew a chewed-up piece of gum into my hair. When I tried to pull the wad out, it got stuck between my fingers. The teacher gave me a nod, my nonverbal permission to leave the room. It wasn't the first time she had to do that. The girls in the class all laughed at me as I ran out. I bypassed the restroom and made a beeline straight to the nurse's office.

"You're not sick," the nurse said to me, cutting the gum out. After a bit of radio silence on my end, she gave up. "Do you want to call your mom?"

I found every reason possible to leave class in the middle of the day, and my mom was used to picking me up. I developed an unspoken habit of calling on her infusion days because I knew she needed me just as much as I needed her.

After a few minutes in the Mustang, the man pulled into the gas station. We thanked him and used the payphone to call a tow truck. Two hours later, a dingy truck pulled into the station, and we asked the surly man to please drive us and our broken-down Ford back to Juniper. He huffed but agreed and spent the entire drive telling us how he often felt like nothing more than a cheap taxi service, constantly rescuing stupid people. "No offense," he said on repeat. The rates are too low, he explained. By the time he paid for gas, he barely had enough to cover his time. Apparently, we were lucky he answered our call for help at all.

When we got back to Juniper, my mom cut him a check, looking like she was handing over her firstborn. Still, he took it, gave half a smile, and left us standing in front of our old house.

"That wasn't so bad." She turned toward me, giving me a triumphant look.

But I didn't see it as a triumph. "We need a cell phone."

"Who would we have called anyway?" She had a point. No one around here had any money, let alone time, to help us. "We're on our own."

2

THE FLOORBOARDS CREAKED, shifting under my feet as I made my way to the kitchen. The early morning sun peeked through the chipped windowpanes. Dust twinkled as it caught the light. Time moved in slow motion on mornings like this. I dragged one of the dining chairs toward the refrigerator, careful not to make too much noise, and reached for my box of cereal. There was no milk in the fridge, hadn't been for days, so I poured the cereal into a bowl and began to eat it dry. My chewing sounded monstrously loud in my ears, and I worried my mom would hear me *crunch crunch crunching* away like a cow. I tried chewing more slowly, testing the frequencies of each chomp to find one that wouldn't shake my eardrums. I was two bites in when small whimpering noises began from Mom's bedroom, which conveniently shared a wall with the kitchen. It was a bad day, best to not keep her waiting.

"Sadie, can you bring me some tea?" she asked, her voice barely audible.

"Be right there." I got up and put a mug of water in the microwave, tapping a minute and thirty seconds onto the plastic display. *Not too hot.*

I walked up to her door and knocked softly. I missed the mornings when she managed to sleep in, because it meant she wasn't in as much pain. But I tried not to think about that.

"Your tea is ready," I whispered as I made my way in.

Her strained face told me she wasn't getting out of bed on her own this morning. At four feet six inches, I was a tiny thing. But my mom never made it past five feet, and there wasn't much to her these days anyway. I had learned that if I locked my arms in a strong, balanced position and planted my feet firmly into the shag carpet, I could be the brace she needed to hoist herself out of bed. I stood ready as she grabbed ahold of me, and we began to walk crookedly toward the bathroom. Her feet were bare and blue.

"Why aren't you wearing any socks?"

"Don't need 'em," she muttered.

We installed ugly steel bars along the walls so she could steady herself, and she shakily latched onto them. Once she was in the bath, I closed the door. Privacy had always been very important to her.

I sat down to my obnoxious bowl of dry cereal. I was hatching a plan for my next collection, a series of pressed flowers arranged by color according to the rainbow. I enjoyed pressing nature in this way, learning how things could be preserved over time, some better than others. I had one collection of all the different varieties of fern and another from the fall that was strictly reserved for the reddest of leaves. Cataloging the forest had become a way to mark time, to anticipate what would come next.

Mom walked into the kitchen smelling like a fresh bar of Dove soap. She used her arms to trace the outside edges of the room, steadying herself with every micro movement. She sat down next to me and cupped her hands around the mug of tea. She loved tea. I, however, only loved the smell of it. I always tasted dirt and struggled not to spit it out. Still, I reached over and took a sip, hoping my taste buds had somehow changed overnight. Once again, a filthy bitter taste washed over my tongue. I did love the names though: English breakfast, jasmine green, chamomile, and lavender. Each one gave me a vision of the English country-side, or rice fields in Japan, or the prairies out west.

When I was little, we used to have tea parties, and she'd always pour hot water from the teapot into her cup and then pour juice into mine from a jug stashed under the table. Out of envy I'd say, *No, Mom, I want the real stuff too,* and she'd laugh and let me have a sip. Dirt. Always dirt. Still, I enjoyed wearing my overly puffed-up girly dresses on those occasions; our baby-blue wrought-iron garden table was the perfect setting for such attire.

But on this day, looking at my mom straining to bring the mug to her lips, I wondered if we'd ever have another tea party. I peered out the kitchen window. The garden was overthrown by weeds, and that beautiful blue paint was chipping off the table leaving nasty black scars all over its facade. Mom took a sip from her cup. Her lips were drained of color and her eyes were red and swollen. But even in this state, she was beautiful. Her long red hair splayed out across her shoulders like kelp swaying in the sea. She looked up at me with her piercing, forest-green eyes, just like mine, assuring me we'd pull through another day.

"I'd like to write a letter to your Aunt Jean today," she said.

Jean, my mom's older sister, was always traveling. Some people in town called her a drifter. With no permanent address, and phones still rare in many of the places she stayed, she often sent postcards. A lost art, my mom said. Thailand, Peru, Morocco... and the list went on and on. Aunt Jean usually wrote something in-the-moment like *Sipping pisco sours. Miss you!* The tradition made for an eclectic box of messages that sat in the basin of our unused fireplace. I always thought of the box as a treasure trove, full of wonders and secrets. Sometimes I'd even use the school computers to research the places on the postcards and imagine myself wherever she was, which was as far away from Juniper as she could get.

"Do we have special news to share?" I pried, curious as to what was so important that it was worthy of a letter.

As far as I knew, nothing had changed for us recently. In fact, nothing ever changed in the Watkins household. The old house had been bought by my grandfather, Louie Watkins, in the late 1950s when it was already well over a century old. It had three small bedrooms and a bathroom upstairs, and a kitchen, living room, study, dining room, and second bathroom downstairs. Last year, we turned the dining room into a bedroom for my mom, so she didn't have to go up and down the stairs anymore. It wasn't much, but those nine rooms contained my whole life.

The house sat on the outskirts of Juniper, past the railroad tracks that divided our town in more ways than one. My grandpa came here from rural southwest Pennsylvania, leaving behind his parents and three siblings to find work. The coal mines in his town had long since dried up, or rather, the companies that once sought the gleaming black rocks had decided to go elsewhere. Grandpa Louie came to Juniper to start something new, and probably never intended for the house to stand this long. But stand it did, just barely, with its slanted porch and rusting tin roof, battered by hailstorms and high winds that whipped off the Great Lakes.

Today there were about ten thousand people in Juniper. There was talk of a Walmart coming in on the north side of town that could bring a lot of new people with it, but those were just rumors as far as I knew. The nearest shopping mall was nearly an hour away, and the girls whose dads worked in Cleveland would take them out there on the weekends to buy earrings and gel pens and whatever else they could buy to rub in my face at school. When I would ask to go to the mall, Mom would say we had everything we needed in Juniper, even though we didn't. The real truth was our car had broken down, and my mom couldn't afford the repairs. Driving anywhere was out of the question, and my mom was trying to make it sound like a new adventure, as if we were just traveling hippies or train hoppers that could get whisked away at a moment's notice. But her storytelling had lost its magic. In fact, everything around me was losing its magic.

They say you lose your imagination when you get older, and I guess that's what was happening. I was growing up. But I didn't expect it to feel so sudden, like something was being ripped from inside me. I wanted to hold on. I wanted to preserve whatever it was that made me a kid and adults something else, press myself like a flower inside a book. But that threshold was so real, and a part of me knew I was just biding my time before I crossed it.

"I was hoping Aunt Jean could come for a visit," Mom said.

"A visit!" I yelled, making her wince. An old teacher, Mrs. V, once told my mom I was an excitable child, and it stuck with me, making me constantly aware of the audible space I took up if I wasn't careful. "That would be nice."

"We ran out of stamps though," she said, a sly smile spreading across her face. "Would you like to buy them this time?"

I hesitated. I had never been to the post office without her. But she was giving me more free rein lately, sensing my growing curiosity about the world.

"Of course, Mama. And when I'm back, I'll make us some lunch."

Before she had a moment to think twice, I ran up the stairs on all fours, as if the thrust from my arms would propel me to the top faster. I dressed to look older than I was, like I wasn't lost in town without my mom.

"Get us some milk at Buehler's, and some bread." She handed me a twenty-dollar bill. "We'll make grilled cheese when you're back."

I dug my bike out of the garage. It was purple and had animal stickers all over it from when the dentist slipped me the entire roll after I got a cavity filled. My mom had held my hand the entire time, my rock when things were scary. But I hadn't been back to the dentist in over a year. I wondered if they noticed.

I road on the berm until I got to Violet Avenue, the main road into town, because the sidewalk didn't go straight to our house. It stopped abruptly when it hit the bridge that signified the no man's land we lived in, as if whoever built this town didn't feel like stretching the sidewalk to our house. It was amazing how a half-mile of broken road and cornfields created such a chasm between us and the rest of the world. It seemed that our house was just misplaced, like if it were plucked up and dropped off one street over then all of our problems would be solved.

When I got into town, I propped my bike on the brick front of the post office and straightened my shirt.

"Hello, Miss Sadie, where's your mama today?" Bill, the postman, asked. I always liked Bill. He had a kind face and a big belly, and he would make sure to give me a cherry sucker on the way out.

"Oh, I'm all by myself today!" I beamed.

"Good for you, girl. What grade will you be in this fall?"

"Sixth grade. I got Mr. Foster."

"Ah I see. And you're gettin' stamps I s'pose?"

I nodded and handed him the wrinkled bill from my back pocket. "Yessir, just one book, please."

"Here ya go, Miss Sadie." He handed me the stamps, embellished with rainbow monkeys. They read *Happy New Year* and had a tiny *2004* etched at the bottom. Aunt Jean would love these.

"Thanks!" I smiled and began to make my way out.

"Hey now!" Bill extended his arm, twirling the candy in his big knobby fingers. "Too old for your sucker?"

I skirted around and retrieved the Dum Dum. I popped it into my mouth, cherry like always, and headed for Buehler's.

I walked the aisles in search of the bread we always got, but I was a fish out of water. The other women in the store were staring at me. So, I made my rounds quickly. The checkout guy, Jerrod, a middle-aged man with a slack jaw and a haphazard shave, lazily moved my items across the scanner. He had one eye glued to the small TV hovering above the counter.

"That John Kerry's got another thing comin'. Gonna pinch us out of every penny we got with that health care plan of his." He spit out his words as he rang up my items, not bothering to even glance at me. "I ain't had health insurance for twenty years and I'm just fine. That'll be $6.72."

As he handed me my change, I could see that he had suddenly become aware of my age. But before he could say anything more, I grabbed the bags and ran out the door.

My mom was sitting in her wicker chair on our front porch, an afghan laid across her lap, strewn with what I guessed were medical bills.

"Time for lunch!" I said proudly.

"Wow, you did good! Where's the milk?"

I looked back at my bike as if the thing could magically conjure a half-gallon of two-percent, but nothing happened. I must have left it in the bagging area when I was rushing out of the store.

"I'm sorry." I felt defeated.

"Oh, honey, it's okay. We didn't need it."

But she was lying to make me feel better. Of course we needed the milk, and now I was going to be eating dry cereal for who knows how long.

"Those strawberries look delicious." She eyed the package in my hands, acting oblivious to my failure.

But that's how my mom was. She was sweet and kind and never hurt a fly. She was proud, despite our house falling apart and her job at the library long gone. She had a way of making everything feel okay, but she also needed me to be okay. So, I fought back my tears. "Bills?" I asked, pointing to the paper in her hands.

"$1,189 for that trial," she said. "And all it did was make things worse."

"I'm sorry, Mom. Can we pull it off?"

"Oh, nonsense, you know we always pull it off. I'll set up a payment plan, and I'll pay thirty dollars a month on it until I die."

She was still rubbing her right hand.

"How's your hand?"

"Numb. No...more like itchy." Her eyes grew wide as she shoved it swiftly into her pocket. "You know what that means."

My mom was big into superstitions, Appalachian wives' tales passed down from her mother. If your hand itched, you had to stick it in your pocket. Something about good fortune coming your way. She would also throw salt over her shoulder whenever she spilled some while cooking. And she'd trace X's into the dust around our house to ward off evil. Sometimes I thought she was making the rituals up just to scare me, but I always listened.

MOM DECIDED TO TAKE AN AFTERNOON NAP. She did that a lot lately. We were settling into this new routine, and I knew she was going to be down for a while. I wasn't sure what to do with so much time and so much freedom. So, I decided to go to the woods.

I grabbed my book from the library and the small red blanket, beautifully embroidered with rabbits, that my Aunt Jean sent me all the way from Hong Kong. In her postcard she said that rabbits symbolized mercy and luck. Her messages always felt so cryptic. I left a note for my mom so she'd know where I had gone, but I doubted she would see it before I returned.

I made my way toward the forest behind our house, my favorite place in the world, the only place I ever felt completely myself. At the edge where our yard met the tree line was a small creek, which we called Leaky Creek, a name my mom and Aunt Jean came up with one dreadfully rainy summer when my mom was about eight and Jean was eleven. The creek had completely flooded Juniper one afternoon, stranding people on their roofs for several hours before help came, if it ever came. My mom told me how they crawled through Jean's bedroom window and sat on the roof above the porch. She doesn't remember much, just that she was equally bored and terrified as she watched the murky water swirl around their belongings. She told me how after the water found where it was supposed to go, the creek took on a new form, swollen and gushing for days. On one of those days, the girls tried to cross the creek. But it was so fast it knocked Jean off her feet before she could even blink and swept her up in its current. She broke her arm and had to wear a cast.

After that, my mom remembered being afraid the creek would swallow the old house whole just as it almost did to her sister. The accident scared them so bad, they didn't cross back into the forest the rest of the summer. Eventually, the rain subsided, and the creek retreated. Several trees had fallen in the wake of the storms, and the following year Grandpa Louie had to reroute the path into the woods so the girls could get through. He said it was safe again, but the girls were not convinced. So, he built a small bridge over the shallow stream that marked the new entrance and carved the words *Leaky Creek* into the wooden railing. He promised them the bridge would keep the creek small, like a belt, and ever since then it had, though Jean never trusted it. My mom tried to convince Jean several times to cross it and come play, but she never did. As I walked over the bridge into the wooded landscape, I thought about what the rushing water must have looked like back then, how it all got there, and hoped Grandpa Louie's promise would hold.

Entering the forest always felt like a return to something greater than myself. It embraced me, making me warm and whole.

The evergreens were so tall I couldn't see the tops. At the right time of day, they seemed to glow and breathe on their own. I tried to tread lightly, letting the moss creep and cover everything in sight, as if I were the one in control and not the other way around. As I got deeper in, I noticed saplings growing up alongside their mothers, the old oaks, shedding the tiniest amount of light onto the forest floor, where aisles of bluebells were unfurling with vigor. Spring beauties were opening their pink petals, awakening the senses of all the creatures who had yet to crawl out from their winter slumbers. As I marveled, I thought of my mom, how she'd walked me through these paths before my feet could be trusted to navigate the creeping oak roots. She'd tell me stories about the creatures that inhabited this place, the magic they possessed. Spring was always our favorite time of year, patiently waiting to see what secrets the earth revealed. I promised myself I would pick a few of the purple flowers whose name I hadn't yet learned and put them in a jar next to her bed, to remind her of those earlier days before it was her feet that could no longer be trusted.

I made my way to the clearing, a large swath of moss and clover next to the creek. In this patch of green you could look straight up to the sky, watch the clouds, and get lost in the canopy. I'm not sure why nothing tall had ever grown in this spot. I suppose the forest needed space to breathe just like anything else. Perhaps that's why it was my favorite spot, because it was the one place where I could find clarity, where I could also breathe.

I sat by the creek, concealed by a massive fallen oak that created a bridge over the water. It was in this very spot that I once saw a golden-brown doe. She wandered gracefully into the clearing and took a sip from the creek. I was only a few feet from her, but she either didn't see me or chose to believe I wasn't a threat. As she sipped, she took quick breaks to survey her surroundings, never once locking eyes with me. But I did want to look into her deep brown eyes. I wanted that moment of recognition when you and the animal have to figure one another out. Ultimately the doe would run as if it could smell a fresh kill on me, but it was that split second when I could try to convince her to stay that made me feel like I wasn't an outsider, that although I would always be a predator to them, I still lived there too.

I unfolded my red rabbit blanket and opened my book, pressing the flowers I had just picked. It was best to do this early, before they wilted. As I flipped through the pages looking at my previous presses, I couldn't help but feel selfish. Selfish for storing these little things away for only my eyes to see. Selfish for forgetting the milk at the store. With everything going on, the last thing I needed was for my mom to worry about something as silly as milk. My mind continued to be busy over it when I noticed a red finch across the creek. My mom's superstition was that a red bird was a warning that someone was watching me. Then I heard a twig break.

Squirrels and other little critters would often forget I was around, and I'd hear them scurry across the leaf litter. But this time there was no animal, and I couldn't shake the feeling that I wasn't alone.

I decided to take a look around. I hopped over the creek and went to a tree I called the Wishbone because its branches split into a perfect V at the base. It was a good vantage point. I sat in the crook of it for a moment, and then I heard another rustle in the leaves near my blanket. This time I caught a small figure running fast between the trees.

I darted over the creek back to my belongings. I was spooked, and I decided I should pack up and leave. But just as I went to put my book in my pack, I noticed a toad poised perfectly on the cover. It was brown and lumpy, nothing extraordinary, and no larger than a nickel. Flustered and in a rush, I swatted at it, but it didn't budge. "Sorry," I muttered to the toad, as if I didn't have any right to do such a thing.

Then I heard something creeping up behind me and felt all the life drain from my face.

"Pssst."

"Who's there?" I shouted into the air, afraid to make a move.

After a moment of no response, I began to wonder if I had made it all up. Then I heard a small snickering sound.

I swiveled around and saw a tiny girl running away from me. Making a split decision, I shot up and rushed after her. But the girl seemed to know the woods almost as well as I did, gracefully turning and jumping at exactly the right times. I couldn't keep up. Then she abruptly turned around and stared me right in the eyes, scaring the heck out of me.

It was that moment of recognition. Her dark eyes cut through me, and I felt like a fawn just taking its first steps on its own. I wanted to run straight for my house, but I held her intense gaze. This contest lasted for an eternity, but the longer I stared at her, the more I had this overwhelming nostalgia. It was like I was daydreaming, like I had met her somewhere else. Then she broke my attention with a wave of her hand and walked behind a large maple. I approached the tree, light on my toes but with wide strides, as if to catch a tadpole in the creek. I was within arm's reach and the anticipation welled up inside me. I jumped around the tree and screamed something primal, not knowing whether I had caught her or she had caught me.

I had jumped all the way around the maple several times before I realized that she was gone. I felt like I might cry. I wanted her to stay, just as I had wanted that golden doe to stay. But the sky was turning the specific shade of lavender that told me it was time to head back, or Mom might wake up without me there. *Unacceptable.*

When I reached the house, I threw off my shoes and left them on the back deck. Mom said never wear shoes in the house or you'd bring bad luck in with you. My bare feet were sticking to the floor as I padded toward her room. She was upright and reading. In my hurry home I had forgotten to pick the purple flowers for her. I was just full of disappointments that day.

"I'm sorry again about the milk," I said, laying down next to her. "It was Jerrod; he creeps me out."

Mom brushed her fingers through my thick auburn hair. "The checkout guy? Oh, he's harmless, Sadie Bug," she said, a nickname she only used for me. "We'll get the milk next time. Are you okay?"

I didn't know how to respond. I wanted to tell her about the girl in the forest, but I didn't want to sound like a child, especially one who needed consolation. Mom needed strength, and that's what I was going to do—I was going to be strong. Still, I let her pet my head. I couldn't resist the feeling that washed over me when she did. It was the best feeling in the world. "When do you think you can come out to the forest with me again?"

"I know it's been a few months." She was staring down at her legs, the useless limbs that could barely get her across a room. "I miss it out there. But Bug, I don't think I will be going back, not in this state anyway."

I heard the sadness in her voice. She loved it out there just as much as I did. We listened to the sound of the spring peepers harmonizing outside the window. "I love you, Mama."

"I love you too." She drifted off to sleep, and I made my way up to my room. Cozy in my twin-size bed, I fell fast asleep. My dreams danced with images of the girl in the woods.

3

THE FOLLOWING MORNING, I found my mom in the study. An oak-paneled room off the back of the house, the study was what I imagined it would be like to live in an old-timey cabin without electricity or running water. One wall was lined with windows overlooking the garden and the other was lined with books collected over time by my Grandpa Louie. Most of them were in various states of decay, and all of them were covered in an inch of dust. Still, there were books on botany, astronomy, and religion. There were books of fiction, war, romance, and other worlds. We may not have had much, but we had those books, and I had been raised to appreciate them. My mom said they were our last connection to him, stored away as if they were our most prized family heirlooms. She believed that you had to spread out the goodness, make things last, and her way of doing that was to simply avoid touching them. So the books stayed in the study and neither of us went in the room unless we had to find an old record.

The smell in the room was dank with mildew, and I swore there were bats or rodents living in the walls, though that theory had never been proven. My mom was sitting in the faded floral armchair by the window, humming as she looked through an old photo album.

"Good morning," I said, perplexed not just at the sight and smell of this old room, but at Mom looking so animated this early in the morning.

"Hi Bug!" Her eyes were bright, and her red hair was particularly flaming this morning. "I'm looking at some old photos of your Aunt Jean and me when we were kids."

I went over and crouched beside her as she turned the pages.

"Oh look, there's me playing dress-up in Dad's clothing," she said. "I can hear him now, scolding me as I clomped around the house in his work boots."

My mom told me that Grandpa Louie was a quiet man. He wasn't mean and he certainly wasn't strict. But he believed there was a proper way to act, and his daughters, Anna and Jean, respected those beliefs, most of the time anyway. He had been married to my grandma, Samantha, for over thirty years, and all the while they lived in the old house. He worked at the Ling-Temco-Vought steel factory and later drove the distance to the Avon Lake power plant for more money. They had a son in the '60s, Louis Watkins Jr., known to this day as "Baby Louie," who was meant to carry on the family name. Baby Louie passed away in his sleep when he was only a few days old, just a few years before anyone knew what sudden infant death syndrome was. According to the stories, Samantha wasn't the same after that. Nightmares haunted her, and she rarely finished a meal on her plate. She had become so quiet that on the rare occasion when she spoke, her voice was rusty and unfamiliar. My grandpa did his best to keep her going, like a vintage car begging to be retired. Then she got pregnant with Jean, something neither of them thought was possible. My grandma worked up her strength, and through the pictures you could see the air of motherhood return to her. It seemed like hope had been restored. Anna, my mom, was born just a few years later, doubling their joy.

"I love this picture." I pointed to the four of them.

"That was Christmas 1978. I was four years old."

Grandpa Louie worked hard. My mom remembers him coming home from the plant smelling like soot. My grandma would complain about washing his uniform, that she felt like it was her only purpose in life, and he would joke with her that the house, the girls, and keeping his uniform clean were all the purpose she needed. Keep the car rolling. But as Anna and Jean got older, she withered. Once again, she stopped sleeping and stopped eating. She died in 1983 when the girls were still very young, but I never asked how. For so long I had assumed that she had just faded away. But now I wondered if there was more to it.

My mom continued to flip the pages of the album, which became increasingly chaotic. Random photographs were haphazardly stuffed in their plastic sheaths, as if my mom had tried to keep documenting even after everything fell apart.

By the time my grandpa retired, his lungs were shot, and soon after he was diagnosed with lung cancer. But he never once blamed the plant. Working there was his biggest source of pride, and he'd tell the girls that they owed their lives to that place. Aunt Jean left the house when she was seventeen, so it was my mom who kept him rolling after that. Then one crisp autumn morning a few years later, Louie didn't wake up. The doctors said he simply stopped breathing, that his lungs had had enough. I was barely three years old when it happened.

The last photo in the album was a fuzzy bluish image of Grandpa Louie holding me, his face beaming with pride. I wished I remembered him.

"Today was their anniversary," my mom said, closing the book. "I miss them a lot on days like today. But, you know, they had a fierce love for each other. They never fought, not once! And usually, it's remembering them together that soaks up all of my sadness."

It was difficult to imagine how the house must have been with the four of them alive in it. Every room was occupied then. A stool in the bathroom where the little girls sat and peered up at their mom getting ready. A humidifier in the linen closet, tugged out whenever Anna had a sore throat. An ironing board that flipped down in the kitchen, used to press my grandpa's uniforms. Every facet of this house was used to support them, until bit by bit the rooms became quiet and dark. Now, like this study, everything was shut up, broken, unloved, or unnecessary.

"Do you want some tea?" I asked, breaking her fixation on the album.

"Not right now. I think I'll stay here for a while." I could tell her strength was waning, and it was only nine in the morning. "Maybe write a bit."

My mom rarely talked about writing. Although she had worked at the library for a number of years, surrounded by books and other people's words, the '80s typewriter usually just collected dust. She had spent the past twelve years surrounded by day-to-day tasks. But now I saw an urgency in her that I never had before. I wondered if we needed some quick cash. Maybe the disability check skipped, but I didn't pry.

"Write, Mom. I can go to the woods."

She set down the photo album and pulled the cover off the typewriter. I couldn't believe it still worked—not everything in the house was broken. I wanted to look inside it and watch the delicate parts move under the weight of her tapping. But instead, I shut the door, letting her ride whatever wave had overcome her.

THE MOTHER OAKS WELCOMED ME as I crossed the bridge over Leaky Creek. Curious about the girl in the woods, I decided the best way to find her was to go back to my spot by the creek.

As I sat nestled next to the fallen tree, I tried to occupy my mind. This was silly. The girl was not coming; she wasn't even real. I sat dawdling with a stick, poking at the rocks to make little pools for tadpoles and salamanders to swim into. The stream was ice cold from the still-thawing ground, and it nearly froze my toes as I let the water rush between them. Then a small whispering noise came from the trees behind me.

I turned around and the girl was sitting in the crook of the Wishbone, dangling her legs to one side, just like I had done a hundred times before her. She looked like a little forest sprite, and I had to blink a couple times to make sure I wasn't dreaming.

"Hi," she said in a small innocent voice.

"Hi." I was more timid.

"What's your name?"

"Sadie."

"Sayyy-deee," the girl said slowly, getting herself acquainted with the sound.

"What's your name?"

The girl hopped off the Wishbone and made her way closer to the creek, her little bare feet somehow aware of every twig and rock ahead of her. Then she jumped over the flat rocks onto the other side of me and sat cross-legged on my blanket. She picked up a pebble and toyed with it in her little pale hands.

"My name...hmm." The girl pondered the question. She was thinking of a response, taking her time.

"My name is...Cali," she said. "Yeah, Cali."

"You don't sound so sure?"

"Well, I always wanted to go to California."

"But what is your *real* name?" I was getting frustrated.

"They have movie stars in California and trees with leaves that look like feathers on top!"

"Palm trees. My aunt sent me a postcard from there once."

Cali didn't seem to care. "You know, it never snows there either. I hate the snow..." She went on about how they have lizards of every color and mountains with hidden volcanoes that could burst at any moment, and how the city mirrors the sky at night with so many thousands of twinkling lights you can't tell where the ground stops and the constellations begin. She used her small hands to exaggerate the scenes she was depicting. I listened and laughed and let her run her course. I liked her.

"How will you get there from here?"

"Maybe I'll walk," she said, thinking hard on it. "I'll get there. You'll see."

Tuckered out and waiting for the next thing to grab her attention, I asked her if she'd ever caught a tadpole.

"Course." Her voice boomed. "Have you?"

"Yeah, loads of times. I usually take them home to my mom,

and we wait for them to turn into frogs and let them go. I like seeing their little legs grow out of their tails, like they're in between a baby and an adult."

"My mom doesn't like when I bring nature into the house." Her voice was kind of raspy, and I loved the care she took in her words. After a pause, she asked, "Do you know the difference between a frog and a toad?"

"No, not really."

"Frogs are slimy. Toads are bumpy. Not much else different about 'em. But, you know, I always liked toads more."

"Why's that?"

"Because they have magic powers." Her eyes grew wide and glittery. "See, no one thinks they are as pretty as frogs. So, everyone likes frogs more. But, if you like toads more, if you are nice to them, they show you what they can do."

"What can they do?" I tried to embrace the idea.

"They can take you places if you follow them. That's how I found you out here."

After every wondrous thing I'd learned about the forest, my immediate instinct was not to go along with her imagination, but to tell her the toad was probably just returning to the creek or hopping away from her in fear. I resisted this urge and tried to get to her level, to feel her same excitement, to believe in such a simple form of magic. After all, why couldn't a toad steer you to water, to opportunity? Why was my mind rejecting such a possibility? "So, a toad led you to me?"

"Oh, yes! Straight to you!"

"Well, then, why did you run away?"

"What do you mean?"

"You saw me yesterday and disappeared."

"I wasn't disappearin'! I was playin'!"

"Playing?"

"Hide-n-seek, my favorite game."

"But you hid so well I couldn't find you."

A cunning smile came across Cali's face, and she let out an uproarious laugh, disturbing everything around us. "Should have followed the toad."

We spent the rest of the afternoon playing by the creek. We caught tadpoles and competed at climbing up the Wishbone. We collected leaves and stones and made a makeshift fire pit, though neither of us knew how to actually make fire. The day passed at a snail's pace, and we were soaking it all up. I didn't think about my mom once, and I was actually having fun. We dreamed up games where Cali was my pet rabbit, and I was her zookeeper. The goal was to not let her get away, but she kept slipping through the make-believe boundaries I had set. They were the same kinds of games I used to play, before everything got so serious. I wanted to hold on to this feeling, and I thought that if I tried hard enough, I could stay a kid. I could give voices to nonliving things. I could play forever! But my stomach grumbled after way too long without a meal, and the afternoon sun told me it was time to go home.

"I have to go check on my mom. I think it's time to head back. Want to join me?"

Cali's smile grew wide and vibrant. She had some missing teeth, and the adult ones were starting to peek through her gums. "Let's play hide-n-go-seek."

Cali had boundless energy, but I had to stop playing at some point or I'd be stuck in the woods all day. I allowed for one more game, instinctively knowing who would be hiding first. I turned my back on her and began to count. I heard the initial tiptoes, like she was trying to hide which direction she was heading, and then nothing. By the time I turned around, Cali had disappeared once again.

WHEN I GOT BACK, Mom wasn't in the study anymore. She was in bed, reading. She looked content, glowing with the satisfaction of a good day.

"I haven't written like that in years. I was so completely transfixed by my thoughts, I hardly kept up with them." Her words quickened. "But when I was done, I realized the whole day had passed, and I hadn't had a bite to eat! So, I crawled to the kitchen like a wild beast and ate everything in sight. We'll have to go to Buehler's again tomorrow."

She laughed and lit a cigarette, discarding the empty green box by her bedside. She loved Newports the most, and she was always careful not to go through them too fast, savoring every last one right up to the butt. I made a mental note that she was smoking more than usual. She told me often how cigarettes reminded her of her mother, who also smoked, although it was usually done in secret after everyone had gone to bed. She had so many excuses for it.

"I'm starving too." I sat down next to her on the side of the bed, a bag of stale chips in hand. "I met a girl in the woods."

"Oh, really? Was she your age?"

"Younger. Maybe eight or nine. She's very small."

"What was her name?"

"Cali. But I think she made it up."

"That's odd, but sometimes kids do that." She put the cigarette down in the ashtray next to her bed and a wide smile grew across her face, like she knew something I didn't. "Well, did you have fun?"

"I think, maybe, she could become my best friend."

I had never had a best friend. I didn't think there was anything different about me. But everyone always chose the opposite of whatever I was interested in. I usually felt isolated at school, and I didn't talk to the other kids much. I couldn't help but wonder what made me so weird. Maybe it was where I lived or how I dressed. Maybe it was because I spoke with a little drawl, the same drawl that most people spoke with on this side of town. Or maybe it was because my mom wasn't married, didn't have a job, and was sick, all things that precluded someone from being well liked in Juniper, even though she had grown up here and belonged here as much as anyone else.

But now, something about Cali was remedying all those hurtful thoughts. I didn't care that she was younger than me or that she made up her name. She loved the things she loved and despised the things she didn't. The childish lines she drew were so definite, and it seemed that she had decided I was on her side of the line.

4

AS THE RAIN HIT MY WINDOW, it leaked through and pooled on the sill. I used a T-shirt to soak it up. The sun was trapped behind the clouds with no hope of escaping any time soon. No hope of going to the forest that day. No hope of seeing Cali. My mind was uneasy thinking she might be out there all alone waiting for me. Cali must have a family, I thought, and she knew her way around the forest. I tried to put it out of my mind.

Distant rumblings of thunder shook the quiet house. God was bowling up there, my mom would always say. The gray misty skies shed no light inside. It was going to be a bad day, of course. With my mom's writing and my time spent with Cali in the woods every day after school, we had been overdoing it. You just couldn't have that much goodness and expect it to last.

The house was dark and musty. I went downstairs and knocked on my mom's door. No response. I pushed the door open, trying not to let the rusty hinges squeal too hard. Mom was lying in bed, eyes closed, a look of strain on her face. This was not a bad dream; this was pain.

My mom had suffered from multiple sclerosis since she was

eighteen, though at first she wasn't aware of what was happening. Her symptoms started as joint pain in her elbows and knees, sometimes her hips. Her body was strained and in constant motion, balancing her schoolwork while taking care of Grandpa Louie on her own. They were always in and out of the hospital. So, whether she was preoccupied or had mistaken the aches as signs of stress, she decided to simply shrug it off. She did this for several months. But then she started to have other symptoms like nausea and irritability, and she became forgetful. Her mind simply wasn't in the right place, fogged by abandonment and obligation. For a few months more she excused all the signs, until one day she left her purse in the front seat of the Ford, and it was stolen. That was when she decided to go to the doctor.

The family doctor in town ran a few tests and came up short on all possible diagnoses at the time. But he did have one bit of information he thought explained it all: She was pregnant.

She was dating her high school sweetheart, my father, Gabe Daniels. His father was a dentist and his mom sold houses. They were authoritarians, strict with high expectations, pushing his three older brothers to go off to big-name schools. Following in their footsteps was Gabe's rite of passage. But as the youngest, he got away with more. He was intelligent and planned to major in English. He read non-stop and worked at the library with my mom. They quite literally had a storybook romance. She told me he asked her to homecoming by slipping a little note inside one of the books she checked out, and she circled *yes* and handed it back to him. She said they'd sneak kisses in the hallway between classes, and he drove her home from school, using the drive to ask her about her day. They talked about books, and college, and how badly he wanted them to go to the same school. They had it all planned out. They were in love.

Gabe had practically become family at the Watkins household. He would buy groceries for them and watch the house when they were at the hospital for Grandpa's treatments. Gabe became very close with Louie and would read the sports section of the newspaper to him when my mom wasn't around.

When my mom found out she was pregnant with me, she was already two months along, still many months after the pain in her joints started, but she had something entirely new to worry about then.

I was going to be born in the spring of 1992. They would stay up all night talking about names and planning their future. There was no option where he could stay in Juniper; his parents simply wouldn't allow it. He would go away to college, and my mom would stay at home to raise the baby and take care of Louie. The cancer in his lungs had become much more pronounced. Once Gabe graduated and had a stable job, he would come back, and they would get married and buy a big house for all of us to live in. Maybe then they might make enough to send my mom to school too. The plan wasn't perfect, but the relationship was, and both were convinced they could make it work long-distance. Gabe ended up getting into Syracuse, his dream school, but over nine hours away from us. They stayed in constant contact for two years, and Gabe would come back every other month to visit. Then my grandpa died, and my mom told me it broke something in her.

Through all of the tumultuous change, her pain never subsided, and she decided to return to the doctor. After several inconclusive tests for a whole range of autoimmune diseases, the doctor gave her his best guess: MS, a debilitating disease with no cure. She never accepted the diagnosis, claiming that she was just sickly, like the runt in a litter, never quite able to get what she needed, but the doctors had to call it something or they couldn't treat it. Still, treatment options were limited. It was quite unpredictable how her life would pan out, depending on how progressive her form of the disease might be. But my mom decided that even if Gabe could afford it, she wouldn't go to college. She wouldn't have more children when she didn't know how long a life she had left. She wouldn't leave the house or the last remnants of her family. Her fate was sealed. So, she continued to work at the library, and she raised me. Not defeated but deflated. Those big dreams washed away, and so did the story of my dad, or at least what I knew about it.

I rarely thought about him anyway. I didn't remember him, but every time my mom told me this story, she assured me he still loved me, as if it were some kind of consolation. When he did cross my mind, I would flip the page up there, so I didn't have to imagine a world where he had stayed, where our house and family were whole. I tried to be like my mom and convince myself we had everything we needed, but looking at her strained face in the gray morning light, I knew it wasn't enough. Everyone had left my mom, including my Aunt Jean. But now it was her turn to be cared for, and I was going to do it.

A FULL WEEK of constant rain had passed, and everything was saturated, including our boredom. We exhausted all of the fun we could have indoors, and we were getting antsy. Then, for the first time in an eternity, the clouds began to drift away, and for a brief moment we felt some relief. We were sitting in the kitchen watching the water evaporate, wrapping everything in a haze. Then a knock at the door broke our fixation.

"Aunt Jean!" I yelled across the house. "Come in!"

"Oh, sweet Sadie, the walls will fall down in this old place if you get any more excited," Jean said as she made her way down the hall.

My mom sat up straighter, pretending the pain in her joints was far less severe than it actually was. "Jean, you look good!" She motioned her in for a hug.

Aunt Jean did look good, and I was reminded how beautiful she was. She'd only visited us a handful of times, never staying more than a few days, always just enough time to start getting used to her presence. It had been almost two years since I last saw her, and she had filled out. No longer twiggy and fidgety, her pale skin was now tanned and freckled, and her strawberry blonde curls bounced on top of her head. Jean was only a few years older than my mom, but looked many years younger and healthier. She was nearly glowing as the sun entered the house with her.

"Looks like you brought the sunshine with you, Aunt Jean."

"Well, I did just come from Costa Rica!" She was stealing glances at the disheveled house. Only learning the day prior that she was going to fly in, we hadn't done much to prepare for her arrival. She pulled out a small box from her giant leather purse and handed it to me.

I untied the twine and lifted the lid. Inside was a painted ceramic frog. It was a deep rusty yellow and had a *Made in Costa Rica* label painted on its underbelly.

"A frog!" I squeaked.

"No, Say, that's a toad! It's the Monteverde toad, or golden toad, and it once lived in a huge colony of other toads like it in a place called the Cloud Forest." Her voice became misty. "But they say it's extinct. The locals have been searching for it, but it's nowhere to be found. I bought this from a local woman who makes and sells them to support their efforts to bring the habitat back. Álvaro says I'm a sap."

I looked at the golden toad in my hands and thought about its disappearance. Could it really be gone forever? No, better to imagine that it was just hiding. Then Cali crossed my mind.

"Whose Álvaro?" my mom asked curiously.

And with that, Jean held out her hand. A small bauble sparkled in the light coming from the windows. "He's my fiancé!"

Jean was always a free spirit, never letting herself get stuck anywhere, so the news of her meeting someone was shocking to both of us. "How did this happen?" Mom asked as she eyed the beautiful ring, a hint of pain in her voice.

"Well, I have more news to share... I'm pregnant."

"A baby!" I was thrilled, and the house felt like it was suddenly flooding with light and excitement. The commotion was exhilarating. Finally, more goodness. I reached out to hug her and all three of us laughed. It was the kind of joyous reunion only Aunt Jean could inspire.

"Well, it's time to celebrate." My mom began to stand up, wobbling a bit as she steadied herself on the table. "What do you say we go get some dinner?"

"Are you sure you're up for that, Anna?" Jean had a way of always knowing things. She could feel others' emotions and practically read their minds. Like my mom, she was also deeply superstitious; coupled with her fascination with medicinal remedies, crystals, and the like, she was a sort of mystic. She was the kind of woman who was going to tell you what you needed whether you asked for it or not.

"Of course, you have to tell us all about Álvaro!" Mom said, playfully rolling his name off her tongue.

"Well, okay, how about Pip's for some of that famous lemonade?" Jean winked, presuming that I hadn't known that Pip's lemonade was only partially made of lemons and was actually mostly vodka. I snuck a swig from my mom's cup the last time we were at the diner, which had been well over a year ago, and it stung my lips.

"I'm getting grilled cheese," I said, squeezing her again. It was like hugging my mom, but a past version of her, when she was healthier, and I was smaller. I always thought of Aunt Jean as my other mom, just living a different life, the kind of life movies are made of. But whether or not that was true, she would never let on. Like Jean, I also had a way of knowing what was on people's minds, and I always sensed a deep pain in her. Even with her smile, she carried the kind of sadness that only someone with so little to cling to could.

After some settling in, Aunt Jean drove us in her rental car, a teal Nissan Sentra. Pip's was a small diner on our side of town, which meant that it was shabby and aging. Those on the north side never came over here, making it a truly local haven away from all the gleaming nonsense that was encroaching deeper and deeper into our territory. When we sat down at one of the torn red leather booths, Pip came up to greet us. He was an old Black man who lived in an apartment above the pharmacy next door. He was as skinny as a twig and always wore outrageously bright and patterned button-down shirts from the '70s. His spine slung back with age and his hips sprung forward, always looking ready for a jive. His arms were often openly swaying to the rhythm of the place, whether there were two people or twenty filling it up.

He acted as Juniper's informal historian and would proudly share his story with whoever asked. I'd heard it so many times growing up it was practically etched onto my brain. He had owned the diner for nearly forty years, opening it at the height of the Civil Rights Movement. He was one of a handful of Black business owners in the area, and he wanted his diner to be a place where people could come together to discuss matters, particularly political matters. But not everyone liked that, and his windows were bashed in one night, the place ransacked. It could have been the end of his business, but some families, ours included, came together to help him fix it back up. Not even a year later, when the Civil Rights Act was established, Pip had a celebration and had framed photos of those first few days hung all over the walls of the diner. We always sat in the booth with the happy photo of Grandpa Louie and Pip together. Pip often talked to me about those days, his glassy eyes traveling to some distant place. Despite the years of hardship our side of town endured, his infectious pride in our shared history kept us all close. For this reason, whenever we had a chance to go out to eat—a birthday or a good report card—Pip's always housed our joy.

"Well, if it isn't Miss Anna and Miss Jean," Pip said as he approached our table. "Who is who, now?"

"Oh Pip, your mind is slippin'," Jean said, bringing him in for a hug.

"Well, I know that sass ain't comin' from Miss Anna." Pip's wrinkled face twisted into an ear-to-ear grin. "Good to see you 'round here, Jean! What'll you have tonight?"

"Good to be back," she replied. "I think we'll get a round of cheese fries and some lemonade for my sis."

"Oh, none for you?"

"No, I'm afraid I'm feeding two now." Jean rubbed her belly, though there wasn't much there yet.

"Aunt Jean is having a baby!" I chimed in.

"Well, I'll be... That's wonderful! We need some babies around here. So, Miss Anna, just the lemonade for you then?"

"You know I can't say no to your lemonade, Pip." Pip left the table, and my mom drew smoke from a fresh cigarette. "So, Jean, tell us about this fiancé of yours."

"Well, he is a carpenter. I met him when I first started traveling through Costa Rica about six months ago. I was visiting my friend Carlos when I ran into Al. He showed me around his part of the country, and I've been staying with him for about five months now. When I found out I was pregnant, he rushed out the door and didn't come back until later that evening. I was so nervous, I thought I had scared him away, and I eventually fell asleep. I woke up the next morning, and he wasn't in bed, but a little pink box was. Inside was the ring. He'd been searching all day for the perfect one, and when I went downstairs, he was cooking breakfast, and a big bushel of lilies was in a vase on the table. My eyes were all puffy from crying the night before, and he said to me, '*Este niño tendrá el mundo.*' It means 'Our child will have the world.' I've been walking on clouds since."

"He sounds nice," I said as I grabbed a handful of fries. "Is he coming to visit too?"

"I'm not sure he will be able to leave his business. But I would love for you to visit us soon," she said, not realizing how impossible that sounded to me.

"So, you won't be staying long then?" my mom asked, sounding a bit worried.

"Well, I'm not sure." I sensed her unsteadiness, as if she might sprout wings and fly right out of the diner. She didn't like to be cornered, that much was obvious. "But I'll stay for as long as you need me."

Jean never stayed in one place for very long. She was already deeply rooted in her traveling lifestyle by the time Grandpa Louie got really sick. And when he died, she came home for the funeral and set off again quickly after. My mom told me she came back one more time after that to pack up her stuff, assuming my mom would sell the house. But Jean never did pack, nor was the house ever sold. She left everything in her room exactly as she had it growing up. Even when she came back the few times since then, she didn't touch her stuff. In fact, she usually slept on the couch. I found a letter from Jean once that had found its way into the postcard box. It disappeared, but I remembered vaguely what it had said. She told my mom how she felt she had nothing to offer. Her emptiness and guilt were overwhelming, and her only promise to my mom was that she'd never settle down. She'd go from place to place, see the world, and maybe one day she could come back and make things right. I know my mom never resented her for staying away; in fact, she seemed to prefer it.

Looking at the two of them sharing cheese fries, no one would ever guess that they weren't best friends. Everything felt comfortable, like the three of us belonged together. Yet, still, something seemed to be gnawing at both of them.

"Can we do something fun tomorrow?" I asked, trying to cut through the tension.

"Sadie, I have my treatment tomorrow," Mom reminded me. "But maybe after, if I'm up for it."

Later that evening, after my mom had gone to bed, Aunt Jean and I got to talking. She asked me a million questions, and I could barely keep up. Making up for lost time, I guessed. I told her how the school year was almost over, how Mom was having a lot of doctor's appointments, and then I let it slip that I had made a new friend. If she knew I struggled with friendships, she didn't let on. I told Jean that the girl's name was Cali, which felt like speaking her into existence. I told her how Cali and I had played for hours, and how I felt like I knew her from somewhere. "Sometimes it feels like I dreamed her up," I said nervously.

"Why would she be a dream?" she asked, cautious not to doubt me, which I appreciated. If anyone was going to understand how I felt about Cali, it was Jean. She always talked about things that seemed like magic. When she was last at the house, she told me she felt my grandmother's spirit. She pointed to the stairs off the living room and said it was like she could see her walking down them, carrying the laundry. Seeing how spooked I was, she told me she'd sprinkle salt outside my bedroom door so Grandma's ghost wouldn't disturb me in my sleep. Sure enough, when I woke up the next morning, there was a thin silver line of salt spread across my doorway.

"Maybe Cali feels like a dream because she didn't seem to come from anywhere," I explained further. "She just drifted into the forest and made up a name like she wasn't staying long, kind of like how you never stay long." I could tell I had accidentally struck a nerve with her.

"Sometimes people don't know when something is worth staying for, Say." She spoke softly. "They don't know how to trust that a friendship is real, that anything is real. Or worse, they *do* know, and they feel totally incapable of handling it, like they'll just screw it up."

I turned her words over in my head, not fully understanding them. Then we heard a crash in the bedroom.

"Mom!" I shouted, and we both sprang up.

Mom was splayed out on her bedroom floor, her hair stuck to her face. She was drenched in sweat. Jean stumbled over to her side. She tried to help her up but couldn't get a good grip. My mom slipped through her grasp and hit the floor. She screeched in pain, and tears began to stream down her face.

"Oh my god. Oh my god. I don't... I can't—" Jean stumbled over her words, her hands shaking.

"I'm here," I said to my mom calmly, leaning in to pick her up. Although it took all of my strength, she still felt so small in my arms. She howled in pain as I moved her over to her bed and tried my best to ease her in. Jean had backed herself into the corner of the room.

"I was nauseous and tried to get to the bathroom on my own," my mom said, resting her hand on her forehead.

I tried not to look toward my fear-stricken aunt in the corner. "It's okay, Mom. We're here. Just relax, and I'll go get some peroxide to clean up these scratches."

After I spent half an hour cleaning my mom up and getting her back to sleep, I went out into the kitchen for a glass of water.

Jean was sitting at the table, her head in her hands.

"How long has she been like this, Sadie?" Her voice was low.

"What do you mean?"

"I mean how long have you been helping her out of bed and cleaning her up?"

I tried some calculations in my head. But I couldn't find the start and stop points. It was like a train that just kept moving, never letting its passengers on or off. I just had to go along with it. "I don't know, a long time I guess."

Jean wiped her eyes and brushed her fingers through her hair. Her curls had flattened. She motioned for me to hug her, and I did.

"It's okay, Aunt Jean. I've got this."

5

THE NEXT MORNING, we got into the Nissan. It had a new car smell that my mom woozily explained made her head spin. She held her hand close to her chest, still nursing it after last night's fall. Jean averted her eyes, probably still embarrassed by how she'd handled the incident.

We drove down the interstate to Memorial Hospital where my mom had been getting infusions for about five years now. The treatments meant hooking her up to an IV for hours while nurses came in and did little more than change the bag and ask how she was doing, to which my mom would respond with a joke about being hooked on the bag, saying something like, "good drugs." But actually, they weren't good drugs. She had run the gamut of medications, each coming with its own set of side effects. The last one she tried caused such a severe response that her legs filled with fluid, becoming twice their normal size. I thought if you stuck them with a pin they might explode. But with every new medication came a new promise she might feel better, so she kept going. They also came with more tests: blood tests, urine tests, tests on her kidney and liver function, scans of her brain, scans of her heart, and so on. The reasons for doctor visits had become so plentiful that it was next to impossible for my mom to keep any kind of commitment like work or community events. Although she was always getting worse, she was never discouraged, or at least she never let on if she was.

The latest medication was just the next in line, another check off the alphabet menu of options, but the treatments were causing near-constant intense nausea. To me, the doctors seemed like they had no idea what they were doing, but rather were just throwing things at her to see what would stick. I often thought about what I had learned in class about the scientific method. If my mom was an experiment, then I was the controlled variable, always present, always observing, but never influencing the outcome.

On that day, we were put in a shared room, which sometimes happened depending on how much available space the hospital had. This meant there was only one television, and that annoyed me. The one source of entertainment now had to be shared among everyone in the room, and sure enough, the other patient was already occupying it with some cheesy soap opera. At least we had Jean to keep us company, but she was already turning green. My mom and I made a secret bet she wouldn't last ten minutes in the hospital and would make some excuse to go outside.

"Hey, I think I'm having some morning sickness," Jean muttered. "I'm going to go wait outside. Maybe drive around for a bit. That usually calms my stomach."

My mom and I looked at each other, trying not to roll our eyes. "Okay, but be back by two o'clock. That's when the doctor comes, and I don't want to be waiting here any longer than we need to be."

"All right, bossy pants." She smiled at my mom and me. "See you two later."

The nurse began to hook my mom up, a mean-looking woman with blonde hair pulled back so tight she looked almost bald. "What's with all the bruises?" she asked, assessing my mom's arm.

"Had a fall last night," she explained. "I got dizzy and tried to get myself to the bathroom."

The nurse seemed to make a mental note but had no additional comfort to offer. When she left the room, my mom and I habitually craned our heads toward the TV and began watching the dreaded soap opera.

"I don't like her much, that nurse," the other patient said, a woman who looked to be about my mom's age. I recognized her from the last visit but didn't want to say anything in case I was wrong. "Doesn't ever have anything to say to help pass the time."

"They never do," my mom replied. "Least they could do is let us smoke."

"You're telling me," the woman said. "Haven't smoked for six years. Lung cancer."

"Yikes. I'm sorry."

The woman looked indifferent. "My name is Helen Jackson."

"Anna. And this is my daughter, Sadie."

"Hi Anna." Helen smiled faintly. "And hello, Sadie. Real nice of you to come here with your mom. My kiddos would rather be at home watching TV."

"You have kids?" I asked her.

"Two of them, both boys, Simon and Hank."

"Are they at home watching TV right now?"

"No, they're probably not." Helen looked upset. "We just moved into an apartment about five minutes from here. No cable."

"Oh," I said, unsure how to keep the conversation going. "Why did you move?"

"Sadie," my mom snapped. "Don't be nosy."

"Oh, she's just making conversation. No worries," Helen said wistfully. "To tell you the truth, Sadie, we didn't have a choice. We got kicked off our insurance about a year ago, and we've been paying out-of-pocket for my treatment. It's so expensive we can't even try to keep up. We're in a mountain of debt. We had to file bankruptcy. It was an impossible decision: my health or the house."

"I'm so sorry." I knew all too well about insurance and the costs of healthcare. This wasn't the first time I'd heard the horror stories people were living. In fact, we were living one too. But because our house was paid off and my mom was single and on disability, the flimsy laws that existed protected us from the worst of what medical debt could do to a family.

"That's horrible," my mom said. "Damn thieves."

"What can you do?" Helen replied nonchalantly.

We were quiet for a while after that, letting one soap opera bleed into the next. The storylines were about couples who'd broken up and gotten back together so many times that it no longer made any sense. Every character had a kid with every other character, nothing was sacred. Even brothers and sisters found out they weren't actually blood-related and would have kids with each other, continuing the vicious cycle. It made my head spin. When two o'clock rolled around, Jean came in with McDonald's.

"God, I miss me some Mickey D's," she said. "Al is always cooking us healthy meals at home. I normally love it, but this greasy goodness is hitting the spot."

Jean scarfed down the Big Mac and offered me some fries. My mom tried not to hurl. Then Dr. Fratello came in, and Jean crumpled up the paper bag and shoved it into her big leather purse.

"Anna, Sadie, nice to see you both," Dr. Fratello said, looking over toward my aunt.

"Jean," she said, holding out her hamburger-greased hand. "Her sister."

"Nice to meet you, Jean. Now, it's been a few months on this new medication. How are you feeling?"

"A little nauseous, but otherwise okay," my mom replied.

"Has your pain decreased?"

"No, not really."

"Any other symptoms I should know about?"

"No."

"Okay, well I want to get some quick bloodwork and then you can head home."

"I have some questions," Aunt Jean piped up.

My mom and I looked at her, astonished. Aunt Jean had never taken an interest in my mom's disease before.

"What exactly are we dealing with here, Dr. Fratello? I know it's multiple sclerosis, MS, but can you give me any more insight into her treatment thus far and your plan for her?"

Dr. Fratello was unphased but gave my mom a quick look, as if to request permission. My mom nodded in return.

"Well, your sister has a chronic progressive form of MS. This means she doesn't experience remission. We're also up against a pretty fast-moving form of the disease, and she isn't responding to any of the treatments we've tried thus far. Now, that doesn't mean one of these medications won't stop the progression, but we are running out of options. The current medication she's on is classified as a chemotherapy drug, and use of it on MS is only advised when other treatments have failed."

"How is a chemo drug supposed to help?" Jean asked. "I thought chemo was only for cancer."

"This drug works by suppressing the immune response caused by her MS. The hope is that whatever switch is turned on in her body will turn off and force her into remission."

"And if it doesn't work, what's your next move?"

Dr. Fratello looked at my mom. "I'm sorry, I should have asked sooner. But should Sadie leave the room?"

"I need a snack anyway," I said. I often glazed over Dr. Fratello's musings about my mom's disease. He had a monotone voice that made me want to fall asleep. I usually wanted him to hurry up so we could leave sooner, but when I left the room, I stood out in the hall to listen. Helen saw me through the window in the door of the room, and I held my finger to my lips, requesting that she not give me away.

"None of the treatments we're trying will reverse the progression of this disease," Dr. Fratello continued. "Your sister is nearing severe disability. Right now, we are trying everything we can to avoid the worst impact of this disease. But these drugs are extremely volatile. I'm afraid we're running out of options."

I heard my Aunt Jean stifle a cry, and I ran off to the vending machine. I didn't want them to know I was eavesdropping; that I knew.

TRILLIUM
Trillium Grandiflorum

6

IT WAS TEACHER WORK DAY, which meant no school. These days were always glorious for me, and I reveled in the opportunity to reunite with Cali. I headed across the bridge into the forest, *my* forest. Everything was soaked from the constant rainfall, and the moss was a luminous shade of green cloaking everything in sight. I walked gently down the path, no destination, no determined time or place, just existing among the giants. Bird calls echoed through the branches, still somewhat bare as the trees had yet to unfurl all of their leaves for summer.

The ground was strewn with clusters of trillium flowers, which I could easily spot because of their three white petals. I was tempted to pick a few and press them—what a prize they'd be in my collection. But I had learned the hard way when I was younger that picking even just one flower meant depriving the root of nutrients and potentially killing the whole bunch. No, trillium was best left untouched. I wondered then about my aunt and how she could have left my mom and grandpa when they needed her most. I wanted to know what had deprived the root of our family, and what caused it to fall apart, but perhaps it was all better left untouched.

My spot by the creek looked different. The heavy rains had washed a lot of the beach away. I walked farther downstream, watching the toads jump in as my footsteps crept by them, looking for signs of Cali.

I kept coming back to this thought that Cali might not be real, that I had somehow made her up. I thought I was too old to have imaginary friends. But if that were the case, why would my mind make up Cali? It all just seemed so fantastic. I had never encountered another soul in the woods, nor was there a reason why I suddenly would. But I ought to know if someone were just a figment. I should have asked her where she lived or what teacher she had, something that could have bound her to this time, this place. But I didn't. My mom hadn't come to the forest with me for months. The last time we spoke it was as if she had decided she never would again. So, when I found Cali, or rather when she found me, I was so happy to have someone to share the forest with again. Cali made *me* feel like *I* was real.

After a couple of hours with no hint of where she might be, I decided I should head back. I didn't entirely trust Aunt Jean to care for my mom. I was worried she wouldn't know how to help her if she needed it.

I made my way up to the back porch and into the kitchen. When I walked in, I immediately got a whiff of pizza—the cheesy, spicy delight that only Little Italy's could provide. But the box was closed on the table, and when I opened it, no one had touched it. I called out, expecting to hear my mom or Aunt Jean tucked away in one of the dank old rooms of the house. Then I noticed a note on the counter. It read:

Sadie, tried to call for you, but we had to leave quickly. Your mom was dizzy, so I took her to the hospital. Call me when you see this. — Aunt Jean

My stomach dropped, and the smell of the pizza overwhelmed my senses. I dialed the number she left me with on our landline. Three rings. Then a shuffle on the other end.

"Mom?"

"It's Aunt Jean, honey. Everything is okay."

"What happened?"

"Your mom and I were about to eat lunch when she started to get dizzy. She said the room was spinning, and when she tried to get up from the table, she fell again. She cut her arm on the edge, and there was a lot of blood. It wouldn't stop."

I turned to see the bloody paper towels in the trash can. "Is she going to be okay?"

"The doctor said she had a case of vertigo, causing her to fall. They prescribed her a new medication that she'll have to take daily. As for her arm, she got stitches and should heal just fine."

I didn't know what vertigo was. I had so many questions and just wanted to be next to my mom. "Can I talk to her?"

"She's sleeping right now. The doctors just ran a couple of tests to make sure there weren't any other problems to worry about. When those come back, we can head home."

After hanging up the phone, I thought I had vertigo too. My head was spinning, and my brain felt like it was pushing its way out of my skull. The sunny afternoon light became glaringly bright. I was never home alone, and I did the only thing I could to keep my thoughts from racing. I cleaned. I started with the obvious things—the dishes, the laundry, the toilet. Then I moved to the floors. I mopped vigorously at the old hardwood, unable to get the water to come back clear. Years of dirt and grime were built into the fabric of the house, and it was infuriating. I washed the windows and the walls. I dusted. I even cleaned the trash cans. After four hours, I was coated in sweat, and the only thing left to clean was myself. I stood in the shower, trying to scrub away the filth. The water began to run cold, and I turned the dial all the way up, attempting to hang on to a few more minutes of warmth.

Thoroughly exhausted, I got into my pajamas and went to the couch. The TV made my ears ring, so I sat in the quiet house, waiting. At nine o'clock, they finally pulled into the long rocky driveway. Aunt Jean walked in first and handed me a bag of prescriptions, then she went back out to collect my mom, who was crumpled up in her arms, barely touching her feet to the ground.

"Mom." I hugged her tightly so she wouldn't collapse onto me. She was dazed and had a huge bandage on her arm. A faint pink outline showed where the blood was still seeping through.

"I'm okay, Sadie Bug. Look, I got a new accessory." She held out a black cane. "Think I'm going to go lie down."

I helped her into her room off the kitchen, and when I came back out, Aunt Jean was sitting on the couch looking exhausted.

"Looks nice in here. Haven't seen the place this clean since my mom was alive."

"Uh, yeah." I thought it strange she would bring up Grandma so casually. Mom and I never talked much about her. "I like to clean sometimes."

"You did a great job. I'm sure your mom will notice in the morning."

"Oh, I'm not worried about it." I tried not to sound like I cared. But I did. I wanted her to notice and to tell me how happy the sparkling floors and smell of Pine-Sol made her, as if my hours of scrubbing could somehow heal her.

"Hey, can we talk for a bit?"

"Sure." I took a seat on the floor in front of the couch. I didn't like sitting in the armchair; my mom said that was Grandpa's spot, and I swore sometimes he was still sitting there.

"So, that was kind of scary, wasn't it?"

"Yeah, I was worried about her. But I didn't mind being home by myself." I tried to make it known that I was more than capable of being on my own.

"You're so brave. But I think you know, Say, things are changing...with your mom."

"You mean her vertigo?" I fumbled over the foreign word.

"Her vertigo is a new problem. But she's sick, sweetie."

"I know. We go to the doctor a lot."

Jean looked defeated, like she had lost a long race and was only reaching the finish line as everyone else had already started walking away. "I understand, and I'm sorry you've had to do this alone."

"I don't know what you mean." I was getting flustered. "We aren't alone. We have each other. Me and my mom."

I watched her as she tried to think of the right words to say. "Well, what she has is not something that's going to go away. She might feel better some days more than others, but it's not like the flu or a cold. She isn't going to get better."

She took a pause, and I wasn't sure what to do, so I looked down at my fingertips, forever finding flecks of dirt beneath them.

"For a while, it was easier for her to take care of herself. But now that she's having more pain, she's more tired and needs more help."

"I know." I wished she'd talk to me like an adult. "So, you're trying to tell me she's going to get worse?"

"Yes, sweetie. It's a sickness that puts her in a lot of pain, and soon her body won't be able to handle it anymore... Does that make sense?" Jean said as tears welled up in her big hazel eyes.

"I guess so." But I couldn't have picked up on the finality in those words.

THE NEXT MORNING, I woke up in a sweat. I had a mad rush of fear and realized I had just been propelled from a dream, but I struggled to piece it together. I was lost in the woods. A thick stormy darkness blocked my line of sight. Humanoid figures stood among the trees. I thought I recognized them as my teachers, the kids at school, Aunt Jean, but I wasn't entirely sure. I couldn't run, my iron feet sunk into the earth. When I tried to scream my voice stretched out like saltwater taffy on a hot summer day. Then I was jolted awake by some unknown force. The morning sun burned my eyes.

I went down to the kitchen and Aunt Jean was sitting at the table. "Morning, sleepyhead," she said softly. She was radiant with her golden curls and soft features, reminding me of the mornings I'd seen my own mom sitting right where she was, sipping her cup of tea before she would head off to work.

"Morning." I noticed a hot pot of oatmeal on the stove. "You made breakfast?"

"I sure did. Go ahead and have some."

I didn't know what to think. I had been making breakfast for so long my mind couldn't register that it was right in front of me. Then I thought of my mom. "Is she still sleeping too?"

"She was awake for a moment. I brought her a cup of tea, but she turned away. She said she wanted to sleep in."

That's my job, I thought, but I didn't want to offend her, especially not after the night we had. It was like a piece of me didn't want her here, as if she were intruding, trying to replace my mom. I didn't want her to see us like this, but I felt like I was making it more difficult for her.

She reached her hand out to me, resting it warmly on my shoulder. "I should have been here a lot sooner. I didn't know how bad she was getting. You don't deserve this."

The same anger I had last night was bubbling again, about to boil. "Will you stop talking like that? I am fine and so is she."

"I understand. I didn't mean it like that." Jean paused, calculating her next step. She got up and washed the oatmeal pot. Yet another thing she was taking away from me. I sat there fuming, unable to even peck at my bowl.

"Hey, I need to go to the store to pick up a few things. Do you want to come with me?"

"I have school." I tried to keep my tone level.

"Oh, right." She grinned. "Do you ever play hooky?"

It was difficult for me to hide my enthusiasm. Missing school always sounded good to me. Besides, something told me I had to get used to her being here. I smiled and apologized and off we went.

Jean and I went to Beuhler's. She was running out of her essentials, so we filled the cart with shampoo, toothpaste, and the like. When we hit the medicine area, she looked brazenly at the vitamins. My mom never liked to linger in that area, as if someone we knew might see us and label her as sick. She was, of course, but she never liked anyone else to think so.

"Your mom has tried these, hasn't she?" Jean pointed to a shiny bottle. "When I was in Tibet, the locals would talk about its healing properties."

I shrugged, inching away from the pharmacy area, a force of habit.

"I need to pick up more prenatals, and some of these." She tossed another vitamin bottle into the cart. I marveled at how much she was about to spend. We were always so tight on cash.

When we reached the checkout counter, Jerrod was once again the lone cashier, as he so often was. The TV was playing the same news station as if the darn thing were broken, stuck on one channel for all eternity.

"Bush has my vote. Kerry's got no spine. Just goes whichever way the wind blows," he said, mimicking the campaign ad we'd all seen a thousand times. He was leering at Jean's chest, but she pretended not to notice. "This country don't need a pushover."

We took our things and left the store quickly. "Nasty man," she said as we sped off in the Nissan. "So inappropriate to talk about politics like that. There are three things you're never supposed to talk about: politics, religion, and money."

"Yeah," I said. "He creeps me out."

"Oh, he's just rude. But I sure do wish there was somewhere else to shop other than Buehler's. I hate to drive all the way up to the Kmart."

"They're building a Walmart," I said. "A supercenter."

"Oh really? Where's that going to go?"

"Right next to the Kmart."

We laughed. "God forbid they give us anything good over here."

When we returned to the house, I checked on Mom. Her bedroom door was cracked, and I eased my way in. "Morning."

"Morning, Bug."

The bandage on her arm was changed out and clean, no longer hinting at the wound beneath. I scanned her body for more signs of damage, expecting her to look worse. She was washed out, her skin gray-looking, like a shadow. But her eyes were bright. "How are you feeling?"

"I'm okay. These new meds make my head all fuzzy." She glanced near her nightstand. A new orange pill bottle stood among the others like a soldier recruited to the army that was keeping her alive. She called the pills her morning cocktail, but I didn't get the joke. "But not that fuzzy," she chided. "It is a Monday. Why aren't you at school?"

"Aunt Jean needed help this morning. School's out in a couple of weeks anyway." She didn't seem to want to put up a fight, so I quickly changed the subject. "Do you need anything?"

"No. I've just been trying to get my bearings after last night."

"Mom, I was so scared. I wanted to be with you in the hospital, and there was nothing I could do."

"Oh Bug, you're gonna be okay." She pulled me into her and pet my head. "We just need to calm down a bit. It was an exciting day, that's all."

I tried to hold back my tears. I hated seeing her mask her pain. Then Jean came into the room. "Ladies, I had an idea for today. How about we clean out my old room?"

My mom laughed a little. "Jean, your room has stayed exactly the same way since you left for college fifteen years ago. Are you sure you can part with your treasures?"

They both laughed, breaking the tension between all three of us. "Oh, now you're making me sound old!" Jean put her hands on her hips.

"I'm pretty sure there's dust older than me in that room," I chimed in.

"Oh hush. If you two are going to be mean about it, I'll just do it myself."

"Fine by me." My mom giggled. "If we haven't cleaned your room for you in fifteen years, what makes you think we are going to do it now?"

"Yeah, I have enough chores," I added.

"Ugh, you two are the worst." Jean smiled and waltzed off.

I HAD NOT SEEN CALI for so long that I decided she must have been a dream. After having such a surreal nightmare that night, I thought my mind could make up just about anything. I wanted to get back to my routine and take my mind off everything. So that afternoon, I went out into the woods, certain I would find some peace.

The creek was nothing more than a trickling stream, and the clearing was inviting me in. When I sat down at my spot, I opened my book and nearly forgot where I had left off. It had been so long since I'd read, and I couldn't wait to sink into the pages. I was born to love reading; my mom worked at the library after all. But it really started with *The Magic Tree House* series in second grade. The teacher would read us one chapter every day after lunch. I enjoyed it so much I didn't miss a single day of school that year because I'd worry about missing the next chapter. I even got a small wooden plaque for no absences, and my mom and I celebrated at Pip's. The library where she worked continued to feed my appetite well through third and fourth grade. The girls at school were always reading *Nancy Drew*, but I preferred reading stories about real-world mysteries like the Egyptian pyramids or Machu Picchu. I could see cave paintings and hieroglyphics and imagine whole worlds. Reading had become a way for me to get out of Juniper, just like my Aunt Jean. Sitting by the creek, lazily flipping through the pages, I suddenly had a sense that I wasn't alone. A high-pitched humming traveled through the trees. It was so faint, I thought I must be imagining it.

I tried to continue reading and let the little song blend in with the birds overhead. But then it grew closer, swallowing up the space inside my ears. I stood up and looked through the trees. Cali was about a hundred feet away picking something up off the forest floor.

"Hey!" I shouted.

Cali looked startled, and she started running in the opposite direction.

"Hey! It's me! Sadie!"

I began to run to her, but once again, she outmatched me. She knew these woods despite my never having seen her in them before. "Hey! Stop!"

After she got far enough away, she turned around and stood as if she'd been caught. I approached her slowly.

"Go away!" she shouted.

"No, you keep coming back here, and I want to know why," I said loud enough so she could hear me.

"I live here! And you're in my spot!"

"Your spot?" I asked, confused. I was about twenty feet from her now. "Don't you remember me?"

"You're Sadie."

"Yeah, and you're Cali. We played for hours the other day."

"That's not my *real* name."

"I know it's not, but it's the one you gave me." I was growing frustrated. "Why are you here?"

"I told you, I live here."

"You live in the woods?"

"No, I live in a house!" She looked upset, her pale little face was flushed, and her dark eyes pierced through me as if I had stolen something from her.

"Okay." I softened my tone, trying to calm her down. "I live in a house too, not far from here."

"Well duh." She began to look less frightened. "Why wouldn't you live in a house?"

She *was* real, her words so matter of fact. I almost couldn't believe it. But there she was, just as solid as the last time I saw her. "I've been looking for you for days."

She smirked. "Well, I can't help it if you are a terrible seeker."

"So, you've been hiding from me on purpose, like a game?"

Cali didn't respond. She looked different than I remembered her. Her tiny posture just the same as before, her hair still a mess, her feet still bare. This time, though, she looked sad, like she had been crying for a while. Her eyes were lost, sunken, and dark like charcoal, glassy and distorting her appearance. "Are you okay?"

"Yeah, I'm just missing my mom."

"What happened?"

"I don't know." She squeezed her eyes closed, holding back more tears. "They won't tell me."

"I'm sorry." I wanted to reach my arms out to hug her, but I was afraid she might take off if I tried. "Do you want to play?"

After a solitary moment of despair, she held out her hand and revealed the small pile of crumpled pink flowers she had been picking.

"Those are spring beauties. I like to press those," I said.

"Press them?"

"Yeah, I collect flowers from the forest, and I put them inside a book and press them into the pages."

"Why?"

I tried not to be offended by her sassy tone; she was just a little kid. "I like to see how things change season after season. I don't like forgetting and then having to relearn what something is all over again."

"You want to pick some more?"

"Sure," I said, happy she was curious about my hobby.

"We can go on a treasure hunt!"

"Treasure? What, like gold coins?"

"No, just things," she laughed. "Old things. You know, the things that have turned up here without any reason."

You mean like you, I thought. Plenty of rubber tires had been abandoned in the woods, although there wasn't a road anywhere nearby. Sometimes I would come across old trash, but I never found the discarded items interesting. Still, I thought I should go along with this for her sake. She needed a friend to help her take her mind off whatever it was that I could tell was still bugging her, and so did I. "Where do we start?"

Cali took the lead and started wandering deeper into the woods. I tried not to focus on which way we were going. We went over fallen logs and got our hair caught on slim branches. Then we entered a clearing.

"Oh, what's that!" Cali said, pointing at something shimmering ahead. She ran over and unearthed a long, thin, rectangular piece of metal.

"I think it's a road sign!" I shouted. "Let's see if we can read what's on it."

Together, we scraped away the dirt, caked on over many years. Most of the paint was long gone, but I made out a few letters, enough to know it said Violet Avenue, the main road on our side of town, the road with the post office and Pip's. For what reason it was buried behind my house, I couldn't begin to imagine.

Soon the objects got more interesting. Each new treasure was fodder for our tales. We started to dream up their origins, making stories about the patch of forest we both called home.

Once upon a time, we imagined there was a village inside the forest. The sign we found belonged to a long-forgotten road. Travelers on their way to Juniper would pass through here, bartering items like furs and knives. We found old cans and glass bottles, relics of a long-gone tavern where the travelers would drink, a pit stop on the last leg of their journey. They'd water their horses and patch the tarps on their buggies. But a new road must have been laid, leaving behind the souls that once inhabited the village. Then we found the sole of an old leather shoe, solidifying our story. We dreamed up the man to whom it once belonged. We named him Thaddeus Glinn, and he was lost too, destined to roam the forgotten landscape in search of his missing shoe.

Our stories became so elaborate I actually grew scared that the items we were turning up might haunt us. Just then, Cali spotted another object in the distance. It was ivory white against the dark expanse of the forest. We rushed over, and I picked it up. It was a skull about the size of a baseball, with beautiful squiggly designs on the top. I thought of my books about hieroglyphics and brushed it off gently, as a real archaeologist would.

"Is it from a person?"

"No, I think it's from a deer or something. You see how the snout and jaw are broken off here and here?" I pointed to the areas where the bones had once joined, how it used to be a whole being.

Cali seemed curious, but she didn't touch it. "What are those squiggly lines on it?"

"I think they're just the places where the skull came together." I thought about what I'd learned in my archeology books from the library. "Our skulls have them too."

This freaked Cali out, and she touched her messy head of hair, feeling for the lines. "Or maybe it's from aliens."

"Could be," I said, laughing. I put it in my pack, and we continued to scavenge for forgotten items, fulfilling our fictional stories. I had more fun than I'd ever had in the woods, and it was mostly due to the company of this small child with a made-up name.

Then, around mid-afternoon when the sun began to wane and my hunger set in, I decided I should go home. Cali knowingly put her hands over her eyes and said, "Your turn."

She began to count, and it was my turn to run. I bolted away wicked fast, pure joy rushing through my veins as I made my way back to the old house. She was real, and she was my friend.

When I got back, I checked in on my mom. She must have been napping, because when I opened the door, she shot straight up.

"Oh, Sadie!" She brought her weak bent hand to her chest. "You scared me."

"Sorry, didn't mean to. How are you feeling?"

"I'm okay." She rubbed her temple, the sign of a headache, which my enthusiasm was probably only making worse. "I feel like I've been sleeping for a week. Did you have fun outside?"

"Yes. I was with my friend."

"The same girl?" She cleared her eyes with the base of her palms.

"Yes, her name is Cali. She's smaller than me, and she lives nearby. We went treasure hunting all day, and I found this." I pulled the skull out of my pack to show her.

"Gross. Sadie, take that outside!" She was horrified by it, pulling away. "It belongs to a dead animal."

"But it's neat."

"It does not belong in the house."

I got upset and left the room. I wasn't going to put it outside, so I ran upstairs and put it under my bed instead. I sat on the floor, trying to calm down. How could she not even look at it? It was as innocent and fragile as anything else in the woods. It reminded me of the golden doe. Maybe it *was* the doe, and that made it all the more precious to me. Then I thought about Cali, and a pit grew in my stomach. I wished she was here. I wished she could come over. I never had a friend come over, and I desperately wanted someone to play with, to share my things with, to tell secrets to, to have sleepovers.

It became very clear to me that I had spent so much of my life so alone. Sure, my mom would play with me—she was my best friend—but I needed someone I could relate to. Someone closer to my age. I was sick of being weird, of being an outcast. Cali was the closest thing to a friend I had ever had, and I wanted it to be a real friendship. She might have been younger, but she understood how to play, how to imagine worlds like me, how to find curiosity in everything. I stared at the skull under my bed, and I began to cry. All it did was remind me of a dead animal. A treasure shared between friends quickly became a reminder that everything comes to an end. It was ruined.

I heard Aunt Jean shuffling around in her room down the hall. I cleared my face of any sign of sadness and decided to go check on her progress. She was stuffing several large trash bags with things and piling them up against the wall. "What's all that?"

"Oh, just old stuff." She was clearing her eyes too. Everyone was sad that day. "No use to anyone. Heard you run up here in a hurry. Are you okay? Did something happen in the woods?"

"I'm okay," I assured her. The walls of the room were a muted pink color, framed cross-stitched art that hung for decades had just been taken down, leaving dark stained shadows where the sun couldn't reach. The bed frame was metal and tarnished and an old afghan was folded over the foot of it. Laid out across the brown shaggy carpet were piles of her belongings. One pile had old college textbooks, a pair of hiking boots that were never broken in but aged poorly just the same, a graduation cap and gown, and some pencils and pads of paper. Another pile had a sky-blue teddy bear whose facial expression was stitched into a sad-looking smile, a series of picture books about a cat, and a baby blanket woven by my Grandma Samantha. "This room has looked the same my whole life. It's weird to see it cleaned out," I said.

"Oh, yeah. It was time though, wasn't it?"

Time for what? I wondered. Aunt Jean brushed her hands through her hair and straightened her flowing blouse, exposing the small baby bump. "Can I feel it?"

"Sure, she's not big enough to kick yet though. She's like the size of a pea."

I tried to imagine a person the size of a pea, resting my hand on her abdomen. I wasn't sure what to expect, but it just felt like a belly. Firm, warm, and smooth. "Does it hurt?"

"No, not really. Most of the time I don't even feel it. Growing life is a very slow process."

"When are you due?" I removed my hand.

"She'll be here around Thanksgiving, I think. Won't that be nice?"

I thought that would be nice except Thanksgiving was always just me and Mom. We didn't even have turkey. We'd just get fried chicken from Pip's and watch the Macy's Thanksgiving Day parade on TV. "You're going to be here for Thanksgiving?"

"Wouldn't you like that?"

I hesitated for a moment. "I guess."

"Something eating at you?"

I hesitated, thinking about the doe skull. About Cali. About how weird it was to be in this room, in this part of the house where memories were locked up, secrets I wasn't allowed to hear.

"I would like to know why you left."

Jean looked uncomfortable. She got up to listen to the house, for my mom, who was probably getting ready to fall asleep. Then she gently closed the door and returned to her spot on the bed by me.

"I…" she was trembling. "I don't know how much your mom has told you."

"I know you left when my mom was still young, that you came back for Grandpa's funeral, and I think one time after that to clean up the house, which obviously never happened. But I don't know why you don't visit more often or why you're only just now getting around to cleaning your room and suddenly talking about Thanksgiving."

Aunt Jean appeared to be sweating, her face glistening. "It's hard for me to talk about it, with anyone."

I felt her closing off, readying herself to take flight, to find anything to keep her from reciting the past. But I wasn't just anyone. "I won't tell my mom, if that's what you're worried about."

Then Jean's face softened. "Oh honey, that's not what I'm worried about. It's just that…this stuff is hard. It's been a long time."

We sat there in silence for a moment. "Well, it was about six months after your grandpa died. You were still very little. The sweetest little girl. You know, you hardly ever cried or whined for anything. Two-year-olds are supposed to be much more rambunctious. But not you."

"I knew that already." It felt like she was avoiding the real question. I waited patiently for her to proceed.

"I came back to clean out the house. Your mom was adamant that she didn't want to sell it. But I thought we could get some money and maybe she could go to school or something with it. But she said she would never leave Juniper. She was so stubborn. I thought if I started at least packing up my stuff, she could be persuaded. But when I came back, she was not good."

"What do you mean?" I pried.

"She wasn't herself anymore. She was…depressed. I mean, she took wonderful care of you. But she had let everything else fall apart. Including her relationship with your dad."

I didn't expect to learn anything about my dad. "You knew him?"

"Of course I knew him. His older brothers were in my class. I even dated one of them once. So yes, I knew him when he was very young. He was sweet, even then, always carrying things for your mom. He treated her like a princess."

So, what my mom had said was true. But it still felt like Jean was avoiding the real story. "I need to know what happened."

"I don't know, Sadie. I feel like your mom should be the one to explain it."

"Bringing it up makes her sad. I don't like to make her sad."

"I understand that feeling." Jean looked on edge. "Okay, I'll tell you what I know. But promise me that you will get the actual story from your mom at some point? I can't give away all her secrets like that. Besides, I only know what I saw."

"I promise." Though I wasn't entirely sure I was going to follow through.

"Gabe, that's your dad's name." I tried not to roll my eyes at her again. She was doing her best to treat me like an adult. "He was over at the house when I came back. I had a bunch of boxes ready to go, and I was trying to sneak them upstairs without your mom seeing me. But she did. She ran up to me and screamed that I just wanted our dad's money, that I never cared about our family or anything that happened to us. Gabe was holding her as she said these things. I did not know how to respond, so I just kept moving the boxes upstairs. Then things in the house grew quiet. The sun was setting, and I remember watching Gabe's car pull out of the driveway. I thought she must have calmed down, so I went downstairs and found her in the kitchen. She was just staring into the fridge, dead eyed, like she hadn't a thought in her brain. I asked her if she was okay, and then she said in a low voice something that I will not repeat to you, and she ran out of the house, into the woods, barefoot. It was a fairly cool evening and I thought she'd get cold, so I chased after her, trying to stop her. But I reached the creek, and I couldn't go past that bridge, I just couldn't. I remember shouting for her for hours and she wouldn't come out. I slept on the couch that night, waiting to hear the back door open, and when it finally did, she was standing there. The blue moonlight falling on her face. I swear she looked just like our mother. It scared the daylights out of me, and I realized then that I couldn't help her. She was beyond reason, and I called Gabe then to come over and check on her... I shouldn't say more."

"I can handle it," I said, not sure if I actually could. It was hard to imagine my mom having that much...rage. She had always been so serene for as long as I could remember. It didn't sound like her at all.

"Well, Gabe came back. He was clearly exhausted, and not just because it was three o'clock in the morning. I could tell he was giving up. When your mom realized I had called him, she threw a fit. She said she was fine, that you were fine, that every-thing was fine. She just kept using that word. But nothing was fine, and I said as much. That's when she told me she wanted us all to leave. She screamed at me to get out of the house. She screamed at Gabe. She told us she could handle it all on her own. Oh, Sadie, I'm so sorry to be telling you all of this. But you deserve to know. I really didn't want to leave you, but I felt like my presence wasn't helping. I felt ashamed I had ever left her in the first place. She was barely sixteen when I stuck her with our dad. It was all my fault. I left that morning, after not even a couple hours of sleep, and I promised her I wouldn't come back unless she invited me."

"What happened with my dad?"

"Oh, I don't know exactly. He probably felt like he couldn't help her either. I could tell he had had enough. He was a young guy. He had a whole life at school. He probably needed space too."

"I don't understand why she would act like that." It was all very hard to hear, hard to believe.

"Well, time has given me some perspective, Say. I think for your mom, that's just what grief looked like. She had lost so much. We both had. I think she needed to go through it on her own, in her own way."

"But it's been ten years. Why didn't he come back? Why did you continue to stay away?"

Jean looked uncomfortable again. "I also handled the grief in my own way. But, Say, I really do think it's best we stop there tonight. I'm tired." She rubbed her belly and kissed me on the head.

I didn't know what to think about what I had just heard. But I went back to my room and looked at the doe skull under my bed. Some things in the world were just harder to fathom. Sometimes the best thing you could do was let time pass until you were ready to try to understand.

7

SCHOOL FINALLY LET OUT, and I didn't miss it one bit. While the other kids signed yearbooks and promised to write to each other or exchanged phone numbers, I sat waiting for that final bell, my sweet release. I was looking forward to an entire summer with Cali.

Jean and I were sitting in the kitchen in a sleepy silence, eating the oatmeal she was cooking every morning, as was our new routine. I was beginning to like having her around because I could get out to the woods quicker. Before I went out, I decided to check on my mom.

She was in the study, turned toward her typewriter. Her fingers were tapping vigorously at the keys, so I decided not to bother her. Besides, I was eager to go outside.

Although it was a perfect sunny day, when I crossed Leaky Creek, the trees took on a deep emerald hue, as if a massive cloud had just swept over, casting an ominous shadow over the canopy above. The thick air had a choke hold on the birds, making for a silence that told me rain was coming, that I should turn back. But I forged on. When I got to our meeting spot by the creek, Cali was already sitting by the fallen oak. "You came!" I said.

"I did, and I brought you this." She handed me a soft little trinket.

"What is it?"

"It's a lucky rabbit's foot. It's my dad's, but he won't miss it."

I inspected the little foot. It was only a few inches long and a dusty white color. The fur was smooth like silk, and I could feel the soft bones inside. I thought it strange someone might carry something like it around on a key chain.

"Don't you want it?" I asked. I looked up at her, dangling the strange gift between my fingers.

"I wanted you to have it. Rabbits are your favorite."

"Well, thank you. I brought something for you too." And I pulled out an old book that had been collecting dust in our study since before I was born. I knew how my mom felt about us touching the books. It was a risk, but I figured it wouldn't be missed for an afternoon. "It's a book about California's bridges. I thought you might like to look at them and learn about them with me." I flipped open the book.

"Look, palm trees! And skyscrapers! And everyone is wearing shiny dresses and suits! And look, there's the big red bridge!" Cali said.

"Yes, the Golden Gate."

"Have you been to California?" she asked, her little hands clasped under her chin.

"No, never. In fact, I've never left Ohio."

"Then how come you know so much about it?"

"Well, I got postcards from my aunt, and I read books. I also watch a lot of TV."

Cali looked puzzled. "I don't have a TV."

"Why not? Everyone has a TV!"

"My dad said they are too expensive, especially the colorful ones."

I wasn't sure what she meant by "colorful," but I was curious to learn more about Cali's dad. "Do you live with your dad?"

"Mhm, and my mom and sister, but none of them come out here with me." Her voice drifted off. "Not anymore."

"Oh..." I paused. "I don't have a dad. I mean I do, but I don't know him."

"I'm sorry. My daddy is really nice. You would like him. Everyone likes him."

"My dad left when I was a baby."

Cali seemed confused or sad, but then just a moment later, she moved on. It was so effortless for her. Her face shifted from a frown to that familiar, playful smirk in a split second. I yearned to know her secrets.

"Want to play?"

"Play what?"

"Hmmm." She pondered, tapping her finger to her chin. "Spies!"

We played spies for a while in the woods that day, investigating for clues, Cali said. Clues that would lead us to the bad guy, a loose cannon come to terrorize our imagined village. After a couple of hours of following her around, we still hadn't found the bad guy, but of course it was all about the chase anyway.

"Cali, I have to go home," I said, sweaty and out of breath. "It's almost lunchtime, and I told my aunt I'd be home."

"Okay, but hide-n-seek first?"

By this point, I knew the drill. I cupped my hands over my

face and began to count. By the time I got to five, Cali's little footsteps had faded to silence. I opened my eyes and was briefly happy for the solitude. I walked slowly along Leaky Creek back to the bridge. When I passed by the mother oaks the sky had shifted; it was bright again, those dark shadows gone. *Must have been a really big cloud*, I thought.

THAT EVENING the three of us sat in the kitchen eating burgers from Pip's. Aunt Jean had swung by to pick them up on her way home from an ultrasound. The baby was healthy. Jean was healthy. "Everything is normal," the doctor said to her, and she kept repeating it at the table, trying to reassure herself.

"Did you get to hear a heartbeat?" I asked.

"Yes, I cried when I heard the little thumps." Jean looked sad. "I miss Al so much."

I didn't want her to leave. But I could tell that time might be coming. She'd been at the house for almost three weeks, the longest she had ever stayed. "Do you think you'll go back soon?"

Mom was silent.

"Well," she paused, rubbing her belly. "I don't think I'm going back at all."

I looked over at Mom. She was staring at her full plate of food, pushing the mac-n-cheese around the perimeter. "You're moving back here? Permanently?" I asked.

"Yes, I want the baby to be born here, and I want you both to get a chance to know her."

My mom was expressionless, as if she were a thousand light-years away, and then she lit a Newport and came to. "We can't wait, Sis. We're so happy to have you here for as long as you like.

But I'm sure it won't be *that* long."

Something wasn't right about her tone. Her words sounded off, like she wanted to say something else entirely. Sarcasm or bitterness, it was hard to tell.

"What's that supposed to mean, Anna?" Jean pushed the cigarette smoke out of her face. "Would you please put that out? I don't know when you picked up smoking, but it is a nasty business. Those things can kill you."

"Been smoking since I was sixteen, since the day you left," she said, picking up her cane and dangling it from her arm. "Are you sure you can handle sticking around here? Things are getting worse, you know, don't want to miss your cue."

The words shot through Jean so fast, I could practically see the bullet hole. "That's not fair."

"You're right. It's not fair. None of this is fair. It's not fair for you, or for Sadie, or for me."

I sat and listened to the two fiercest women I knew, my two mothers in this lonely world, like the sun and the moon, waging war on each other.

"Anna, I know you blame me for leaving you with Dad, but think about it."

"I don't want to have this conversation right now." My mom exhaled another cloud into the room as if she could smoke us out. "Not in front of Sadie."

"Well, you brought it on. Besides, I think we have to. It's been ten years since we lost him, and we're still dancing around it."

"You're right, Jean. It's been ten years, and you've been home, what, three times? Thanks, but I think I'll stick to the postcards. They have a way of making me feel a whole lot better about this situation. Nothing screams 'I'm sorry for abandoning you' like a photo of the Mohave. You're ridiculous."

Jean looked intense. Her freckled skin was reddening, and I felt sick. I couldn't understand why Mom was being so cruel. This was all completely out of character, or so I thought, thinking back to what Jean had said a couple of weeks back. Then I thought about the doe skull under my bed and how she had swatted me away. Maybe this side of her was returning because Aunt Jean was back, or worse, maybe this was part of her disease. "Maybe we could all just go—"

"Anna, you may have taken care of this place for ten years, but I was the one taking care of it long before you," Jean said, cutting me off. "Don't you remember? I was the one who packed your lunch, who washed your laundry, who helped you with your math homework. I held it all down for so long. I needed to leave, and Dad was the one who told me it was okay."

"Well, I'm happy you got permission to be free."

"You know I'm not free, Anna. I carry this pain with me every single day, but coming back here hurts worse. This place, you, it's all a shadow of the past. Why didn't you move? Why didn't you get on with your life? You can't blame me for the fact that nothing has changed. You can't blame me for your disease. You had permission too. No one made you stay here."

My mom was crying now, and she snubbed the lit end of her cigarette onto her paper plate. She looked so weak. "Stop," I said to Aunt Jean. "You're upsetting her."

"Oh really, Jean? I could be free? Knocked up at eighteen with one dead parent and the other running to the grave to join her? No money. No future. Just this old house, a baby, and a truckload of medical debt. Yeah, I could have had it all."

"What could I have done?" Jean was exasperated. "Seriously, what do you think I could have done for you? I was a mess. I had no idea who I was, and I had to figure it out."

"I suppose you've done that now. You've figured it out, and now you've come to save the day!"

"Yes, I have." Jean was stern, lifting up her chin. "I am ready to take this on."

"Well, good for you. I'm so happy you have decided to grow up."

The two of them fumed for several minutes. None of us flinched. But my Aunt Jean wasn't going to let her have the last word, and she dealt the final blow. "I think it's time for bed. We're upsetting Sadie."

With that, she left the room. Mom and I sat listening to her feet plod up the stairs as she made her way to her reclaimed bedroom. My mom broke down in a sob. I had seen her cry so many times, but never with such vigor. These were tears built up over a lifetime, and I couldn't do anything except pet her head. I ran my fingers through her hair just like she did for me. She was so small in my arms, and it frightened me. She was withering away. But I held tight. We sat for a while, listening to the summer night song of crickets fill the room.

LATER, AS I LAY IN BED trying to fall asleep, Jean thrashed around in the room adjacent to mine. She was murmuring, and I went out to the hall to put my ear to her door. "She's bad, Al. We have no choice. I have to do this."

A long pause.

"But you can't leave your business."

Another pause and some muttering in Spanish.

"*Te amo.*"

When she hung up, I waited a moment and then made it sound like I had just opened my door. Then I knocked on hers.

"Come in," she said in a low voice.

"Hi."

"Hey, Say. Did I wake you up? I'm sorry. I was talking to Álvaro."

"How is he?"

She rubbed her belly but had lost her calming nature. She was frantic and flustered, like all the light she usually brought with her had been drained out. "He's good. I miss him so much."

"I'm sorry," I said. "What was that all about at dinner?"

"Your mom and I had a bit of a fight earlier this morning when you were out in the woods. Old wounds."

"Aunt Jean..." I hesitated, thinking about the best way to get her to reveal more of those old wounds, to tell me more about what happened. "Can you tell me about Grandma?"

Jean looked at me with wide, tired eyes. "You never talked to your mom about her? Doesn't she tell you anything?"

I shook my head. "No, I didn't want to hurt her."

"Oh baby, you are such a sweet girl. I understand. You know, your mom was so little when it happened, I don't even know if she remembers everything."

Then, after a moment, she told me the story. Grandma and Grandpa had some trouble getting pregnant. For a while, they thought something must be wrong and they gave up. Louie came to terms with it, but Samantha didn't. She was stuck on a step, unable to enter the next phase of her life. Without children, her world would be empty. She thought it must be her, like she had drunk some poison when she was a girl and now she was doomed to never be a mother. When she finally got pregnant, she was the opposite of thrilled. She worried constantly that one small move might snuff the baby out. She lay in bed the entire pregnancy, hoping not to disturb the life growing inside her. If she could just hold the baby, everything would be okay. Until then, it wasn't real. When Baby Louie was born and she got to hold him, she could finally see her future laid out. She vividly saw his first steps and baseball games. She saw him on the playground and at school dances. She saw everything he could be and knew it would all be okay.

And then, on the third night of his life, he slipped out of this world almost as shockingly as he had come into it. Samantha's grief was all consuming, a knife stuck in her chest, and she didn't know how to keep moving. She didn't leave his crib for the entire day. She just sat watching his lifeless body, hoping it might take in a breath. When my grandpa came home from work and found her broken over the blue little infant, he was horrified. It was God's worst punishment, and he didn't understand why his wife had to endure it. What learning was there from something like that? He, along with the house and their marriage, grew quiet. There was no Christmas that winter. There was no Easter that following spring. He went to work, and she lay in bed. It was the darkest year of their lives, and it did not get much better in the years to come.

Samantha eventually got out of bed and started to look for answers. She attended church, although Louie no longer went with her, and she spoke to doctors. She met other mothers who had lost their babies, and she found solace in their support. She sought to help others through the same thing and formed a small community of mothers going through loss. Together they'd knit blankets for children's caskets. Still, she grappled with her own loss. She rarely slept through the night, thinking she'd heard the baby cry. When she ate, it was morsels.

Then in 1971, Jean was their miracle baby, and this time, Samantha wasn't going to lay in bed and let it happen again. She was active right up until her water broke, gardening, cleaning, and preparing their house. By the time Jean was born, the old house had been transformed, and the baby brought a new sense of life into it. This baby would walk, she would speak, she would go to dances, and Samantha would do whatever it took to make sure she had the world. Then Anna came along, and Samantha and Louie decided to put their past behind them. The single black-and-white photo of Baby Louie was crowded by a mantel full of memories. Samantha made it her mission to make every moment with the girls magical. They had beautiful Christmases full of tinsel and snowball fights. They had Thanksgiving dinners with huge turkeys.

They went on like that for years, until Jean and Anna started to grow up. Once the girls were both in school, Samantha struggled to stay connected to them. She got restless with the day-to-day chores and would talk to Louie about going back to knitting with the ladies. He told her that was a morbid idea, knitting blankets for dead babies. So, Samantha's hands, and her life, grew idle once again. By the time Jean was twelve and Anna was eight, she had stopped sleeping and stopped eating altogether. She would lay in bed for days at a time. Louie tried to revive her spirit. He told her she could knit if it meant keeping the past in the past. He told her they could move. He'd sell the old house and they could go someplace warm. But she dismissed it all.

She became increasingly removed from their lives until one day, she left a note explaining her pain. She had been living with it for so long, even before Baby Louie was born. She wasn't meant to be a mother, it was all a mistake, and she felt like she was putting on a show. She told them she'd spare them her troubles. She signed and dated it. Then two days later, a search party found her in the woods. She had wandered out where no one could save her and poisoned herself, making true what she had assumed about herself all along: that she was toxic, deadly, no good, and that everyone else was better off without her.

When Aunt Jean finished telling me the story, we sat together for a while taking it all in. Suddenly so much of my life made sense, and my brain was rewiring itself. My grandma didn't just fade away, she died by suicide, and my Aunt Jean was left to pick up the pieces. She cared for my grandpa and my mom for so long that by the time she was eighteen, old enough to leave, she had already lived an entire lifetime.

"I'm so sorry." It was all I could think to say.

"It was a long time ago," Jean said wistfully.

"So, is that why you said it hurts to come back here?"

"Yes," she replied. "It hurts, but that doesn't mean seeing you and your mom hurts. It's just this town, this house, this bedroom. You'll understand when you get older."

"The tea set," I said, thinking about the juice under the table. The nasty dirt taste of my mom's tea.

"What?"

"We used to have tea parties, my mom and me, but now the table has rusted over. When I see it, it makes me upset."

Aunt Jean pulled me in and stroked my head, just like my

mom. "Oh Say, you're too young to already understand this."

A wave of anger rose in me again. "Why do you keep saying things like that? Like I don't deserve this? Or that I shouldn't have to do this?"

"Because, Sadie, I had to do the same thing when I was your age. I had to grow up fast. I had to take care of your grandpa and your mom. I had to clean the house, cook the food, and go to the grocery store. I didn't know how much of a strain that put on my mind until years later. It smothered any chance I had to learn who I really was. It hurts me to see you going through the same thing."

"But I love my mom," I said, pulling away from her. "I don't see it that way."

"That's because you are your mother's daughter. You are kind and caring. You put others before yourself."

"So are you, Aunt Jean."

"Maybe I was once, but all those years of neglecting my own needs rubbed me down to nothing. All that was left was bitterness and selfishness. That's why I left. I had to figure out what I needed, or I wouldn't last long."

She was finally speaking to me like an adult and not just some child who needed things simplified. "Is that what you meant when you said you were ready?"

"Gosh, yes," she said, smiling. "I really want to be here now. I hope your mom can see that. You know, you are such a good listener. That's a good trait to have."

"I guess so," I said. "I've never thought about it."

"Well, I want you to think more about it. I want you to think about all the things that make you who you are, even the not-so-nice things. The more time you take to discover yourself, the better off you'll be. I'm only just now at a point in my life where I understand who I am and why I've done the things that I have. I'm thankful I gave myself the space to do it. I just wish it hadn't meant leaving you and your mom behind. I can see everything so much more clearly now, especially my future with you and this baby."

"I am worried about my mom," I said, noting that Jean didn't include her in this vision of the future. "She's in constant pain, I can see it in her eyes. I am worried she won't get better."

"Sadie, you have to be honest with yourself and your thoughts. Neither of us knows for sure what will happen with your mom. All we can control is our own actions right now. We can do our best to make sure she's cared for. But we also have to make sure she has the freedom to make her own choices too. We can do our best to make sure she's cared for, but we have to respect whatever choices she might make, even if we disagree."

Pools of tears welled up behind my eyes. My cheeks got hot, but I didn't want to cry. I wanted to be strong. I shut my eyes to stop the tears.

"It's late," she said. "I think we both need to get some sleep. I love you so much. And I promise, no more fighting."

I hugged her so tight I thought I might hurt her. For the first time, my thoughts weren't bad. Aunt Jean gave me a gift, the gift of trust. It was trust in myself, in nature, in God or whatever it was that put us all here. It was trust that everything would be okay.

8

THE NEXT MORNING, I woke up with a sense of peace. My midnight conversation with Aunt Jean was still buzzing in my head, replaying the things she said. Was I brave? Was I selfish? Was I smart? I had never considered how I might make an impact on the world, only how the world was impacting me. How the girls at school treated me. How I was lonely most of the time. How I didn't have what other people had. But I now had an opportunity to think differently.

I went downstairs to find my mom and aunt sitting at the table. They were watching a blue jay on the feeder out back, their heads moving in the same motions, following the bird as it fluttered from one spot to the next. I wanted to be like them. "Good morning," I said, hugging them both.

"Morning, baby," my mom said. "We wanted to talk to you a little bit today."

I sat down at the table with them.

"Aunt Jean is officially moving in. She's going to help out. It'll be really nice to have her here, especially when you go back to school."

"What about Álvaro?" I asked, tripping over the rolling cadence of his name.

"Al is making plans to move here, too," Jean chimed in cautiously. "He will be here in a few weeks."

I thought about what it'd be like to have a man around the house. I had never known any man very well. I was nervous, but I needed to embrace the change.

"The baby is going to need a room," I said. "She can share with me."

"That is so thoughtful of you, Sadie," Aunt Jean said. "I think she'll be okay in my room for a while. But we'll think of something."

"Aunt Jean and I are going to go to an appointment today," my mom added. "Think you'll be fine on your own here?"

"Absolutely," I said, thankful for an opportunity to be alone.

I WENT OUT IN THE WOODS that day hoping I might find Cali. I clutched the soft rabbit's foot in my pocket, which she and I had come to believe through one of our stories was a lucky talisman. As long as I had it with me, we would find each other; it would always bring us back together. Sure enough, when I reached the creek, Cali was waiting. "Hi," I said cheerfully.

"Hello," she said. She didn't look so great.

"What's wrong?" I asked.

"It's my mom," she said, crying. "They told me she's gone."

We hugged for a while, and I tried to think of what to say. I wanted to know the facts. "Did she run away?"

Cali sniffled. "I don't know. All they said was that she's not coming back. Ever."

I wondered what kind of mother would leave her child. I thought about how with some animals, if you touch their babies, the mother won't come back. But what does the mother fear? Is it that she will be risking her own life if she stays? Is she afraid the human will come back for her baby and hurt her? Or is it just that the baby is changed now, something less recognizable, something startling and unknown? Maybe she feels like she can't care for it anymore, like she's incapable of loving something that's been changed by the outside world.

"Well, you still have me," I told Cali. "I'm not going anywhere."

Cali continued to weep. She looked so small; I couldn't help but cry with her. "We don't need to play today. We can just sit here and listen."

"Listen?"

"Mhm," I said, scooching close to her. "To the birds. Let's see how many we can count."

She nodded and we both looked up at the sky. We heard the rapid-fire chatter of finches, the rattling squawking of crows, the echoing jays, all creating a symphony above us, soothing our aching hearts. The best kind of medicine.

After some time, she turned to me and said, "Do you ever think about running away?"

"No," I said, thinking back to my conversation last night with Aunt Jean. "I want to be here. I don't want to miss a thing."

"She still loves me, doesn't she?" Cali said after some time, looking lost in thought again. "My mom?"

"Of course she does. You know, I think about my mom leaving too," I said, not believing I just said it out loud. "She's really sick."

"I'm sorry." Cali hugged me tightly. "Maybe my mom was sick too. Maybe she left so she can go get better."

"Maybe," I said. I felt like crying, but couldn't. It was like my body wouldn't let me.

Cali's face twisted. "Or maybe, she died."

"Don't think like that," I told her, but it didn't seem to slow her train of thought.

"Where do you think moms go?" Cali asked. "When they die?"

"I think moms go somewhere really pretty with lots of flowers and babies everywhere, so they don't miss their own."

"That sounds nice," Cali said, no longer crying. "I hope your mom gets better."

"Me too," I said. "I know I have to be brave, but it's hard."

"You don't have to be brave. You can just be sad like me."

She was right. I could just be however I needed to be. I could even cry if I wanted to, I could even scream...and then I did. I screamed so loud I was clearing the entire forest around me. The finches and jays all flew with abandon. Then, Cali joined me and gave her own powerful roar. We stood up, hollering at the treetops together like two wolves lost from their pack. I didn't care if someone heard us. Let them listen. When my voice finally cracked, I began to laugh, and Cali did too. I tried to catch my breath, letting my body release the energy. Tears dried on Cali's flushed face. Then she screamed once more, so piercing I could sense the pain inside of it, and she fell down crying. Her anguished little spirit incapable of any more hurt.

I hugged her desperately, hoping she would stop. "Cali, it's okay. You're going to be okay."

"I know," she said between sniffles. "I just needed to let it out."

"Me too."

"You are brave, Sadie. You will get through it too."

"You are much braver than me."

We collected ourselves for a moment. "You know, I think you are my best friend," I said.

"You're my best friend too," she said in the smallest voice.

"Can I tell you a secret?"

"Yes!"

"Sometimes I think I don't know how to pretend anymore," I admitted. "It's like my brain forgot how, and I've been struggling to get it back."

"What do you mean?"

"I mean I can't always see what you see. I can't see the village. I can't see the bad guy. I can't follow the toads. I can't believe juice can be tea. I can't even imagine myself being anything other than what I am. I used to be able to, but as hard as I try, as much as I love our stories, that's all they are. It's like something is broken in me, like I can't pretend anymore."

"That's because you're big," she said in her practical way.

"What?" I asked her.

"You're older. You're kind of in the middle. But you're not little like me."

I thought about it for a moment. Perhaps the loss I was feeling, for my imagination, for the way things used to be, was just part of growing up, of becoming older. But I still wanted to feel like I used to feel for just a little while longer. "Cali, do you think if I think my mom will go to a happy place with flowers and babies, like if I believe it, then that's where she'll go?"

"Yes, I sure do."

"But, what if it's not real?"

Cali looked hurt. "But what if it is?"

Sometimes I forgot how much younger she was than me. "It's real then."

"Everything is real," she said with might.

"I just want to know for sure," I said.

"You don't know anything," she teased.

"You're right. I don't know anything except what is right in front of me. Like you!"

"And like you!"

Together, we named all of the things we knew. Cali knew the birds above us were finches. She knew the water in the creek was cold. She knew that the forest was alive and would protect us. I knew all that too. But I also knew my mom was sick and Cali's mom was gone. I knew we were both growing up. I knew things were changing. I knew I was brave and strong. I knew I wasn't alone. I knew she was my best friend, and I knew I was hers.

THAT NIGHT, I wanted to be with my mom. I had been avoiding her since the night she got back from the hospital. I didn't want to confront the new pill bottle, or the cane, or the fact that Aunt Jean and her baby and Al were all going to be living here with us in this tiny old house.

"Mom, are you scared?" I asked her, laying down next to her in her bed.

She looked at me with her soft emerald eyes that so perfectly matched mine. "No, not really," she said, knowing exactly where my mind was.

"What do you think will happen next?"

She pondered the question for a moment. "I think it doesn't matter. All I know is that my life here with you is beautiful, and when it ends, I'll be happy for every moment of it. Where I go next is out of my control, isn't it?"

"But, what about me?" I asked. "Where will I go if you leave?"

"Well, honey, where do you want to go?"

"I don't know. I don't want to be like Grandma Samantha. I don't want to be sad my whole life."

My mom inspected my features like she was trying to decipher my thoughts. "Sometimes I forget how much you've grown up."

We were silent for a moment. I wondered if she was thinking about her own mother. "You know," she said, "I don't know if your grandma recognized she was loved, or if that was enough. She didn't realize her own strength and capabilities. She was always trying so hard to be something she wasn't. Changing her emotions to be what she thought we needed her to be, to be the perfect mother. In the few memories I have of her, she was mostly angry. She wanted to be doing the opposite of whatever it was she had in front of her. She couldn't make peace with anything, and I think she bore responsibility for things that were out of her control. Like my little brother passing away. I know she blamed herself; it was obvious in every action she took. But there was something deeper to her guilt. A restlessness and a fear that I think were with her long before any of that happened."

My mom adjusted her pillow and weakly laid her hands out in front of her. "You know, there was also a beautiful lesson in all of that too. I saw very clearly that I could go down the same path. I could try to right the wrongs, or I could accept what I had been given. So, I chose to accept her death a long time ago. And when I found out I was pregnant with you, I accepted that as well. Now, I've accepted this disease..." Her words trailed off and she hesitated. "And I've accepted that your father left."

"Do you miss him?" I asked.

"Oh, I don't know if I miss him. I think I just saw the struggle I would have to endure taking care of you on my own. It made me angry. I accepted that we fell out of love. I accepted that it wasn't meant to be. But it upsets me that you don't get to have that same kind of closure, that you are left wondering, and I worry about it all the time. I want you to have a wonderful life, and I want you to see that these things that are happening aren't things you have to fix. Some things are just out of your control."

The conversation so closely mirrored what my Aunt Jean had said the night before. Faced with an impossible set of circumstances, they both chose a different path to survive. I thought about the wood frog and how it survived the winter. Its entire cellular structure froze over, even its eyes. Its heart stopped beating. Its brain stopped sending signals. It didn't let in a single breath. The frog allowed winter to run its course as ice swirled through its veins. It knew, deep down, that nothing was permanent, even death. But there were some animals that didn't even attempt to stick it out. The goldfinch flew thousands of miles away, sometimes all the way to Mexico, just to avoid the cold. To chase the sunshine.

My mom and Aunt Jean simply chose different ways to adapt. My mom chose to hunker down and wait for better days. My aunt chose to fly away. But all at once, spring returned, and so did both of them. Despite their long, challenging journeys, both of them woke up in this house this morning. Both found their own kind of peace with the past.

I found comfort in that, as if neither was the right or wrong way to cope, that there were no mistakes or missteps. They were both just doing the best they could with the situation they were given, and everything ended up being okay.

"Mom, I think I do want to meet him."

She looked at me with such love that I knew this decision didn't hurt her but released her. "I will think about it," she said.

MILKWEED

Asclepias syriaca

9

IN JUNE, when the sun weighs heavy on all the tiny and fragile things, milkweed thrives. The grass might be turning brown, and the creek might be nothing but a damp streak of bare earth. But milkweed, with its lanky stalks and sweet pink puffs, blooms with fervor. As I carefully plucked a few stems for pressing, I thought about how love, like milkweed, can survive in even the harshest conditions. That's how that summer was. A time to grow and heal even when everything was stacked against us.

Aunt Jean was on her way to pick up Álvaro at Columbus International Airport. It was a four-hour round-trip drive, so Mom and I tried our best to kill time by cleaning up the house. She was moving around better, still with her cane, but motivated, nonetheless. The three of us had spent the past few weeks having fun, and the tension between my mom and aunt had subsided. We cleared out the entire house. Jean and I painted the walls and fixed the kitchen sink, which had been leaking for years. She was proud of her plumbing skills. There wasn't a single photo of me anywhere in the house, so we printed some off and hung them all over. One above the stairs, another on the mantel, and one of the three of us that was taken at a park a week ago, which was now hanging in the kitchen. My mom and I even planted some flowers, the first time we had touched the garden in years. Our house had new life, ready for new memories.

I was nervous about Álvaro living with us. But it was how things had to be. Having Al meant having Aunt Jean, and I needed Jean. She was doing so much for us that my life was veritably transformed. We always had milk in the fridge. I hadn't gone to any of my mom's doctor's visits for nearly a month. She was even applying for jobs in town to help support us, but there were either no jobs or no places that wanted to hire a pregnant woman. She didn't let that stop her though. She had incredible patience and negotiated a better deal for my mom's disability aid and found a program that helped us repair some of the more major problems around the house. She even set us up with internet access, which I was particularly excited about. I only used the computers at school for homework and rarely had a chance to roam free on the internet.

On the night of my first foray into surfing the web, I clicked and scrolled by the dim blue light of Aunt Jean's compact laptop. I searched so much in that midnight glow, my brain overflowed with the stories and information I was able to conjure from the interwebs. Something about it felt wrong though, like I was sneakily stowing away scraps of others' lives, and if I told anyone about it, they'd take it all away. I disturbed myself on more than one occasion when I researched my mom's disease. I learned about the different types of MS and tried to gauge where she was on the spectrum of life and death. I suspected from her symptoms that she had a form of MS called primary progressive, and I drew an assumption that she would soon lose all mobility in her legs. I learned she could lose her sight, which is when I started hoping for a swift end to things rather than a slow crawl. This only led to more nightmares about losing her, and I knew I needed to stop scrolling.

My nightmares about my mom commingled with the excitement of seeing Cali. With Aunt Jean running things, Cali and I had spent time together on an almost daily basis. On the days when one of us wasn't around, we left little trinkets for each other to say *I'm still here.* We had grown to believe the best way to maintain our friendship was in secret, which was easy for me because no one ever asked. I had complete freedom out in the woods, and I was discovering so much about myself. I was testing the confines of my entire persona, learning and unlearning new ways of connecting with the world. Cali was too. Though she was younger, she had a striking ability to catch on to whatever I was trying to accomplish. Little kids are smart like that. They don't overanalyze everything. They can just live in simplicity, and it was precisely this simplicity that made her the perfect sounding board for whatever was on my mind. One day I asked her, "What would you do if you couldn't walk anymore?"

She pondered the question for a moment. "I would get a cool car, and I'd tell everyone to drive me places like a lady in the parade," she said unhindered, waving her hand like a pageant queen.

"What would you do if you couldn't see anymore?"

"I'd fall off a cliff, and I'd smack into the dirt," she said dramatically, clapping her hands together. We laughed. "What about you?"

"I don't know," I lied. "I try not to think about it."

"You don't know anything."

It was her favorite phrase to use with me. But I didn't mind. She was right. I was still only twelve. But I couldn't help but feel light-years beyond my age sometimes.

JEAN ARRIVED WITH AL that afternoon, pure joy spread across her face. He was handsome, with a dark complexion and silky black hair sculpted into a smooth wave. Slight wrinkles showed around his eyes and mouth in a way that made him look kind, like his face was set into a perpetual smile. They made a beautiful couple, and Jean's whole demeanor changed in his presence, like she was somehow more whole and complete. "Álvaro, this is my sister, Anna," she said. "And this is my niece, Sadie."

"*Hola*," he said shyly. "You can call me Al."

My mom smiled, her entire demeanor changing too. "So nice to meet you, Al."

Everyone's eyes then fell on me. I had to say something, but Al's shyness made me shy too. I wasn't sure what I was expecting, but he was so much more real now that he was standing in our living room. So, I just stood still and smiled. Then Jean swooped in.

"Sadie, we're going to go put Al's things in my room," she said. "Then do you want to take him on a tour of the Watkins household?"

I nodded and noticed that my mom was looking at me like I was being funny. I always had my words out in front of me, but now I was lost for them. But by the time Jean and Al came downstairs, I had found them again.

"Thank you for the frog," I said to him abruptly.

"Frog?" He laughed, making the shallow wrinkles on his face deepen.

"She means the golden toad, Al," Aunt Jean said. "Remember the little figurine?"

"Ahh, *sí*! The Monteverde. That's a very sad story."

"What do you think happened to it?" I asked, knowing full well after an extensive web search that it had likely gone extinct.

"I grew up in Monteverde. My father was a fisherman, and he knew all the best spots for trout. When I was a little boy, he would take me to a special place in the forest that he said only he knew about. We would go every spring, hoping to find them. I remember the only time I saw them, there were thousands, glowing like a sunset. Oranges and yellows, shimmering so bright! It was the most beautiful thing I'd ever seen. But they were so hard to find. When scientists came to study them and turned up nothing, they declared they were extinct and linked it to global warming. My father laughed when he heard those scientists' stories. He said the toads simply did not want to be found." Al's face softened and his gaze grew long. I stared at him hoping he would say more, but he was far off at that moment.

"What a beautiful story. I wish I could have seen them."

"Jean tells me you go to the forest a lot too," he said. "I bet you have a secret hiding place too."

"I do," I said. "But nothing like that."

"Well, how about one day we go visit Costa Rica and try to find them?"

I nodded and felt my cheeks flush. It was like I had known him for years. I wanted to hear him speak more. He had such a rich accent, like nothing I had ever heard. Yet, I was able to hang onto his words effortlessly. I could see why my aunt loved him so much. "Would you like a tour?"

We traversed the various corners of the house together. He was careful with each step, his hands clasped behind his back as he walked, not peering beyond the doors, taking special note of each photo and memento. He was respecting the time and history of the place. No judgment, no questions. He was just happy to receive any information I gave him. I thought it might not be so strange to have him around after all.

"How's the tour going?" my mom asked when we reached the kitchen. She politely put out her cigarette.

"Very well!" I said. "Al, this is my mom."

"Yes, we met earlier." He smiled and not at all in a way that made me feel embarrassed for forgetting. "Nice to meet you, Anna."

"Are you hungry?" she asked. "I think Jean was hoping we could stay in and cook tonight."

"What's that about cooking?" Jean said, coming into the room. She put a hand on Al's back. Their affection toward one another was magnetic, and I realized I had never seen anything like it. I wondered if my mom and Gabe were ever like that.

"I'm hungry," I chimed in.

"Well, I bought some fish and fresh vegetables," Jean said. "How's that sound?"

I had never had fish, but I wanted to explore everything at that moment. "Sounds wonderful!"

DAYS PASSED, and Al fell perfectly into step with our life in Juniper. It wasn't that there was a missing piece he had filled; more like he had inserted his way into our lives, finding a space for himself. He made several trips into town and always came home with more tools. We gave him the garage, which he used as his temporary shop until he was able to get some business going. He intended to build an entirely new crew and start his carpentry business from the ground up. I was shocked to see him so undeterred by the obstacles put before him. I learned Al had already lived in America for several years, in Miami, before moving back to Costa Rica to take care of his mother. I learned his father, the fisherman, lived to be eighty years old and fished right up until the day he died. At fifty-two, Al was considerably older than Aunt Jean, but I never would have guessed it. With his jet-black hair and bright cheerful eyes, it seemed to me that he was ageless. The only giveaway was those faint wrinkles that made his whole face smile when he was happy, and he was always happy. He was happy when he was working, when he was relaxing, and especially when he was holding Jean in his arms. He told me he couldn't wait to have a family of his own, that he'd wanted one for so long, but he was just waiting for the right moment, which happened to be about seven months ago when he ran into Jean at a local shop.

He told me about that day. Jean had just finished touring the Cloud Forest with a group of friends and was digging through her bag for spare change to buy a bottle of water. Al wasn't going to wait for her to find it, and he pulled out all the change he had in his pocket and said, "*Aquí*, for you." She didn't know Spanish but gave him her best *gracias* and paid the man at the counter. Al said she was beautiful, her sun-kissed skin glowed, and the humidity caused the thick tendrils of her curls to spring wildly from her head. He asked her to have dinner with him at his house, which might have thrown anyone off, but Jean was equally taken aback by his beauty. That very same night, she went to his home, a small peach stucco house outside of town. They talked for six straight hours over a bag of chips and never got around to cooking a decent meal. Jean said she knew she was in love that night because she didn't realize how hungry she was until she got back to her friend Carlos' place and ravaged his kitchen. They went on like that for two weeks, spending all of their time together, talking, dreaming, and laying the foundation for their future. Within a month, she was living with him, and a few weeks after, she found out she was pregnant and they got engaged. Al beamed when he told me that "everything just fell into place," and he would do whatever he needed to do to be with her, including moving all the way to Ohio. The story made me so happy I went and asked Aunt Jean to give me her recount so I could hear it all again.

THE SUN WAS RELENTLESS, draining the last drop out of every living thing in sight. The flowers dried up. The leaves wilted, and the grass was crunchy and brown. I found Al outside under the hood of our broken-down Ford, which hadn't moved since the tow truck plopped it down that spring. His arms were elbow-deep in the belly of the old beast, and it looked like it might swallow him whole. When he came up for air, he saw me staring and motioned for me to come over.

"*Aquí*," he said, pointing to the setup. "This belt here has snapped. The serpentine belt."

He showed me the floppy strip of rubber, and I was almost embarrassed seeing it crumble away in his hands, as if the car were a depiction of our life: desperate and in serious need of repair.

"You see these pulleys here," he said, pointing to a few black dials. "And this here, this is the crankshaft, the brain of the operation. When the belt snapped, it cut off the power to your battery and the car died. But it should all be fixed now. Want to test it out?"

"Me?" I questioned. "I can't drive!"

Al laughed and had me sit in the front seat. I could barely see over the dash. He turned the key in the ignition and said, "Just press your foot on this pedal," pointing to the gas.

When I pressed the pedal, the car groaned to life. I squealed with excitement.

"*Fantástico*, you did it!" he said, his whole face grinning.

"I didn't do anything," I said bashfully.

"But you did! I knew you would be the perfect helper."

"What's all this?" my mom asked, hobbling over with her cane to check out the result.

"All fixed," Al said, cleaning off his hands.

"I can't believe it!" She looked exhausted but impressed. "Thank you so much, Al."

"No problem," he said, his happy face changing to one of concern. "Hey, you're not looking so good. Do you need to sit down?"

My mom's face flushed, and she steadied herself on the car. "I'm fine, it's just this heat."

"Let's go inside," I said. As we walked, I braced her right side, hoping to keep her upright, but she kept stumbling, her legs shaking and giving out beneath her. Al followed behind and gently pressed against her back so she wouldn't topple the other way.

"I just don't get it," she said, sitting down in the kitchen. Al left the room gracefully, giving us our space. "I feel okay, my mind is clear, but ever since I fell a couple of months ago my legs just haven't regained their strength."

I recalled my search history and was ashamed to know what I knew about the disease, as if she had never done her own research. "Mom…" I paused, trying to figure out how to broach the conversation.

"I think it's time for a wheelchair," she interrupted.

She took the words out of my mouth, but I couldn't reconcile her tranquility as she spoke them. "Are you sure?"

She reached out to hold my hand. "Sometimes things are out of your control, right? Sometimes even our own bodies. But a chair will restore some of my freedom. Truthfully, I haven't been doing as much as I normally do because I've been afraid of falling."

"Why didn't you tell me?" I was a little angry that she would hide something so serious. She used to tell me everything.

"Well, I wanted to give you some room to breathe. With so much changing around here, I didn't want you to worry about me."

"But I always worry about you."

"Well, Bug, that's not always necessary. You have to trust that I know what's ahead, and I am not afraid. You shouldn't be afraid either. Everything is going to be okay."

She smoothed my hair and wiped the tears from my eyes. She had such bravery against this ugly, brutal disease. Her strength, though physically waning, was astonishing. I wanted to learn to emulate it, as if I too could come out on the other side unscathed.

10

WE SPENT THE NEXT FEW WEEKS adjusting the Watkins house to my mom's wheelchair needs. The hallway into the kitchen was too narrow, so Al built a new door off the living room. The bathroom that connected to her bedroom was too small to wheel into, so we installed more bars along the bedroom wall, which my mom used to stand and maneuver herself around the room. The front and back porches needed repair after years of weather damage, and Al built new ramps and decks on both sides so she could enjoy the garden, which I was religiously watering even though it was mostly weeds. My mom said Al was a godsend, joking that it was fate Jean should marry a carpenter. Jean said he did this kind of thing for fun, that he was a person who needed to stay busy.

My mom got pretty good at wheeling around, but there were some things we weren't going to be able to accomplish because of the size and layout of the old house. She accepted these limitations with grace and patience. Still, we tried to make it as comfortable as possible. I was going to town a lot more often on my own, mostly because the buildings in town were not all wheelchair accessible. We had made enough wasted trips, finding out too late that she couldn't go in, so I decided it would be best to handle some of the errands on my own. I made sure to pick up new books at the library for the both of us, so she would have fresh reading material at her bedside. She was devouring the stories at an impossible rate, saying that without the need to go grocery shopping, cook, clean, or even walk, reading was the only thing that kept her mind occupied during the long summer days. That, and writing her own book, which she hadn't seemed to lose her focus on. I was curious to know what it was she was typing away at, but I figured she'd tell me when she was ready.

I was reading a lot too, always at my spot by the creek. I hadn't seen Cali for a couple of weeks, and no little trinkets either. Still, I carried the rabbit's foot key chain and hoped for her return. Our secret friendship had been my lifeboat through the tumultuous changes with my family, my home, and my own self-discovery. I didn't realize how much I needed her until she was no longer there.

When I got back to the house that day after a morning out in the forest, I was surprised by how much our house had changed. I couldn't believe the difference a few upgrades could make. It almost didn't feel like ours.

"Hey Mom," I said, checking in on her in the study. Her red hair was shading her eyes and she was sitting perfectly still with her book laid across her lap. "Mom?"

She stirred, and my heart skipped a beat. I approached her and pulled her hair back. "Mom, are you okay?"

"Oh hi, Bug! Yes, I'm okay. I guess I just dozed off. This book is boring," she said, closing it.

"I'll get you some new ones tomorrow at the library."

"Sadie, I have to tell you something." She looked at me with sudden concern. "Your father called."

I was stunned. I didn't know what to say, so I waited for her to keep going.

"He apologized for taking so long to return my call."

"I didn't know you reached out."

"I didn't want to tell you about it until he responded."

She was hiding more from me. First the wheelchair, now the phone call. I thought I should start keeping a list but tried to put my anger aside. "What else did he say?"

"He said he'd love to visit. He said he could come up this weekend...on Saturday."

"That's two days from now. Why so soon?"

"Well, he said he could visit tomorrow, but I told him we had a doctor's appointment."

"But your physical therapy is on Monday."

"I was trying to buy us some time. I know you must be nervous."

I sat down and tried to imagine my father walking in the room at that moment, as if it were a normal thing to have him around. I couldn't do it. I had never been able to.

My mom looked uneasy, fidgeting with her fingernails. "He was very eager. He has been thinking about you for so long, he just needed to work up the courage. He doesn't want to wait."

"He thinks about me?" I still hadn't fulfilled my promise to ask her what really happened between them. But Aunt Jean didn't know that.

"He loves you, Bug," she said. "He always has. He is your father. But we can tell him to hold off until you're ready. I want to make sure you're comfortable first."

I felt sick, like I might keel over if I let myself think about it.

I didn't want him to visit. I wasn't ready. I had a million thoughts. What if he made my mom upset? What if he didn't recognize us? What if he didn't think I was all that great? Or worse, what if he did? I tried to tell myself I didn't care what he thought. I had everything I needed.

"I don't know. It's not a very good time."

"Sadie, I've been thinking a lot about this," she said. "I need to see him too. I need to apologize."

Now it was making sense. Gabe's return was bigger than just me and him. My mom wanted her reunion too. That's why she didn't tell me about calling him. She needed to be sure she was ready.

"What on Earth would you have to apologize for?"

"For kicking him out of our lives."

"Mom, you didn't do that. You didn't do anything wrong." But I didn't actually know whether or not that was true.

"Well, he didn't do anything wrong either. I want you to know that. Things might have gotten heated between us—we both said things we didn't mean—but he didn't do anything wrong."

"But that was so long ago," I said, anxious to pry. "Why didn't he come back if it was just a fight?"

"That's the thing you don't realize yet, Sadie. As you get older, time doesn't feel so linear. It feels like I just saw him yesterday, like I'm both stuck in time and being pushed forward at a thousand miles a minute."

"The law of inertia," I said, recalling a book I was reading on science and the universe.

"What?" she said, perplexed.

"I read about it in one of my books. Inertia is that feeling you get when you're driving in a car. You're sitting in one place, but the car is moving. That's why you can throw a ball in the car, and it won't fly back at you at sixty miles per hour."

"Gosh, you are smart," she said. "Time does feel like that sometimes."

"Well, it doesn't feel like that for me." I let my anger slip out. "He's missed my whole life."

"I'm sorry, Bug. But your dad will not do or say anything you don't want him to. I know it. Trust me, and remember, we're doing this together. I'll be with you the whole time."

"I'm not scared," I said, trying to sound brave.

"Of course, you're not."

SATURDAY MORNING ARRIVED, and I lay awake in my bed, staring at the sticky stars on my ceiling, still faintly glowing in the gray morning light, wondering how long they had been there. Who put them there? I began to question everything in my room. Where did my bed come from? Who bought me the stuffed bear I had slept with every night since I was little? I thought of my father doing all these things, as if he had never left, like he would open up the door and come in to wake me up any minute. It was a strange feeling, wondering what he would smell like, if he would hug me or not, if his hugs would be as good as my mom's or Aunt Jean's. The kind of hugs you felt safe in. I wondered if he liked mac-n-cheese as much as I did. I wondered how much of myself could come from him, never having known him.

I went downstairs, and my mom was already up in her chair. She was delicately applying a mauve lipstick, the one that brought out the green in her eyes. Then she combed through her faded curls with her fingers.

"Mama? What are you doing?"

"Oh, Bug!" She shuffled the makeup around, embarrassed. "I just thought I should look nice today. All things considered."

"You look pretty."

"Thanks, honey," she said as she pushed a fallen scarlet strand of hair out of her face. It had been so long since I last watched her get ready. "Are you ready for today?"

"I guess." But I didn't know how anyone could be ready to meet their father.

The four of us sat around, trying to occupy ourselves, unable to focus on anything other than our soon-to-be guest.

"How are you?" Al asked me, leaning in. He was so gentle with me.

"I'm okay, just nervous."

"You know, I think you're a great kid," he said. "Any dad would be lucky to be your dad."

"Really?"

"*Sí.* You are smart, and you take such good care of your mother. I had to take care of my mom too, and I know how hard it is."

"I'm sorry." I hoped for another one of his stories to calm my nerves. "What happened to her?"

"She was an old woman. She got diabetes and had a stroke. She needed lots of extra care," he said with sadness in his eyes. "She was an incredible woman though. She had so much wisdom and read the land. She always knew when we were going to have heavy rains days before anyone else. She knew which plants and flowers were safe to eat and which ones weren't. She made the most delicious food."

"I love identifying plants. Actually, I press them and put them in collections."

"I'd love to see them sometime," he said kindly.

"I'm sorry about your mom. I wish I could have known her."

"Well, in a way, you do. You see, she's always with me. So is my father." He put his palm to his chest. "Everyone you've ever loved is with you right now. Your father is always with you too. Trust me, he has not forgotten you, and he never will."

Al always had a way of saying just the right thing at the right time. I hugged him freely and openly, thankful to have him close by.

Just then, a black BMW pulled into our driveway. The windows were dark, and the luxury of his car clashed with the worn-down surroundings of our side of Juniper. Then a tall, bulky man stretched out of it. He had on a pullover and sporty sunglasses. He kept checking his cell phone and putting it back in his pocket, not aware that we were watching from inside. Aunt Jean opened the door and ushered him to come in. "We're in here!" she said across the lawn.

When he entered the house, his whole posture softened. Still, he towered above the rest of us. "Wow, it's like stepping back in time," he said in a deep voice. He kept his eyes fixated on Aunt Jean, unable to look at us. He was nervous. "Look at you! You're pregnant! When are you due?"

"In about four months," she said, giving him an awkward hug. "How was the drive?"

"Good, good, good," he kept saying, almost stuttering as he looked toward my mom. "Anna..."

Mom boldly wheeled up to him, and he leaned down to hug her. "It is so good to see you." She looked different in his company, more whole. I couldn't help but imagine what the two of them must have looked like back then, young and healthy. And then they both turned to look back at me. It was strange to see them, both of my parents, looking down at the little person they had created together.

I shot a quick glance at Al, and he tipped his chin down as if to say he had my back. Then I looked at my dad. Right in the eye. Drawn to him, I stood up and walked closer, feeling smaller with every step. Suddenly I was a young child again. The whole person I had come to be over the last few months fell away under his gaze. He had been a figment of my imagination, and now seeing him in real life was like entering a dream.

His eyes were glistening with tears. "Sadie," he said, reaching out his big arms and scooping me in.

I pressed my hands into the smooth nylon fabric of his pullover. "My beautiful girl. Look at you." His voice was soft, and he smelled like fresh leather. "You look just like your mother."

I was quiet, unsure of what to say.

"Do you know my name?" He was waiting to hear me speak.

"Gabe," I muttered.

"That's right. I'm Gabe Daniels, your dad."

"Dad," I echoed him, testing out the new word.

"How are you, Gabe?" my mom interjected, relieving the pressure in my ears.

"Well, I'm doing all right. I'm teaching at Ohio State, and I'm trying to finish up a new book."

"Good to hear," she said. "Why don't we go into the kitchen? Al is going to cook."

Gabe turned to Al and reached out his hand. "Gabe," he said.

"Álvaro," Al said, returning the handshake. "I am Jean's fiancé."

"Right on," Gabe said. "Nice to meet you."

The five of us made our way to the kitchen. My mom wheeled in from the bedroom and swept her chair gracefully under the table.

Gabe was taking note of the house. "I love all the changes you've made, Anna. It's so light in here."

"Oh, it's all been in the past couple of months. Al and Jean have really brought new life into the place. Can't say I noticed before, but now it feels so fresh and new, doesn't it?"

"It does," he said. "And look at the garden. It's beautiful!"

"Thanks," I said, chiming in.

"Did you do it all by yourself?"

"Well, we usually do it together, mom and I," I explained. "But this summer has been harder. That's all we could manage this year."

Gabe's expression shifted away from the flowers. "So, you'll be in sixth grade?"

"Yes. I have Mr. Foster."

"Blast from the past!" he said. "Rick Foster was my neighbor growing up! He was a couple of grades ahead of me, but sometimes we would hang out."

"I forgot about that," my mom said.

"Where did you grow up?" I asked.

"I grew up off Whitmore on the north side of town. I haven't been over there in ages. My parents and brothers have all relocated to Columbus."

"Did you know they're thinking about putting a Walmart in on the north side?" Aunt Jean chimed in.

"No, I did not. Not surprised, though. All in the name of progress, right?" he said. "What else has changed?"

There was a long pause. My mom looked to be struggling with a response. "Doesn't seem like a whole lot, I guess."

"Is Pip's still in business?" he asked.

"Of course," my mom said. "It wouldn't be Juniper without Pip's."

"What about The Joon?"

"Oh my gosh." My mom was blushing. "I haven't heard anyone talk about The Joon for ages."

"What's The Joon?" I asked.

"It was an old bar we used to hang out at," she said. "Near the police station."

"A clever spot to put a bar," Jean said. "Right under the cops' noses."

All three of them laughed.

"Do you remember that one time my brother snuck in and tried to get that older woman's number? The cops busted him almost immediately."

My mom started laughing, truly laughing. Then we all started laughing, even Al, who had been quiet that evening. It took several minutes for the commotion to die down.

Gabe gave out a long sigh. "Good times," he said, and the ice that had frozen over everyone for years was finally broken.

We all ate lunch, and then Jean and Al said they were going to go for a drive, leaving my mom and me with Gabe.

"How are you?" Gabe asked her. I stood up and started cleaning around them.

"I'm not so bad," she said, poking at the remnants of her lunch. "Got these new wheels a few weeks back." She rubbed her palm against the metal frame of her wheelchair. It was a manual wheelchair, all that our insurance would cover, and certainly noth-ing fancy. I sensed she was embarrassed by the condition of it.

"Anna, I'm so sorry to see you like this," he said. "I wish you would have called sooner."

My mom looked uncomfortable. "I didn't see the point."

"I could have sent money. I could have done so much."

"You have a life of your own now, Gabe. I didn't want to intrude. I've never seen you in that way. Like some kind of fall-back. We've made things work."

"Okay, but I would like to help now," he said. "What do you need?"

"Really, Gabe." She leaned back into her chair and crossed her arms over her chest. "We're fine."

Gabe looked like he had something he wanted to say, but it was stuck inside his throat. "Is it bad?"

"Is *what* bad?"

"I mean, are you going to make it out of the woods?"

What an odd expression, I thought, as if the woods were a bad thing. The woods were my haven. I was beginning to feel defensive, and my mom shot a glance at me as if to tell me *I've got this*. "Gabe, we're all getting along the best we can. Now, say what's on your mind."

"You know me so well," he said, looking down at his hands.

"Of course I do."

"I want to apologize." His voice cracked. "For everything."

My mom sighed and smoothed out her shirt. "I'm sorry too. For everything."

The exchange was terse, robotic, like they had both rehearsed so many ways to say something so impossibly simple. It was hard for me to stay focused on the dishes, and I felt like leaving the room. But my mom said we'd be next to each other the whole time, so I couldn't back out on her.

"You don't have to apologize, Anna. This was never about you. I had so much happening at school. My grades were slipping and every weekend I came home, I got more and more distracted. I reached a point where I had to decide whether I was going to stay in school or come home and be with you. It tore me apart for months. And then when you told me not to come back, which hurt at the moment, it was the release I needed. Thank you so much for that. But it doesn't negate the fact that I left my family, and it eats away at me every day. I feel like I live two lives. There are two people I could have become in that moment: the person I am now and the person I could have been if I had come home to you. I am always thinking about what my life would be like if things had gone differently."

My mom reached out, and they hugged. He held her so tight, his fingers in her hair, and he sobbed into her embrace. I had never seen a man cry. It felt like something secret, like I shouldn't have witnessed it. My mom, on the other hand, was expressionless. She gingerly pet his head like she pet mine.

"It's okay. It's okay," she repeated in a soft voice. "You didn't do anything wrong. I think about it too. But not like that. I don't imagine a scenario where you came home. I think about the life I could have had if I never had gotten this disease. I think about how you and I probably would have broken things off anyway. We were so young. I would have found a way to go to school, find work, marry someone, have more kids, move out of this old house. You have to understand that I fell out of love with you when I got this disease. I fell out of love with everything. So, we never would have made it, you see? You have to give yourself permission to let it all go."

Gabe was still crying when he leaned out of her arms and back in his chair. "Anna, that's the most heartbreaking thing I've ever heard. I hate seeing you like this."

"Well, frankly, Gabe, I hate seeing myself like this too. But honestly, it's only because, for the first time in ten years, I feel like I can see things clearly again. I may not have lived the life I had intended, but I have lived a beautiful life. Watching Sadie grow up has been my greatest joy, and if I had gone into a busy career, or married, or moved out of this house, I wouldn't have been able to see our child grow up into the smart, beautiful young girl she is today. She is my light and my best friend. She's everything I need, and when the time comes for me to part with this world, I won't have any regrets. I am at peace, Gabe, and you should be too."

Gabe seemed like he wanted to protest, but looking at my mom's face, she was telling the truth. "It's all gone so wrong."

"Not from where I am sitting. Everything happens for a reason. That's why I called. I wanted to see you and tell you it's all okay."

Their eyes landed on me.

"Sadie, I think you and your dad need to have a talk now, in private. Is that okay?"

I nodded, feeling queasy, and sat down next to him at the table.

"I'll just be in the other room," she said, wheeling herself away.

"Thanks, Anna," Gabe said. "For everything."

We waited for the door to shut and then Gabe turned toward me. "Sadie, I am sorry if I've made you uncomfortable. I don't usually cry like this."

"It's okay," I said, aware of all the empty space around us. "I cry sometimes too."

"You do?"

"Well, yeah, about a lot of things."

"Like what?"

"I cry when I can't see my friend. I cry when Mom is in pain. I cry when I think about what's coming."

"Oh, Sadie," he said, reaching out to grip my shoulder. For the first time, I noticed he wore a wedding band. "You are so brave for facing all of this head-on."

"I don't feel brave." I suddenly felt the empty space closing in, like the house might consume us whole. "I'm just going along with what everyone tells me. I have nightmares sometimes."

"I know how that feels. But I can tell you're doing an amazing job handling such a tough situation. It's not fair."

"I hate thinking about what's fair." Rage began boiling up inside me then, like I was going to burst. "I don't think it's fair that you got to leave. My mom might. But I don't."

"I know. I owe you an extra big apology."

Extra big apology. He was talking to me like I was a child.

"I know you won't understand." He was choosing his words carefully. "But seeing you all grown up reminds me how long I've been gone. It does not feel like ten years at all. I feel like I only just got out of school. But when I stand time up next to you, I realize I should have never let it go on this long."

"Do you have kids?" I asked abruptly.

124

"Well," he spoke softly. He was leaning in with his elbows on his knees. "Yes, I have a son. He turned one last month."

"Are you married to his mom?"

"Yes." He cleared his throat. "Her name is Julia."

"Does she know about me?"

"Yes, she does. She knows you're important to me. I met her four years ago when I was finishing up my master's. We got married two years ago. She has been urging me to visit you throughout our entire relationship. So, she is really happy I'm here."

"What's your son's name?"

"His name is Henry, after my dad."

"Do your parents know about me?" I continued to interrogate him.

"Yes, of course they do. But they aren't very loving or warm people. They were very much focused on my success. They were always talking about a better life for me and my brothers, your uncles. They're good people, but they aren't sentimental."

I was close to having all my questions answered, close to finishing this whole ordeal. I wanted nothing more than for him to leave, so I dealt my final blow. "Do you still love my mom?"

He leaned back in his chair and glanced back at the shut door like he knew my mom was on the other side listening. "I do, but not the way you're thinking."

"What do you mean?"

"Well, I will always love your mom. She was my first love, and nothing changes that. But I've changed, and I'm not the same man I was when I left you. I guess you could say I've grown up. Just because you're an adult doesn't mean you stop growing up."

I began to release myself from the conversation, from the shut-up box that had become our kitchen. Then one more question shot out so fast I couldn't stop it. "Do you still love me?"

"Ohhh, now that one is easy. I love you so much, Sadie Bug. So, so much. Do you know how much I loved you when you were a baby? Oh man, all of my friends at school thought I was nuts talking about a baby all the time. But I didn't care. I had pictures of you framed in my dorm room."

Thinking about him as someone else, someone who loved me, only made his words hurt worse. I couldn't listen to any more of it. In fact, I stopped hearing him after he used my mom's nickname for me. "How do you know about my nickname?"

"Sadie Bug?" he asked, and I nodded. "Well, that's silly. I made it up."

A huge rush came over me. So much of what I feared had just come true. Perhaps I was a little like him and some things stuck even without him around. He was with me the whole time, and I was with him, just like Al said. "I didn't know that."

"Yes, we started calling you Sadie Bug when we went into your room one morning and found you standing up watching a ladybug crawl along your crib. You were mystified by it. I said to you, 'That's a ladybug,' and you looked at me, and you pointed at yourself as if to say 'Me?' and I said, 'No, you're a *Sadie* Bug, that's a ladybug!' You were so smart, even then."

Sadie Bug and ladybug did sound very similar, I thought to myself and laughed. "I wish I could remember."

"Oh hey, it's okay. You know, we can make a lot of new memories now if you want."

I had been dreading this moment; I still did not feel ready.

126

I decided I needed to be honest. "I would like that, but not right now. There's too much going on right now. I start school soon, and my mom has so many appointments, and Aunt Jean's baby is coming."

"I understand." He looked disappointed. "I don't want to rush you into anything. Take your time, and when you're ready, I'll be here. I'm always with you, Sadie. I love you. I really do."

"I know," I said, and he leaned in and hugged me.

"Well, I think I should probably go. It's getting late, and I want to be back by bedtime."

"Where do you live?"

"I live in Bexley. It's a little town right next to the city. We have ice cream and a movie theater just like you do here. It's a nice place."

"I'd like to see it one day."

"You are always welcome to visit. I'll even come pick you up and take you down there myself. Henry would love to meet you."

I felt pressure building in my ears again.

"Whenever you're ready. The offer stands forever."

GABE LEFT BEFORE DUSK, and even after everyone had left the room and gone off to bed, I watched the spot where his black BMW had pulled out of the gravel driveway, as if he would rematerialize from the dust. I was feeling so much. I just wanted to talk to Cali. I thought if I ran out there now, I could be back before it got too dark to see my way home, never considering whether she would be out this late. I quickly threw on my sandals and made a mad dash for the forest. I ran right up to our spot by the creek. The mosquitoes were starting to come out and the sky was pink.

But Cali was there, sitting on the fallen oak, dangling her feet over the water. Golden shafts of light beamed down on her. She hopped off the tree when she saw me coming toward her.

"Cali!" I shouted. I ran up to her and hugged her, squeezing her little frame tightly.

"I missed you," she said.

"I know, I missed you too. I haven't been coming out as much. My dad visited today."

"I haven't been out here much either." There was a weight behind her words, but then her tone shifted. "You met your dad?"

I was so relieved to have my friend that I didn't notice the sun was setting. "Yes, it was so awkward," I began to ramble. "He cried a lot and my mom pet his head just like she does mine."

"My mom used to pet my head too." She scratched her scalp.

"He told me he has a wife and a son, and they know about me. For some reason, I thought he'd kept us a secret."

"Why would he do that?"

I thought about it then. "Well, kind of like you and me. We keep our friendship a secret."

"That's true. It's better that way."

"So, why haven't you been coming back here?" I asked, finally catching my breath.

"I don't know." She grew shy. "I got scared."

"What were you scared of?"

"I thought you weren't real anymore. I thought I made you up, like a dream."

"I felt that way too. I never see anyone out here. Never. So, when you showed up, I thought you must be lost."

She nodded her little head to agree.

"Well, I'm glad we're both here now." The sun was nearly gone. "Hey, I have an idea."

"What?"

"Let's carve our names into the tree." I pointed at the fallen oak. "That way every time we see it, we remember we were here."

"I like that idea!"

We searched around for a sharp rock, which didn't take Cali long. She found a perfect piece of slate already shaped into a wedge and began to carve her initial into the tree. I followed her "C" with a plus sign and an "S" and we left it like that.

"Should we add anything else?"

"No, I think it's perfect." We stood back and stared at our handiwork.

"Now we won't forget each other. Never ever. This is our best friend tree. This deep in the woods, no one will ever find it."

"I should be getting back," she said. "It's almost dark. My dad will be worried."

"I know, me too. It's your turn."

Cali closed her eyes and started to count. I sprinted off, and the last thing I remember was tripping over a log—a log I didn't recall being there before—and smacking my head on the hardened earth. I rolled onto my back and saw small white lights dancing across the sky like a million shooting stars rattling in my skull.

11

I WAS SAILING ON THE WATER with a young woman whose appearance kept shifting. One moment it was my mom, the next Aunt Jean, and the next Cali. All of their faces swirled together, transfiguring into a solitary being. The waters were murky, furiously whipping the coast. Then a colossal wave nearly toppled the boat, and we struggled to regain control. When the wave's crest had receded, the shape-shifting spirit went out to the deck and started to climb over the railing, preparing to jump. I watched in horror, unable to let go of the wheel, screaming for her not to jump, but no words came out of my mouth. The waves continued to crash down around us. Water flooded the deck. Before I could steady my focus, the spirit had disappeared, and the water grew frighteningly still. I released the wheel, now nothing more than a stationary toy, and ran out to look over the railing, only to find I was no longer on a sea at all; it was just darkness. There were no waves, there were no stars, and everything around me had vanished. It was like I was inside of a vacuum on an abandoned plane of existence. I began pinching myself. *Wake up!* I shouted, trying to find my way back.

"Wake up!" said a distant voice. "Sadie, wake up!"

The voice and a face came into focus. It was Al. He looked concerned. Other voices were scattered around the woods, bouncing off the trees. For a split second, I thought they were the voices of the lost souls of all the villagers Cali and I had dreamed up.

"*Ay, Dios mío*," the voice rang out. "Sadie, are you okay?"

"Al?" I recognized his accent.

"*Sí*, Sadie. It's me. We've been looking for you for hours."

"Sadie, oh my God!" a woman shouted.

"She's okay, Jean," he said. "She fell and must have passed out."

Jean shuffled over and picked up my head and rested me on her chest. I sank into her warmth. "We've been looking everywhere. We've scoured the entire forest. All the way up the creek, down the trails, off the trails, were you here the whole time?"

"I was with Cali and then it got too dark, and I couldn't see my path home," I said. "I must have fallen. What time is it?"

"It's 3:00 a.m.," she said.

Then another voice approached us, and a harsh light beamed across my face, making my head throb. It was an officer, and he made his way over to us. "We found her," he said over his walkie. "She is safe. Tell the mother." He hooked his walkie back into his belt.

"Young lady, you scared the bejesus out of us. Were you hurt? Let's take you to the medic."

"I'm fine." But my head was still swimming. A large knot was forming above my hairline, pulsating in pain.

The three of us and the officer walked quickly toward the house. When we got inside, my mom cried out. "Sadie! Where were you?"

"I fell. I'm sorry."

"I was so worried," she said, stubbing out the butt of her cigarette in a tray full of dozens more. "We called the police and they've been searching for you for hours. I felt so helpless."

It seemed like hundreds of people were on the lawn and in the house, crawling around like ants. Then a woman in a white uniform came near us and sat me down at the kitchen table. After checking my heart rate and temperature, she shined a light in my eyes and started poking and prodding across my body.

"You have a concussion. I think you're going to be okay," said the medic. "But we can take you in to run some tests just to make sure."

"No," my mom said. I knew we couldn't afford more medical bills.

"All right," she replied. "Just ice that lump on your head. And *don't* fall asleep."

"Thank you," I said. "I won't."

"Why were you running around in the dark?" she asked.

"We've had a very eventful day," my mom interjected, looking defeated. "I should have kept an eye on her. But I fell asleep."

"Sadie, the officers want to know who your friend is, the one you've been hanging out with," Aunt Jean chimed in.

"Her name is Cali." I applied an ice pack to my head. "She lives near here."

"How old is this woman?" the officer with the walkie asked. The EMT began packing up and my mom followed her out of the kitchen, weakly wheeling behind her.

"She's a girl," I said, feeling dizzy again. "She's younger than me."

"Does she have any family?" he continued. "Anyone we might be able to contact?"

"She has a dad. But I don't know his name."

"Do you know her last name?" The officer continued.

"No, it's just Cali, and it's a made-up name anyway," I said, getting increasingly frustrated. "I want to go to bed."

"You can't go to sleep," Jean said. "Answer the questions for us. Please, Say."

"Almost done," the officer said. "Do you remember what she was wearing?"

"No. She's usually barefoot though," I said. "Is she missing too or something?"

"We're just trying to get the facts straight," the officer said, aggressively scrawling notes onto a small pad.

"Am I in trouble?" I asked.

"Sadie, you're not in trouble. We are," Jean said. "We lost you, and they need to make sure you're okay."

After a few more minutes of questions, the officers packed up and we followed them as they headed out the door. Everything was happening so quickly.

"Sadie, you know you can't stay out in the forest that late," my mom snapped at me as we watched the crew load up their trucks. "Anything could have happened out there, and I'm not able to go out and look for you like this."

I knew she was talking about her chair. I thought about how helpless she must have felt, how her helplessness made me feel helpless too. "I am fine on my own," I snapped back at her, hurt and frustrated.

"It's still early. Maybe you should go back to bed," Al

suggested, putting a hand on Jean's back. "You both should get some rest. I'll stay up with her."

Al and I waited in the living room while the house and the lawn cleared out, all the ants back to their holes. When the house was empty, we sat on the couch watching as the sun began to rise, flooding the house with yellow streaks of light. He changed my ice pack.

"How's it feel?" he asked.

"Like I got hit by a truck."

"Was it something to do with your dad?" he asked gently. "Why you went out there, I mean."

I nodded. "I just wanted to clear my head."

"You know you could have come to me," he said. "I would have been happy to listen."

I paused, looking at his kind familiar face. He looked exhausted. "I'm sorry," I said. "It's a lot all at once. You, Jean, the baby. Now my dad. It was just me and Mom for so long."

"We all love you, Sadie," he said. "We are all here for you."

I didn't know how to take this. Part of me assumed the parade of people entering my life was merely here to see my mom, to say their goodbyes. And when my mom finally did leave, I'd be left on my own. But now it made sense. They were preparing for the inevitable, carving out space so the stray could have somewhere to go. I never thought about what would happen if my mom were to die, but at this moment it all became clear. These decisions were being made about my life because my mom was dying, and soon.

Later that morning, Aunt Jean switched places with Al, and he returned to their bedroom to sleep. She and I sat quietly on the couch, neither of us quite sure what to say.

"I'm sorry for scaring you," I finally uttered into the silence.

"I'm sorry I left you and your mom with Gabe," she replied. "Did he say something to you?"

"Not exactly." I hesitated. "He was telling me how I could come to visit him in Bexley and meet his son, and I got overwhelmed. I wanted to see Cali, I thought she might be able to help. She always knows exactly what to say to get my mind off things."

"Honey, can you tell me more about Cali?"

"I guess so," I said. "What do you want to know?"

"Well, how old is she?"

"I don't know, she's smaller than me."

"So, maybe ten?"

"Maybe younger."

"And what does she look like?"

When I tried to create a picture of Cali in my mind, all that would come up was that horrid dream of the shape-shifting woman. It was as if, once again, Cali wasn't real, that she was just someone I made up. I began to question myself, my head throbbing. "Sometimes my memory of her fades as if I haven't seen her for a hundred years, like I have to dig her up out of my mind like a fossil that's been buried for a very long time. Then when I do see her again, it's like I never forgot her at all. Is that weird?"

"I think you may have just hit your head really hard." She reached out to inspect the bump on my head. "And what do you two do together?"

"We mostly play by the creek. You might know the spot. The clearing, where the fallen oak is? We play pretend games and treasure hunt. We play hide-n-seek. We go on adventures."

"She sounds like a good friend," she said. "But Sadie, you can't go out that late anymore. Something really bad could have happened. Something bad *did* happen."

"I know. I'm sorry I scared all of you."

"You know, when your grandma took her own life…" She paused, her strained face looking down at her belly. "She did it out there. She did it in the forest."

"Yes, I know," I said, recalling our conversation a couple of months back. "Aunt Jean, I wouldn't do that."

"I saw her body as they brought it out of the woods." Tears welled in her eyes. "It didn't look anything like my mom."

"I didn't know you saw her," I said. "That's horrible."

"It was horrible. Your mom and I used to play out there by the creek all the time. But after seeing my mom like that, I thought the woods were cursed. I was only twelve years old, the same age you are now. Going out there tonight to find you was the first time I had been back in more than twenty years, and I didn't know what I was going to find."

"I'm sorry I made you go back." The guilt I felt was causing the pain to grow worse. "I didn't mean to fall."

"It's okay. If I'm going to live in this house again, I have to face it. You helped me do that. You reminded me that being in the woods, in nature, is the safest place in the world. Usually…" she said, looking at the ice pack on my head. "Sometimes I think that's why my mom did it there. I think she did it in the one place where she felt safe from all the madness of the outside world, where she felt most at peace."

"Really?"

"Yeah, she would play with your mom and me all the time

there. She'd say we didn't have much, but we had a castle in the woods."

"A castle?"

"Well, you know, it didn't make sense to me either when she said that. But now, I realize, it is quite like a cathedral when you first enter it, with the ancient trees high above you. And Leaky Creek is kind of like its moat."

"It *is* kind of like a moat." I giggled.

"Sadie, I want you to show this baby girl the forest for me. She's going to need someone to watch out for her, to be her friend. Can I count on you?"

"Yes," I said, honored by her request. "I will protect her and show her everything there is to know about our castle in the woods."

I couldn't decipher what ached more that morning, my heart or my head. I recalled what my dad told me about always growing up, and I thought about how my mom and aunt were just like me. They were each limited in their own ways. My mom because of her chair, and my aunt because of her past. I forced them to confront those limitations when I fell in the woods and, in the process, created more for myself. I realized all of these new people in my life loved me, and that love now formed a responsibility in me, a responsibility to be cautious, to think about all of them before I made reckless decisions.

Later that morning, Al came back down and started cooking breakfast. The three of us ate together and tried to forget the scene in the house just a few hours prior.

"I'm going to check on Mom." I went into the bedroom and found her sitting up in bed. "How are you feeling?"

"I should be asking you that," she said.

"I'm fine, Mom."

"What happened with your father last night? You two were fine when I left the room."

"He wants me to visit him," I said, unable to come up with a better answer, to explain how the room had closed in on me during my conversation with him. How I felt like I needed to run out of there before my head exploded. How I knew I needed to talk to Cali and it would all feel better. I rubbed the bump at my hairline.

"And you don't want to do that?" She could tell there was more to it.

"Well, I do…I think…But not right now. I don't want to leave you."

"Bug, visiting your dad would not be the same as leaving me. That's not how it works."

"I know." I was growing frustrated by all that I could not say to her. "But I don't want to go there any time soon."

"Well, that's okay. You don't have to. But one day you should. I want you to know him. His family is your family, okay?"

"Okay."

"He's not so bad, right?"

"He's all right…He cries a lot."

We both began laughing. My mom looked relieved at that moment, but I worried the stress I had put on her had done too much damage. "He told me you never stop growing up."

"I'd say there's some truth to that. I think what he means is that we never stop learning about ourselves, about the world. There's always room to grow."

"Sounds like a lot."

"Well, it can be." She stroked my hair carefully. "But that's what life is all about. You can't be afraid to take on new experiences or you'll get stuck. I was stuck for a long time…" Her voice trailed off and her eyes went somewhere else.

"Are you stuck now?"

"No, not anymore," she said, snapping back. "Quite the opposite. I feel free, like I'm floating away."

"Is it scary?"

"It is, but only because I am going somewhere new."

I WENT OUT TO THE WOODS that afternoon to try to recount my steps. I swore I had tripped over a tree, but when I returned to the spot where I had fallen, there was only a decrepit old trunk just off the trail that looked like it had fallen twenty years ago. There was moss growing over it, and the wood fell to pieces in my hands. The spot was close to the path, as if I had been running parallel to it. If I had been ten feet over, I would have made it home without any issues. Without Cali, the forest was just sticks and dirt. But with her it was different, more magical, as if it really was our castle. As if dangers lurked beyond it, monsters and dragons, and things so strange they could only be found in dreams.

I wandered over to our spot by the creek and saw our initials in the oak. The C and the S had looked so vibrant in the grain of the massive tree last night, but now they were faded and barely visible. Clearly, I thought, we didn't carve deep enough. I looked for our sharp piece of rock so I could touch it up, but it was nowhere to be found. I pulled out my rabbit's foot and used the keyring to etch back over our initials. There, I thought, now it looked fresh and new again. Time wasn't going to stop, and I was just going to keep growing. Some part of me needed to remain here or I'd lose myself entirely.

I didn't expect to see Cali. Something told me she had also been out too late. I hoped she made it home, wherever her home was. When I thought about Cali in any other context, going to school or the market, the images were fuzzy. It was as if she only existed when she was in the woods with me, like I was the imaginary one.

I had a sinking feeling I shouldn't be spending so much time in the forest; I was needed back home. My mom, Aunt Jean, and Al were probably so afraid. I couldn't believe how ridiculous it was that I not only got lost in the woods but that I hurt myself doing it. I was supposed to be safe in the forest, among the mother oaks, so why had they betrayed me? I decided I wouldn't go back for a few days, and I left the rabbit's foot on the log above the initials as a sign to Cali that I was okay. I hoped she would understand the symbolism, that this wasn't a message of goodbye, just a see-you-later. As I made my way back to the house, I thought about my mom and how distant I felt from her. She was going somewhere new, she said, and I knew the place she was going didn't include me. My heart felt like a frigid little stone at the bottom of a well, never to be touched or seen again. If this was how it felt to lose someone you loved, I didn't want to get close to anyone ever again, especially not my father.

As I exited the woods and crossed Leaky Creek, I took a look back at the tall pines. The same trees that always seemed to invite me in looked like they were guarding the forest, like an impenetrable wall I couldn't pass.

12

A FEW WEEKS PASSED, and the last gasps of summer were permeating everything. The days were long and sweltering and the nights offered no relief. It was the time of year when my body yearned for crunchy leaves, hot cocoa, and most of all, snow. But I knew we were months away from that. Still refusing to go into the woods, I buried myself in other tasks.

I slipped into a nice routine with Al in the mornings. He and I would prepare breakfast and tea, and he would bring his tray up to Jean. Her belly had doubled in size, and she was waddling more than walking. She complained of swollen ankles and spent a lot of time lounging because of it. So, Al would bring Jean her breakfast, and they'd pass a couple of hours together, laughing and whispering, no doubt about the baby and the joy it would bring. I would bring my mom her breakfast and try to spend time with her too. I had resolved to spend as much time with her as possible, not because she needed me, but because I needed her. She was the only thing that made me feel like I wasn't slipping away, even though that's exactly what she was doing. She no longer got out of her chair, except to get into bed. Her legs trembled fiercely every time she tried, and she would say something like, "What's the point, anyway?" which always made me cringe. She was so casual about her circumstance. It became too much for me one morning, and I asked her why.

"I have made peace with it," she said, about her disease. "Can't go back now."

"But how can you make peace with something so..." I searched for the right word. "Brutal."

"Brutal?" she retorted. "I don't see disease as brutal. It's a fact of life, Bug. Everything must go at some point. It's the way we go that sometimes makes it seem so harsh. I honestly don't remember a day when I wasn't in pain. I don't remember what it's like to dance or run. And I don't miss those things either. If anything, I'm just happy I was once capable of those things. I loved living the life I did, to feel everything I've felt. To create everything I've created. I want the same for you one day."

"I don't think I can do any of it," I said. "I feel like I'm inside of a shell, a little tiny seed buried in the earth."

Her face deepened into a frown when I said this. "Seeds grow, they always do. It might not seem like it now, but you'll soak everything in, and you'll bloom. You'll live a full life, Sadie. I know it."

I couldn't imagine how I could possibly make it to the other side of my life, the side without my mom in it. It felt like an impossible gap to jump. I needed more time. I needed everything to stand still. But things would inevitably shift again soon. School started in a couple of weeks, and at times I felt excited because I knew the classroom would be a welcome distraction from the longing I had to return to the forest. But every time I looked out at the tree line, I shriveled up inside. I now equated the woods with danger. *Don't go in there or your mom will die*, my thoughts screamed. When I had a fleeting concern about Cali, I hardened over like the bark of a tree before winter. *You don't need friends. You don't need anybody.*

13

SCHOOL WAS A WEEK AWAY when Al presented me with an intriguing idea. We were making breakfast, moving around each other in the kitchen like synchronized swimmers. We had it all perfectly timed; our legs danced as our arms floated from the microwave to the cupboard to the stove to the sink. I thought it would probably be an impressive performance for a spectator.

"I think we should go to the mall, you and me," he said, stirring the oatmeal with a wooden spoon.

"The mall?" I repeated, pulling the hot cups of water out of the microwave.

"*Sí*. We need things for the baby, and you need things for school."

"I guess you're right." I lazily plopped the tea bags in the cups. English breakfast, like always.

"Want to go this afternoon?"

"Okay," I said, handing him his cup. "Just you and me?"

"Mm-hmm," he said smoothly, pouring the oatmeal into the bowls.

I hadn't been to the mall in over a year. Between the back-and-forth trips to the hospital and the fact that our Ford had broken down, there simply wasn't a good reason to make the trek. But Al was right—I needed things. Last year's shoes were too small, and my backpack had a broken zipper. I thought about the girls at school and their name-brand clothes. I wouldn't be able to keep up with their trends, and I wished so badly I could go to school without worrying about how I looked. But I was a short, noodle-thin kid. My hair always looked like it needed to be brushed, and I rarely found clothing that didn't have a stain or a rip somewhere on it. Most of the time it didn't matter, but my anxiety about the first day of school was getting to me all the same.

Al drove us in his truck, and we parked outside the JCPenney, already crawling with people. Women had armfuls of clothing, and their young children lagged behind, looking miserable. Groups of teenagers hung out by the food court, and men were walking so fast they might as well have been running to get out of there. A polished-looking man with a suave haircut tapped Al on the shoulder and asked him if he had a few minutes. Al, not understanding the setup he was about to find himself in, nodded. The man jumped into his pitch about hand lotion. Then he took Al's hand and began rubbing the lotion into his cracked carpenter's calluses. Al was perplexed by this man dancing with his hand and didn't know what to say. He looked back at me with a desperate expression that said, "Save me," and I swiftly jumped in and said to the lotion man, "Sorry, we're not interested."

As we quickly walked away from the lotion man, Al held out his greased-up hand. "Honestly, that was pretty good stuff."

I laughed and told him we'd get him some Jergens the next time we went to Beuhler's. Then we passed the store all the girls would be shopping at. I gazed inside but dared not enter. It was dark, and the scent of artificial flowers overwhelmed my nose. Music was blasting from the entrance, and a lone woman stood outside in extremely short shorts.

"You look like a model!" she said to me.

"Me? No. No way," I said, blushing.

"Hey, why not?" Al said, patting my back. "Want to go inside?"

"No, not really." I shifted my body away from the entrance.

"Didn't you say you needed clothes?" he pried.

"Yes, but not from here. It's too expensive."

"*Qué tontería!*" He exclaimed. "Silly!"

"Al, I don't think this place is for me."

"Are you sure?" Then he walked inside, past the giant palm trees, and was out of sight. I had no choice but to follow him.

The walls were neatly lined with clothing, folded and sized perfectly. I ran my hands over a stack of T-shirts with the store's logo written across the front.

"Do you like that one?" Al asked.

"It's very… pink."

"Well, how about this one?" He pointed to a dark gray V-neck.

"Really, Al, it's too much."

"I want you to look nice on your first day of school."

I held the V-neck in my hands. The soft cotton felt like luxury. "I'll get this one then."

He took the shirt straight to the register and bought it. As we walked around the rest of the mall, I got to carry around the brown bag and felt so special. I had never owned anything so nice. When we were done shopping, Al bought us pizza in the food court, which he did not seem to like one bit.

"You don't like it?" I asked him.

"No, no, no, no." He pushed his plate toward me. "All yours."

I laughed and happily took his plate. "Thank you for taking me to the mall."

"It's no problem." He shifted in his seat. "I notice you haven't been going to the woods since that night."

No one in the house had talked about the night I fell in the woods until now. It was swept under the rug as if it never happened. I was uncomfortable bringing it up, but I knew I owed him an explanation. "It's not the same."

"I understand," he replied. "Shortly after my mom died, I couldn't do anything I loved either. I wanted to lock myself in my house and never leave."

"I'm afraid if I'm not near her..." I struggled to finish my sentence. "She's going to leave without saying goodbye."

"Oh, Sadie. She's not going to do that. You need to free yourself from those thoughts."

"I can't. It's all I think about."

"What about your friend?"

"I don't have any friends."

"Sí, yes, you do," he said. "Cali?"

I looked at him and saw how much he cared. But I wanted him to stop. "Cali isn't real," I lied. "I made her up."

"Why would you make her up?"

"Because I wanted her to be real. I wanted a friend."

Al's eyebrows furrowed, and he looked stern. "I know this

time must be confusing for you. But you also have to see the good that is happening. The baby will be here soon, and school has so many possibilities. How about joining a sports team, maybe?"

"Ha! What sport? I suck at everything."

"I've seen you climb trees. You're strong."

"I'm small," I corrected him. "No one is going to be intimidated by me. Besides, sports require money...and parents."

Al looked at me for a moment, then smiled. "I can teach you how to play *fútbol.*"

"Football is for boys."

"No." He shook his head. "I mean soccer. We call it fútbol where I'm from."

"Oh, right." I thought about it for a moment. "Do you think I'd be good at it?"

"I think you're a natural leader and would be great at offense. A forward or a striker, maybe."

"I don't know what that means, but I'll take your word for it."

"You know, I'd make sure you got to every game, and I'd help you with your training."

"I don't know, Al." I folded my arms. "I've never thought about it before."

"Well, just go to school next week, and let me know. I think you'd love it."

I finished eating the forsaken pizza, and we left the mall. When we got home, Jean was on the front porch fiddling with an electric fan.

"It's hot, but I can't sit in bed anymore. Did you two have fun?"

"I got everything I need for school! Al got me everything!"

Jean smiled and kissed Al who was in the midst of lugging our bags into the house. "Everything?" she asked him, smirking.

"Everything!" I shouted.

Inside, my mom was in the living room. She had wheeled herself in front of the TV and was watching the evening news. I hated the news. The anchors always looked like paintings with their makeup all caked on, and the stories droned on. Troops killed in Iraq, a hurricane about to hit Florida, the presidential election, and the debates that ensued. It was never anything good. Even when it was supposed to be good news, like a deer being rescued from a swimming pool, it still made me sad. The deer only got stuck because it thought the pool was a pond. It was just thirsty.

That night, the four of us ate dinner together, and I regaled them with the story of Al and the lotion man. We were all laughing so hard. Still full of the food court pizza, I didn't touch my dinner. But I did take a moment to appreciate the food, the night, enjoying time with Al and Jean and my mom. I tried not to think about how many more nights we had like this before everything changed. I tried to let the happiness fill me, but it poured down the well, so far down, like I might never be full again.

I SAT IN THE HOUSE watching the forest, wanting to go in and enjoy the last quiet moments of summer break. I thought about Cali. It was as if she were luring me in. Her little hum reverberated in my head. So much of this summer felt like it was all in my head. I spent so much time dwelling on the inevitability of everything, my mom's decline, my dad's return, and my aunt's baby. Everything was flying at me full-force, and I'd been barely equipped for any of it. The pressure to stay close by was intense, as if leaving the house might lead to ruin. Yet all I wanted was to run away, straight through the forest, until my lungs gave out.

I watched the minutes pass on the digital clock on our stove, which was mistakenly set four minutes into the future, mocking me. I thought I could just go to bed and wake up the next day. Then, Al came in with a big black-and-white soccer ball. He was grinning so wide, and it took everything in me to smile back. I had hoped he wasn't serious about me playing sports. The thought of taking any kind of field and turning it into a game sounded preposterous. I really had lost all my childhood imagination.

"Time for your first practice!" he said gleefully.

"I don't know," I replied.

"Something better to do?"

I couldn't argue with him. This, too, was inevitable. We went out to the yard and Al stood against the tree line of the forest.

"You're going to kick the ball with the inside of your foot," he said, tapping the bridge of his foot. "Like this," and he sent the ball whizzing toward me.

I went to retrieve it, feeling awkward as I ran. My arms flopped and my head was dangling too low. But I felt the ball with the toe of my shoe and kicked it. It zagged into the creek, and I immediately felt red hot to the touch.

"Don't worry about it!" he said. "Use the inside of your foot, remember? It gives you more control over the direction of the ball. Try again." He kicked the ball back to me with another effortless motion.

I tried again. And again. And again. I did get better at aiming for my target, which Al said was his feet. We were teammates, and it was our mission to get this ball to the goal together. After a sweaty practice session, we went inside, and I was delighted to see a whole hour had passed by on the stove clock.

"How are you feeling about school tomorrow?"

"Fine, I guess," I lied.

"Jean calls them jitters," he said. "Funny word. She had them when she was flying home to you guys. Did you know that?"

"No," I said, relieved he was switching the subject.

"Oh yeah, real bad jitters," he made a freezing, teeth-chattering motion, and it made me giggle.

"Those are shivers, not jitters," I said. "But all the same."

"Well, she wanted you to be happy when she saw you. She wants to be here, to make this work. And so do I."

Now he looked like he had the jitters, as if he were asking for my approval. I didn't know what to make of it. Adults seemed to live by their own rules. I didn't think I had a say in how anything went. I sat silently, shooting glances at the stove clock.

"Do you want me to stay?" he asked.

Al was possibly the only man I had ever *really* known. Boys were an enigma to me, and I realized Al was the first man I had ever formed a relationship with, though I wasn't sure what kind it was. Sometimes it felt like he was trying to be my dad, and other times it felt like he wanted to be my friend. But I looked into his eyes and all I saw was love. The labels didn't matter.

"Yes, I want you to stay. This is our home: yours, Aunt Jean's, the baby's, and mine," I said, shooting another glance at the stove clock. Four minutes into the future. The future where there was a picture of us, and I realized I forgot to put my mom in it. But I didn't correct myself. I told myself I was being realistic.

"Well, that's good to hear," he said shyly. "Because I want to stay too."

"Will you miss Costa Rica?"

"No. There's not much for me there. My parents are gone, and the rest of my family is spread out. I only moved back to take care of my mom, and when she died, I was just waiting. I didn't know what I wanted to do next until your aunt came along. She spoke about everywhere she had ever been, but she never spoke about Juniper. Then, one day I asked her about it, and it's like her eyes went dark. She showed me a small box she carried around, and it had all these letters in it. It had pictures that you drew, too. You and your mom mean so much to her."

So, Aunt Jean had her own treasure trove. That made me feel special, like our bond was nothing new, like she had been with me all along. "Did she want to come back here?"

"Well, when we found out she was pregnant, we knew we didn't want to settle our family in Costa Rica. But there wasn't anywhere else we wanted to go either. Then, your mom sent that letter, and I never knew what it said, but she told me she needed to go to Ohio. It was the first time I saw her eyes light up when speaking about it. She looked so sure, and I knew she was ready. I told her to go right away. I didn't want her to lose that spark. So, she bought a ticket and was on a plane in less than twenty-four hours. I told her I'd catch up. You know, I didn't just shut down my business. I sold my apartment. I sold everything. I never intended to go back."

"So, you really want to live in Ohio?"

"More than anything." He looked like he had one more thing to say.

"What is it?"

"I think it would be good for you to go back to the forest."

I shook my head. "No way."

"Sadie, you have to trust yourself."

Going out in the forest felt impossible. Everything felt impossible. "I can't."

"You love it out there. I could tell how much you wanted to go in when we were practicing today."

"But..."

"I promise nothing is going to happen here. Everything will be okay. Do you trust me?"

I may not have been able to trust myself, but I realized then that I could trust Al, and that did count for something. I looked out back to the tree line, the mother oaks calling me in.

Al reached out and put a hand on my shoulder. "You will be okay."

He was right. The forest was my sanctuary. It was time I took it back.

I HOVERED AT THE BRIDGE, hesitant to go in. I had built up so much resentment toward this place. I felt it had betrayed me, pushed me out, and told me I didn't belong there. Then I noticed a patch of Queen Anne's lace on the other side of the creek. I laughed inwardly; the forest was always trying to tell me something. When I was younger, I'd often wished I was small enough to sleep atop one of those delicate white blooms. Its softness was comforting, a sign of safety. I remember picking them for my mom one year, and she told me how they were her mom's favorite, how they symbolize Heaven.

I crossed Leaky Creek and instantly felt held, warmed by the familiarity of the mother oaks after so long apart. I reached the clearing and my spot by the creek where everything was just the same as it had always been. The birds were chirping overhead, singing just to me. I took a seat and marveled at the trickle of the creek, how it could still push on with so little feeding it.

Then, I heard rustling behind me and knew all at once what, or rather *who*, was there.

"Please come out," I whispered. "I'm sorry."

Cali revealed herself from behind the Wishbone. She took a seat beside me. "I waited for you."

"You did?"

"M-hmm," she said. She seemed hurt. "Why didn't you come back?"

"I had a bad fall the last time I was out here with you. I realized I needed to be more careful. I have to think about my mom. She needs me."

Cali didn't look anything like the girl I knew just a few weeks ago. She looked deeply sad, and that sadness had aged her. She wasn't snapping back into the proud, spritely kid I once played with. She was changed, and then I realized, I was too.

"Cali," I tried to find words. "I know we don't have much more of summer left, but what would you say about making the most of it?"

"I'd like that a whole lot."

We spent the rest of the day together, going deeper into the forest than either of us had gone before. We slowly tracked our movements, bending branches and documenting odd trees and rocks, anything to help us navigate our way back. The farther away we walked, the more intense the challenge became. I started to wonder what might happen if either of us got hurt. I felt simultaneously responsible and also like I had no chance, if something did happen, of ever finding my way back. We were a very long way from the old house when I finally felt like I couldn't take another step. "We'll get lost."

"No, we won't."

"How do you know?"

Cali pointed to the trickle of the creek. "Because we've been following the creek the whole time."

She was right. Although we had documented our every move, we had a backup plan all along, or rather, Cali had a backup plan. Time and time again, this small child with a made-up name surprised me with her wit and fortitude. Her confidence in herself and her beliefs was not just that of a naive child, but of someone who had true inner strength. She trusted herself. She trusted the forest. If only I could emulate her. "I'm ready to go back."

"Just a little farther," she pushed. It was as if she didn't want to go home.

I followed her deeper into the woods, unsure of how much farther we could go before we reached the other side. Suddenly the sounds started to shift. The trees swayed a little heavier, leaves swishing together like waves in an ocean. The bird calls echoed. And I noticed a slight ridge just ahead.

Cali and I kept walking, more cautious with every step. Then we saw it—a ravine, and just beyond that a large system of caves. Cali immediately ran in, leaving behind the stream without a care in the world.

"Cali!" I shouted after her. "Where are you going?"

Cali's figure grew smaller and smaller as she ran deeper into the dwelling. Then I heard her scream. *Oh no.*

This was why I hadn't come back. I knew I should have stayed home. But it was too late now. I had to follow her. She needed my help.

I ran into the large rocky expanse; it was cool down here and the walls were closing in. I felt claustrophobic then, like I might be sick. I called out for Cali with no response and kept moving. *Please let her be okay.*

Then the caves began to open into a wide expanse, and there, standing in the center of it was Cali, arms outstretched as a thin clear veil of water fell around her.

"It's a waterfall!" Cali shouted. "A real waterfall!"

I couldn't believe it. It was beautiful. It was all ours. I dropped my pack, took off my shoes, and ran toward her. Cali let me take her place inside the water, cold as it struck my back. I felt invincible. I realized it wasn't the forest that had betrayed me, it was my own fear stopping me. The forest was telling me what I should have understood all along. I needed to trust myself, to listen to my intuition.

By the time we made it back to the clearing, the day was nearly over. The peach sun cast down on the newly bloomed goldenrod, a reminder that fall was coming. A sign of new beginnings. I hugged Cali tightly. Her friendship that summer, and the memories we made, were my greatest gift.

GOLDENROD

Solidago ohioensis

14

IT WAS THE MUCH ANTICIPATED first day of school. I was wearing my new shirt from the mall, and I felt as good as any kid could after three long months at home. Mr. Foster was the teacher everyone wanted that year, so I already had a good feeling about my class. We were envied among the other kids in our grade, and I hoped that bond might unite us.

I found my seat near the back. They were always alphabetized for the first few days until the teacher learned our names. As a Watkins, I sat second to last next to Jacob Williams, who hadn't changed much over the summer. But still, not seeing someone for so long changes your perspective of them.

"Hi, Jacob," I said quietly as I took my seat.

"Hey, Sadie," he replied with melancholy. Some kids hated the first day just as much as I did.

Mr. Foster came into the room and everyone's back straightened. We all looked around at each other smiling. He was our star!

"Welcome back, kids!" he said enthusiastically. "I hope you all had a wonderful summer."

With that, the learning commenced. The day went by slowly, and I couldn't help but think about Cali, about our final days in the woods spent playing and exploring.

When the class let out for lunch, I snapped out of it and was filled with instant dread. Without a friend, I was unsure where to sit while I ate. All the kids had their groups, and I never knew if I was wanted in any of them. Some of the girls would sit together, and all they wanted to do was talk about the other girls, gossips of the worst degree. Others would talk about TV, movies, and books, mostly anime, which I had no interest in. Some were sporty, and it didn't seem to matter what sport they played, but even though I still planned on trying out for soccer, I never felt I could belong with them. Then there were the brainy kids. They were the good ones, the nice ones, and I admired them for never gossiping and making others feel bad about themselves. But, when it got down to it, they didn't necessarily make me feel good about myself either. So, instead, I would sit alone, a few seats down from one of the groups. I got used to being the loner after some time, but the first few weeks were often painful, watching all the kids carve out their designated areas. I felt like I was in the way.

As I followed the line through the cafeteria, I locked eyes with a few others who looked as lost and concerned as I did. Then I'd watch as their eyes found the faces they were looking for, and they were instantly at ease. If Cali were here, she'd be who I locked eyes with. Then I felt stupid for thinking about her. She was so much younger, she wouldn't be at this school, let alone in this cafeteria.

"Hi, Sadie!" a soft voice called out from ahead of the lunch line. It was Emmi. She and I were a lot alike, but never quite clicked. She was also raised by a single mom and lived in an apartment above a shop on our side of town. She didn't talk much, and I knew very little about her. When I asked about her mom, Emmi would say she had long nights at work and slept during the day. But I never knew what it was her mom did for work, because further questions only made Emmi quieter.

"Hi!" I said back, surprised. She waited for me to get through the line, and we both stood with our trays as if we were waiting for someone else. "How was your summer?"

"Good," she said. "I babysat for a family on Hill Road. I made five dollars an hour!"

"Neat! What are you going to do with the money?"

She shrugged. "I just gave it to my mom."

Emmi grew quiet after that, and I didn't know how to keep our conversation going.

"What did you do this summer?" she asked.

"Oh..." I had prepared for this question a thousand times. I even searched the web for what I could say instead of talking about how my mom was in a wheelchair, how I met my dad for the first time, how a search and rescue team found me in the woods, but I came up with nothing. "Nothing really. My Aunt Jean moved back, and she's having a baby."

"That's so cool!" she said exuberantly. "Are you excited?"

"Yes, we think it's a girl. I'm going to be like her big sister."

"I've always wanted a younger sibling."

"What about Devon?" I asked about her little brother a couple of grades below us.

"No, I mean like a baby brother or sister," she swooned. "I could cuddle them and take care of them. Hey, by the way, I like your shirt."

"Thank you!" I beamed. We didn't say much after that. I think we were both just grateful to have someone to sit with.

When I got home, I found Aunt Jean and my mom in the kitchen. They had chips and pop on the table, Mountain Dew, my favorite.

"You're back!" Jean said. I hugged them both. "How was your first day?"

"It was all right, nothing special."

"Tell us all about it," my mom said, patting the open chair next to her.

"Well, you know, we didn't learn anything."

"How was Mr. Foster?" my mom asked.

"He's good. He's going to let us pick twenty minutes a day to talk to him about whatever we want. I think that'll be cool."

"*Anything*?" she asked suspiciously. "Sounds risky."

"Well, like about the world, science, how things work. We have to put the slips in the box, and then he'll pull out the questions he likes best and answer them for us."

"Okay," she said. "Safer to do it that way, I'm sure. What are you going to ask him first?"

"I don't know." I shrugged, thinking about it for a moment. "Maybe the Inca or the Maya."

"So smart," my mom said. "Did you see any of your friends?"

I tried not to roll my eyes. My mom knew the answer to that one, but she couldn't help but remain hopeful. "I ate lunch with Emmi."

"Oh, Emmi! Sweet girl. Jean, Emmi has always been so nice to Sadie."

"So, we like Emmi," Jean chimed in. "What's she like?"

"Quiet, mostly. She tends to keep to herself. What have you two been doing all day?" I asked, noticing how happy they both were.

"We had a girl's day!" my mom said. "Al has been out all day on a job, and it was just us. We started off on a bad foot when Jean tried to take me to the grocery store. We couldn't get that good-for-nothing wheelchair to unlock, and so she left me in the car like a dog."

They were laughing, but I couldn't imagine why. "What's so funny about that?"

"Oh, nothing. It was horrible," Jean said. "It was so hot. I felt awful about it. But then when I went inside, I saw a motor scooter, one of those the seniors ride around in, and I took it! I drove it right up to the car, and I told your mom to hop on!" They busted out laughing. "Then when we went inside, another one was free, so I grabbed it! I said, 'Move out of the way, I'm pregnant!'"

"The two of us raced the scooters around Beuhler's so fast, I thought I was going to have a panic attack. You should have seen your aunt, Say, she looked ridiculous. Hair flying everywhere. Pregnant belly popping out. We looked like complete loons."

"But it was a blast!" Jean retorted. "You'd think someone would say something to us about leaving the scooters for those who really need them, but nope, everyone stepped out of the way. Parting like the sea for us to go down each aisle."

"Quickest shop of my life," my mom said.

As they continued to recount the events, our laughs grew bigger and bigger. I was so happy to see my mom laughing. Then Al walked through the door and came to join us.

"Al!" We all shouted simultaneously.

"*Que pasa?*" He smiled and matched our energy instantly. "You all seem happy."

"How was your day?" Jean asked, methodically rubbing her belly.

"Hard work," Al replied as he leaned in to kiss her head. "My crew works so hard, and I can't give them much. Need bigger jobs. Hey, Sadie, how was school?"

"Boring," I said, not wanting to think about it. Except Al looked hurt, like he genuinely wanted to hear about my day, and my one-word response was a way to shut him out. So I said, "We never learn anything on the first day anyway, but I did eat lunch with my friend Emmi."

He smiled and said, "Excited for tryouts next week?"

"More like nervous—" but before I finished my sentence, I turned to see my mom's eyes rolling to the back of her head. She was still for a moment, and then her body began convulsing. "Mom!" I shouted.

Her body went rabid like something was trying to claw its way out of her frail frame. We tried to hold her in place, careful to make sure she wouldn't fall out of her chair. Al held her shoulders, and I held her head and neck and brushed her hair trying to get her to calm down. Jean went to call the doctor's after-hours number.

"Call an ambulance!" I screamed as she walked into the other room with the landline.

After a couple of minutes passed and the jerking finally stopped, my mom's head bobbed downward. She looked to be asleep. Jean had disappeared from the scene but came back in just as things started to slow down.

"Are they coming?" I asked desperately.

"No, honey," she said, holding the phone to her chest.

"Why not?"

"Because, the truth is, this already happened once today. And it happened last week when you and Al were at the mall, and a couple of other times before that…that I know of."

"I don't believe you!" I huffed.

"You just haven't seen it yet, and Al has only seen it once. We think it may also be happening in her sleep."

"Well, what is it? What's happening to her?"

"They're seizures. She also doesn't always convulse like this. Sometimes she'll stare into nothing, or her eyes will roll back and her body will go stiff. But it's being caused by a bunch of things. The medications she's on list seizures as a side effect. Lack of sleep might be another factor. But…" Jean trailed off.

"What?" I was growing impatient.

"It's most likely being caused by the damage to her brain. It's the disease. That's why I didn't call the ambulance. The doctor said she will continue to get them more frequently due to lesions on her brain that are impairing her ability to function and do basic things. It's why she can't walk, and why she slurs her words sometimes or—"

"She does not slur her words!" I screamed, trying to protect my mom from the embarrassment.

"She does," Jean said firmly. "Especially when she's stressed."

"So, there's nothing we can do?"

"Not really. We just have to make sure she doesn't hurt herself while she's doing it, like bite her tongue, or fall, or scratch. If it lasts too long, she may need to go to the ER. But they usually only last a minute. This was a particularly bad one."

Then my mom groaned, and her head began to sway. "Mom, are you okay?"

But she didn't respond.

"I think maybe we should put her in bed and give her some dark time," Al said. We agreed, and he wheeled her into her room and laid her on her bed. It was so effortless for him to pick her up.

I sat back down at the table, and Jean joined me. "Why didn't you tell me sooner?"

"Sweetie, she's been going downhill so fast. I wasn't keeping it from you. I just, well, I don't want you to have to understand all of this. It's so scary."

Then she began to cry, and suddenly our roles were reversed. She needed me, so I hugged her tightly.

"It's just so hard," she said. "I hate this. I can't stand seeing her like this. I wish it was me. I wish it was me. I wish it was me."

"Aunt Jean, we need you. It can't be you. What about the baby?"

"But we need her!" she wailed. "What are we going to do without her?"

"It'll be okay." I continued to hug her. We sat in the dimly lit kitchen. The sun set through the trees, turning everything gold. Tears dropped from Jean's eyes onto her belly. I cried too, but my tears were more contained. The kind of tears that make your eyes water, but not gush.

"I promise I'll make it okay as much as I can," she said to me. "I know I'll never be your mom. But I promise you I'll be there for you, and I'll do all the things you need me to. All of them."

"I know you will," I said. Al came back into the room and said my mom was regaining consciousness. I went in and laid down in bed next to her while Jean stayed put in the other room. Al shut the door.

"Mama," I whispered.

"Hey, baby," she said groggily.

"What was that like?"

"I honestly don't remember. It's like I dropped out of the world for a minute."

"It was such a long time," I said. "How often do you think this is happening?"

"Well, I forget so much these days," she paused. "Honestly, it's been happening all summer it seems. I can't remember how I got into a room, or where I left off in a book, or whether I already shampooed my hair when I'm in the shower. But I don't know if that means I'm having a seizure or if my brain is just fried."

"I don't want to go back to school," I said. "I want to be home to take care of you."

"Sadie, you have to go to school. It's the law, so I technically can make you," she said in her usual playful tone. She reached out her hand for her Newports, weak and trembling.

"It's not funny," I said, putting the box of cigarettes in her hand. "I could do all of my studying and assignments at home and drop them off with the teachers."

"I won't allow it. I've got Jean and Al."

"But they're not me. They're not paying attention."

"Of course they are," she said. "Stop your worrying. Your only priority should be going to school right now, nothing else."

We laid in bed together, letting time pass. I thought she might be asleep, and I whispered, "Do you still feel ready?"

"More than ever," she said. It was a soft blow, but it crushed me all the same.

I listened to her breathing grow heavier as she drifted to sleep, running my fingers through the red waves of her hair, looking stringy and bleached, as if it was thinning out. It's like her image was becoming less sharp, blurry, like she might vanish into the dusty air of the old house. I let my tears fall freely now. This was a new stage, one where my strength was needed not to keep her going, but to let her go. If she was ready, I had to be too. We all did.

I WOKE UP in bed with my mom that morning, and when I opened my eyes, she was watching me. Her green speckled irises just the same as mine. She was so beautiful then, like an angel with the morning light pouring over her. I knew it must be well past my alarm, and I knew Aunt Jean knew as well because I smelled the remnants of a cup of coffee in the next room. Still, we didn't speak. There was nothing to say. We laid there in silence, letting the morning pass by.

Aunt Jean came in after some time and told me I didn't have to go to school. My mom looked at her with a disapproving eye.

"It's infusion day," Aunt Jean said. "You don't have to go; you can stay here if you like."

"I want to go," I said, holding onto my mom.

We packed up the Ford and made our way down the interstate. The same drive we had made a thousand times. But today felt different, like we were soldiers going into battle. I didn't want to leave my mom's side no matter what. This medication had to work.

We reached the counter at Memorial Hospital and the nurse handed us a clipboard. We had to fill out our information every single time we went in. Name, address, insurance provider, etc. It infuriated my mom, and she'd always talk to the nurses about why she had to keep filling it out. *Didn't they have a database for this kind of thing?* But after the seizure she had no fight in her, so I filled out the clipboard. By this point I had every field memorized. I handed it back to the nurse.

The infusion went much the same way it always did. They struggled to find a vein, bruising her arm to an alarming purple. But she didn't complain. We were in a shared room again, and about an hour into my mom's treatment a familiar face entered the room.

"Helen," I said. "Is that right?"

"Oh," Helen said. "Yes, that's right. I remember you. What's your name again?"

"Sadie," I reminded her.

"Sadie, right," she said wistfully. Her spirit seemed to have dimmed significantly since the last time I saw her just a few months ago. "Beautiful girl. How are you today? Shouldn't you be in school?"

I shrugged in response. "How are your boys?"

"They're okay. We finally got cable again, a small consolation for their mom dying."

"I'm so sorry, Helen."

"We've lost everything." She began to weep. "My job, the house, one of our cars, even our dog has to stay with our old neighbor because the new apartment won't allow pets. They've been so strong for so long. I don't want to put them through this anymore."

My mom had fallen asleep, and Jean was off making a phone call, still unable to handle the hospital visits. It was just Helen and me, so I went over and held her free hand. "It's not fair."

"Oh, child," she said, squeezing my hand. "One thing you're gonna realize real quick in this world is that fairness has nothing to do with it. We live in a world where people profit off of disease, where your life is at the mercy of companies that can't even remember your name. Unless you can work and contribute to society, you're cast aside, a nuisance. We're at the will of the system." She began to cry more vigorously. "But what am I doing telling you this? You know all of this. I know you do. Look at you, not even at school, taking care of your mom. You know better than anybody."

I held her cold bony hand and her body began to relax. We sat together in silence, watching the newsreels tick by. The election was picking up steam, and the headlines pointed to Iraq, to federal tax hikes, to rising oil prices, to a so-called bubble around the housing market. There were eighty-nine people on two planes flying out of Moscow, taken down with bombs. It was never anything good.

"I wish we'd find a way to focus less on killing each other and more on healing each other," Helen said. "But what can you do?"

My mom's infusion ended without complication, and I waved goodbye to Helen. I had a gut feeling I wouldn't see her again and tried my best to shake it off. Aunt Jean rejoined us in the lobby, and we headed up a few floors to Dr. Fratello's office. It was a routine visit, and we thought maybe we should skip it because my mom could barely stay awake. But we marched on.

"Good to see you all again," Dr. Fratello said, nodding at each of us. He was being extra formal today. "How is the vertigo?"

My mom sighed. "Between the vertigo and the seizures, I couldn't tell you which way is up and which way is down, and I'm so tired I feel like I could sleep for an eternity. I don't think this new medication is doing it."

"I see," he said, jotting down some notes. "Well, we got some alarming results from your panel last week, and I wanted to touch base. We found a bit of blood in your urine. Now, that may be an infection, and we'll give you something to treat it. But your white blood cell count is very low. Again, that could be pointing to an infection, but I'd like to run a few more tests in the meantime just to make sure."

"And if it's not an infection?" Aunt Jean asked.

"Well, I am concerned," Dr. Fratello said. "Last time I told you how this medication is seen as a last resort. That's because it comes with a number of risks, including cancer."

My Aunt Jean took in a sharp, deep breath. "How can a chemotherapy drug cause cancer? That seems contradictory."

"Well, the medication is volatile, and it has a tendency to damage healthy cells," he explained. "That's why it's a risk. If we're not careful, it can damage her healthy tissue and cause complications."

"That's ridiculous," Aunt Jean said, growing irate.

"Jean, I knew the consequences when I went into this," my mom said. "We were prepared for this outcome."

"Then why—"

My mom raised her hand, cutting her off. "We'll talk about it later."

We wrapped up with Dr. Fratello and headed back to the car. The tension between my mom and aunt was molasses thick. It was as if heat were radiating from them.

"Why would you pursue a treatment option that could kill you?" my aunt asked after some time on the interstate. I counted the mile markers, attempting to soothe myself in the backseat. *Sixty-two, sixty-three, sixty-four.*

"Jean, not now."

"But wouldn't it have been easier to deal with the pain and the symptoms of the disease, let it run its course..." Jean was being gentler now. "Why take such drastic action?"

"I don't know," my mom said. "I thought if I could force my body into remission then I could go back to work."

Aunt Jean looked at her suspiciously. "What's the real answer?"

My mom was silent, standing her ground. "Wouldn't you do everything you could too?" she asked. "You're a mom now too. Almost."

DINNER WAS QUIET that evening. Al tried peacemaking, but he was up against less anger than fatigue. A long battle was lost, and they were licking their wounds. I did not understand everything my mom and Aunt Jean were talking about. They were dancing around their words so much lately, shielding me from some unknown entity. But their armor was cracking. They were spilling out left and right, and I was the one figuring out how to clean it all up.

Aunt Jean came into my room before bed, staying in the doorway. "I'm sorry about last night...and about today."

I was quiet for a moment. But before Jean could walk away I said, "We're losing her, aren't we?"

"I can't answer that," she said softly, taking a few steps into the room. "But it sure does feel like it."

"It feels to me like she was fine just a few weeks ago," I admitted. "I don't understand."

"Sometimes I think the only reason she's able to let go is that I'm here now," Aunt Jean said. "Like if I left again, she'd keep fighting."

For a split second, I feared she might go back to her old ways, run off to a foreign place where no one knew her. I wanted to hold on to her, but I didn't know how. "Don't leave me, okay?"

"Sadie!" she said, coming to sit next to me on the floor, which wasn't easy with her ginormous belly, but I appreciated the effort. "That's not what I mean. I would never leave you. Not again. Not ever!"

She held me tight, and I could barely breathe. I saw our whole future together. Al, Jean, the baby, and me. We'd play in the living room, and we'd eat in our cozy little kitchen. We'd run through the forest, and we'd go out to eat at Pip's. It would look normal on the outside, and that thought gave me some comfort. I always felt like my mom and I stuck out, like people would look at us and know we were poor, or sick, or abandoned. They'd see our house and think, *yes, that makes sense*, like we were just two forgotten souls inhabiting this derelict place. But now things were changing. Yes, everything was falling apart, but we were also coming together. Funny how I could still feel grateful in the midst of such tragedy, but I did. I felt so incredibly grateful that I didn't have to do this alone.

15

DESPITE MY MOM'S WORSENING CONDITION, I managed to go to school for the most part. I was on autopilot most days, waking up with my alarm like a robot. I tried to pay attention in class and did my best to do my homework. On the days I missed, Mr. Foster never asked why. But on this particular day, the day after I had missed my fifth full day of class in the month since school started, he didn't just accept my homework.

"Sadie," he said firmly. "I know I don't need to ask. I know about your mom's condition." He cleared his throat. "And we both know you can't keep missing so much school or you'll never make it through the year."

"Mr. Foster, I—"

He held up his hand. "You don't need to explain," he said. "You are not in any kind of trouble. But I did find this question in my box the other day, and I'm almost certain it belongs to you."

I stared down at the crumpled piece of notebook paper, not entirely sure if it was mine, but willing to bet he was right.

"It asks, 'What happens when you die?' Did you write this?"

I stared at the floor for a moment then nodded.

"What did you mean by this question? Do you mean what happens after death?"

"No…" I paused. I thought the questions were anonymous. "I mean, what happens during dying. Like, does the person feel it? Does it hurt?"

Mr. Foster looked at me with kind, sad eyes. "That's what I thought. I don't think I should answer this in front of the whole class; it might make them upset. Do you understand why?"

"Not really. We all die, don't we?"

"Well, yes." He looked unsure of how to proceed. "But most children aren't prepared for the answer to a question like this. You see, it can frighten them. Most children don't see death for a very long time. In fact, some people go their whole lives never seeing it until it happens to them. And the truth can be unsettling. No one wants to think about this kind of thing, not even adults."

"I'm sorry. You don't have to answer it for the class. You don't have to answer it at all. It's just that I tried to search it on our computer at home, and I didn't come up with anything that made sense. So, I thought you might know."

He looked down at the floor for a moment, my note wilting in his hands.

"I do know. My father died last year. It was dementia. It took a long time. In the end, I had to put him in a home. He was there for about six months, and I visited him every day, thinking it would be my last time seeing him. Then one day the nurse told me it was time, and I asked how she knew. I could tell you what she said if you want."

I nodded. He began speaking in a hushed, soft tone. He appeared anxious, but I needed to hear it.

"The nurse told me our bodies are built to die. I thought that was such a strange way to put it. But thinking back, they are built to grow, to learn, to age, to love, to eat, to sleep. All of those things come so easily to us, like instinct. So, why not dying? That's when she told me that during this process there is no pain. The body slowly shuts itself down. First, the body stops eating and drinking and begins sleeping a whole lot. It's a time of release, to let go of the things it no longer needs, which includes sadness, and grief, and fear. There's also this huge release of natural chemicals in the brain. Remember me teaching you about dopamine and serotonin last week? Those chemicals help them relax, and it's not painful at all. Sometimes, they even have dreams, visions, like they see things beyond the room."

"Visions of what?" I asked.

"Well, it's different for everyone. But in the last days with my dad, I saw him talking at the wall. He said he saw his parents and his childhood dog. He was so happy, so at peace. It was like he was between two worlds. And when he did finally go, he left this world with a smile. It was the most peaceful thing to watch. He just drifted away."

"That sounds so nice. Thank you for telling me."

"I hope this helps you, Sadie." His eyes began to water, and his voice started to crack. "I really hope it helps. And you know, the world does just keep moving, and you will too, right along with it."

We sat watching the students trickle in, and just like that, our exchange was over. I took my seat at my desk in the back and class carried on. Everything just kept moving.

I thought about Mr. Foster's words, how someone might have visions before they die. It seemed like that might be a greeting from the other side, an invitation to whatever came next. But I struggled to piece together what that might look like. We never went to church. My mom said they stopped going after Grandma Samantha died. The kids at school would ask me why I didn't go, and I always felt uneasy answering them, like I might say the wrong thing. I asked my mom about it once on one of our trips to the hospital. She told me she didn't ever plan on going back. I sensed some hostility, and I didn't pry further. But it left me with an awful feeling of being disconnected from the thing that all the other kids at school seemed to have: God.

I didn't know what to think about a man in the sky, about how he made all of us and everything around us. When I was younger, and I still played with dolls, I used to think of myself as a kind of God, controlling their fates. Maybe that's how it was; maybe we were all just inside of a dollhouse. But if that was the case, then why would God hurt me? Why would he take away my mom? I couldn't rationalize it. Now that I was older and no longer played with dolls, I felt that if there was a God, he wouldn't take my mom away. My mom was all I had, and surely he knew that. It was easier to imagine there was nothing.

When I got home that day, I caught Al on the porch. He was sipping a pale-yellow beer and watching the cars roll by. "Hola," he said calmly. "Want to join me?"

"Sure," I said, taking the chair next to him. "Where is everyone?"

"Oh, your mom is asleep. Jean is also asleep. It was a hard day. I'm just giving them the house for a while."

"What happened?" I dreaded the answer.

"Nothing. Well, it was a bit of a mess. Insurance."

"Oh. I hate insurance."

"Me too. We were on the phone for hours today and never got a response."

We sat idle for a moment as I worked up the courage to ask, "Al, are you upset with me that I chose not to do the soccer tryouts?"

He looked over at me and smiled. "Not at all," he said, his whole face smiling. "You'll do things when you're ready. It's your choice."

"I do appreciate you teaching me though. I would like to keep practicing with you. Maybe I can try out next year."

"I'd love to keep teaching you. But not right now." He lifted his beer to his lips, looking worn out. "Why don't you go to the forest?"

I got up, left my backpack on the porch with Al, and went straight for it.

"Be careful," he said.

The late September sun was beginning to turn the leaves a golden brown, and the path was crunchy beneath my sneakers. A warm breeze rolled through, swishing the leaves and causing a few strays to detach and float down. I sat by the creek, watching as they collected on the surface of the water. It wasn't long before Cali joined me. She asked how I was.

"My mom isn't doing well," I admitted. "I don't know what to do."

Cali was quiet for a moment. "The kids at school don't like me," she said solemnly. "They aren't mean or anything. But I can tell they don't want to be near me. I think it's because I don't have a mom anymore."

"I feel the exact same way," I said. "Who's your teacher?"

"Mrs. Vincent," she said.

"I had Mrs. V. She's so old," I teased, trying to cheer her up. "I hate that bell she rings at recess like we're a bunch of cattle being herded."

Cali laughed a little. "She's not *that* old."

"Are you kidding? She's ancient, and her silver hair is so long, her braid is all the way down past her butt!"

"Mrs. V has short black hair," she contradicted.

"You're kidding. She cut it *and* dyed it? Sounds like an extreme makeover."

"Be nice," she reminded me. "One day you're gonna be an old lady too. You're already way older than me!"

We both laughed and lay down, looking up at the trees.

"I am sorry about your mom," she said.

"It's okay," I said. "I learned today that sometimes when people die, they see visions, like of those they've lost."

Cali thought about it for a minute. I appreciated that she didn't seem scared off by the subject. Then she said, "I wonder what my mom saw. I hope she saw her mom and dad."

"We'll never know, I guess. But we have to keep on moving."

"I don't know how," she said, and for the first time I saw doubt in her eyes. "How do you keep going when you lose someone you love?"

"I wish I could tell you. But I think we all do it in our own way. Maybe it just means holding the things you have even closer."

Cali folded her arms across her tiny frame. "I wish I could just run away."

"Where would you go?"

"California," she said, smirking.

"Of course. How could I forget?"

"Where would you go?"

"I just want to stay here. I don't want to run."

We played around for a while, but the sky was turning peach, warning me it was time to go home.

"Winter is about to come, Cali, and I don't think I'm going to be around much anymore. I need to be with my family. I need to be close to home, just in case."

"I understand," she said. She reached her small arm around to her back pocket, pulled out the rabbit's foot, and gave it to me. "You left this a while ago."

"I know." I rubbed the soft fur between my fingers one last time and handed it back to her. "It belongs to your dad. You should keep it."

She put it back in her pocket and we sat together for a long time, not saying anything. "Hey, remember our initials in the log?"

I had almost forgotten, but we walked over to the log and sure enough, they were still there. It really hadn't been that long since summer, even though it now felt like ages. Our initials reminded me that we remained. "Secret friends?" I reminded her.

"Secret friends forever!"

We hugged and got up to part ways. This time, it was my turn to count, but instead of closing my eyes, I peeked at her through my fingers, watching as she ran away. The strangest thing was that she was running toward the bridge, the same path I always took. I assumed she lived in the opposite direction, on the other side of the woods. But she knew every rock, every swerve, and soon she was out of my sight. I turned back to look at the log over the creek, thinking about the glorious day we followed it to the waterfall. Golden leaves speckled the surface, swirling in kaleidoscopic shapes, waiting to be carried to that beautiful place. And I knew that like leaves on a stream, I too would carry on. The release was the hardest part.

AFTER MY CONVERSATION with Mr. Foster, I had a new resolve to go to school, and my mom took note. At least I wasn't letting her down by skipping my classes. Education was always important to her.

Emmi and I continued to eat lunch together and our friendship was budding, which helped me get through most days. We started hanging out outside of school, a first for both of us. We'd go to the park, and Al would come pick me up after he was done with work. Sitting on the swings, Emmi and I treaded lightly over the various components of our lives. When I missed a day of school, I'd tell her it was doctor's appointments for my mom, and more often than not it was. Emmi knew enough about my mom's condition that she didn't pry, and I was grateful for that.

But Emmi was so private that I often longed for Cali. I missed the stories we made up, how she inspired me to dream up new places. Together, she and I escaped the confines of the forest. Or rather, the forest helped us live beyond our current circumstances. Cali understood what it was like to lose a mother, and that bonded me to her. I began to wonder if anyone would ever understand me quite like she did.

I told Al I wouldn't need a ride home. I was going to spend the night at Emmi's, and we were going to go back to school together the next day. I was so excited to have my first real sleepover. We both were. I packed my bookbag to the brim with pajamas, my toothbrush, and whatever else I thought I might need. When school let out, our first order of business was to pick up Devon. He was at the elementary school next door, for grades one through four. The kids were lining up outside the building and Mrs. V was monitoring. She rang the old bell, and the kids began to file in line in front of her.

"I hate that bell," Emmi whispered to me. I nodded in agreement.

Mrs. V's hair was indeed silver, and her braid flowed down past her waist, just as I remembered. She wore an ankle-length corduroy skirt and a vest with little gold moons imprinted on it. She looked like a witch you might see in a Halloween movie, fit for the season. I couldn't help but wonder what Cali meant by Mrs. V having short black hair, then I realized that Cali might be standing in that line with Devon. I scanned the crowd of children for anyone who looked remotely like her, but I couldn't find her.

As much as I wanted to see her, the idea of crossing paths at the school unnerved me, like our friendship couldn't withstand a collision of the outside world with the one we had created for ourselves in the forest that summer. I ran up the sidewalk and waited for Emmi to pick up Devon and catch up with me.

"What was that all about?" Emmi asked, Devon in tow. He didn't talk much either.

"Nothing," I said, catching my breath. "I just thought I might see someone I didn't want to see."

"Who?"

"No one," I said, squirming.

Emmi dropped it, and we continued walking toward Main Street. Their apartment was around the corner from Pip's diner, Buehler's, and the other small shops that made up the old town of Juniper. Living so close to everything was a luxury I had never considered, but despite its convenient location, luxury was not the word I would use to describe Emmi's apartment. It was above the auto parts store, and the whole place smelled of rubber and motor oil. There were two small rooms, one shared by her and her brother, and her mother's, the door shut. The kitchen was small and had an electric stove a quarter of the size of a regular stove. The living room was nothing more than a couch, a small box TV, and a single barred window overlooking Main Street, making it feel like a prison. The whole place felt cramped, and I began to realize my house, old as it was, at least had windows you could open and immediately smell fresh air wafting in from the forest. I realized that in all my life I had never spent a night away from home. I yearned for my bed and, more importantly, my mom. Emmi put a pot of water on the stove so we could make mac-n-cheese for the three of us, knowing it was my favorite. Devon sat on the couch and flipped on cartoons, and we watched from across the bar. I could tell Emmi felt exposed. This was the first time either of us had ever had a friend over.

"I like your magnets," I said, eyeing the collection that engulfed the entire face of their refrigerator.

"Thanks. They were here when we moved in last year. We kept them."

"Where did you live before this?"

"Another apartment just up the street. Section 8."

"What's that mean?"

She shrugged. "Means we're broke."

We were silent for a while after that. The water came to a boil as the cartoons blared artificial laughter throughout the place. We ate the mac-n-cheese and headed to the bedroom, leaving Devon in front of the TV.

Emmi and I started talking about the kids in class, and she got oddly avoidant when we started talking about Jacob Williams, the kid I sat next to. "Can I tell you a secret?" she asked in a hushed tone.

"Sure!"

"I kind of have a crush on him."

"On Jacob?" I was embarrassed by the idea of anyone having a crush. "Why?"

"I don't know." Emmi giggled. "He's cute."

"I guess," I said, trying to sound more mature about it.

"Do you like anyone?"

I had never given it much thought. Honestly, most of the boys in our class were mean to me, and not in the "oh, he just likes you" kind of way. No, they were actually mean. "I don't think so."

"That's okay. Boys are weird anyway. Hey, do you like board games?"

"I don't know. I've never really played one."

"What about Monopoly?"

"Nope. But we can try it."

Emmi's face lit up, and she went to grab an old thin box. Its edges looked like they had been chewed, and the pieces inside were a jumbled mess. It took us several minutes to sort it all out. But Emmi loved teaching me as we set it up. It was the most I'd ever heard her speak. She held up a miniature silver dog and said,

"This one is my favorite, this is the one I always use. Now you have to find one that speaks to you. Which one do you like?"

I inspected the little tokens—a ship, a hat, and a car. I ended up choosing the shoe. I thought of Thaddeus Glinn, the lost traveler Cali and I had dreamed up, and for some reason I thought the shoe could bring me luck. As our pieces moved along the board and we exchanged colorful bills for houses, our minds eased. We became absorbed by the game, and before we knew it, it was nearly midnight. Devon had passed out on the couch in front of the cartoons while Emmi and I continued to play. Then we heard the doorknob out front jiggle, and Emmi looked at me, startled. I thought it might be an intruder, someone breaking in, but then I realized it was probably her mom, and she forgot her key. We heard a thump, and it was quiet. Emmi looked like she didn't want to get up. She was glued in position.

"Is it your mom? Should we go help her out?"

"No," Emmi said. "I've got it. Just stay here, okay?"

Emmi got up quickly and opened the door. I could hear scuffling and Emmi telling her mom to get up. She was struggling, and I thought I should go help. When I went out to see what was going on, Emmi's mom was on the floor, her head stuck halfway between the doorway and the hall.

"Is she okay?" I asked, lunging to help pick her up. Emmi didn't respond. We dragged her mom to her bedroom and flopped her body on the bed as best we could, but half of her was hanging off. She was a lot heavier than my mom. I noticed a bunch of empty liquor and pill bottles scattered about. It was a mess. When we got her situated, Emmi practically pushed me out of the room. We went back into her and Devon's bedroom, and Emmi threw the

Monopoly board across the floor, scattering our riches. She began to cry.

"What's going on?" I was unsure of how to comfort her.

"Can you just leave?" she asked me desperately.

I knew she meant it, and there was no way to salvage the night. I picked up my backpack and went into the kitchen. I used their landline to call home. I could hear Emmi shut the bedroom door.

Al picked up. "Hello," he said groggily.

"Al, it's me. Can you pick me up?"

I gave him the address and decided to sit in the living room next to Devon while I waited. I flipped off the TV and laid a blanket over him and his eyes fluttered open. He didn't say anything. He just sat staring at me, both of us cast in the white moonlight coming through the barred window.

"Is there a girl named Cali in your class?" I whispered. "With Mrs. Vincent?"

Devon shook his head. "There's a Casey."

I shook my head and remembered then that Cali was probably lying about her name. "She's shorter than you, pale, and has dark eyes. Her hair is light."

Devon shook his head again. "I'm the shortest one in my class."

I walked back to the window and peered down to the street below, and when I saw the headlights of Al's truck pull up, I left the apartment without saying another word.

EMMI WAS LATE TO CLASS the next morning, so I couldn't ask her what happened. Then at lunch, I tried to approach her, and she turned away. It was as if she was mad at me. I thought maybe I had done something wrong. Maybe I shouldn't have left. When I got out of the lunch line she was nowhere to be found, and to my own shame, I ate by myself, feeling the eyes of the entire cafeteria on me. *The weird girl without any friends.*

As I sat there eating my bagged lunch, I grew furious with Emmi. How could she do this to me? And worse yet, how could I let myself get close to her? To anyone? I was not meant to have friends. It was as simple as that.

We dodged each other at all costs for two whole weeks. I made a deal with Mr. Foster that I could eat in his classroom during lunch as long as I didn't make a mess. He was in the teacher's lounge during this time, so I sat at my desk and read in solitude. I zipped through three chapter books in that short timeframe, and it ended up being my favorite time of the day. It was the one time when I didn't have to be surrounded by students, teachers, or my family, and I could be alone. It was in these quiet periods that I returned to the person I was before our Ford broke down, before my mom got so much worse, before Jean and Al moved in, before I met my father, and before I met Cali. I was reminded of how much I loved to read, how much I needed that "me time" to collect my thoughts. I was fortifying myself, hardening my shell against all the change.

16

IT WAS ELEVEN O'CLOCK when the whole house woke to Jean screaming. We all rushed to get my mom in her chair, get the overnight bags, and load everything and everyone up into Al's truck. Al drove wicked fast down Violet Avenue and hopped onto the interstate without skipping a beat, as if he'd been practicing. I had never counted the mile markers so fast. When we pulled up to the hospital, Jean was panting fast and sweating like she'd just run a marathon.

Al and I got her into the lobby, and the staff quickly wheeled her into the maternity ward. Then we went back for my mom, plopped her onto her wheelchair, and flew right back inside. Al left us in the waiting room and went back with Jean. My mom, barely awake, kept saying, "Has it happened yet?"

It was Election Day, and the results were still coming in. We watched CNN as the points ticked up. The map was almost entirely red, signifying Bush was likely going to win. The people in the waiting room seemed happy about it. But some states were still holding out, and the numbers were close. Wolf Blitzer kept remarking on the technological advances of this election, how some states still had punch-in ballots and others had machines tabulating their results. There was some big fuss over Ohio, and the newscasters kept saying it was the most crucial state of all. Without Ohio, Bush couldn't win. It made me feel special; of all the states, we were the wild card.

Around 3:30 in the morning, an analysis team was writing down the numbers from Ohio, counting the votes one-by-one they said, and they *still* weren't ready to call it. They kept talking about how it was a vote for American values. I turned to my mom, who was barely hanging on to the waking world, and asked her what she thought about all of it.

"Honestly, if your little cousin wasn't being born, I'd be asleep," she said in her sarcastic way. "None of these people give a damn about me."

By six in the morning, we were both so delirious we started making games out of the infomercials. There were ads for Depends, Regis Philbin on CD, and OxiClean.

"Every time he says the word *clean*, hold your breath," I said. The two of us looked like whales ready to blow. We were turning purple at the will of Billy Mays when Al ran out into the waiting room in a pink gown.

"It's a girl!" he said. We both let out our breath and laughed.

"Finally!" I screamed, jolting an older man in the corner awake.

When we got into the room, Jean was holding the baby to her chest. She looked exhausted but strong. My mom wheeled herself right up to the edge of the bed, and the two of them looked at each other with such intensity. All I could do was watch as these two sisters spoke to each other with eyes alone. There was a moment between all of us, almost imperceptible, in which I think we realized change wasn't just coming, it was here. When the silence lifted, the first thing Jean said was, "Would you like to hold her?"

My mom shied away, folding her arms into her lap, shaking her head. "No, no, I'll drop her."

Aunt Jean wouldn't have it. She handed the little bundle over to my mom, and she took her in and held her close, right up to her chest, and leaned back.

"She barely weighs anything," my mom said.

"Six pounds, two ounces," Jean said. "She is tiny."

"Tiny but mighty, right, little one?" my mom said softly to the baby. Then she looked at me. "Would you like to hold her, Bug?"

I wanted nothing more than to hold my new little cousin, but I didn't know how. "How do I do it?"

"You have to support the base of her head. She's not strong enough to keep it up on her own. Cradle her like this," she explained, her movements so gentle and slow. "Then, if you want, you can hold her right up to your chest, like this."

I stretched out my arms and pulled the baby in. She was so small, no bigger than a rabbit. And warm. She let out a gurgle and twitched her arms. Her little hand was reaching, and I met it with my finger. When she clasped her hand around it, our bond was sealed. This was instant love, and I knew no matter what I would protect her and teach her everything I knew. "What's her name?"

Al and Jean were holding each other. Then Al said, "Her name is Lily."

"Lily Samantha," Jean added.

"After Mom," my mom said warmly. "It's beautiful."

"Lily," I said to the baby still holding my finger. "It's nice to meet you."

After a couple more hours together, Al drove my mom and me home and immediately went back to the hospital to be with Jean and the baby. My mom and I were energized from the night's events, but when we finally got inside, we realized we hadn't slept for nearly a full day. I helped my mom to bed and decided to stay up for a little while longer. I rarely had the house to myself anymore, and it was such a peaceful morning. I walked from room to room, thinking through the changes we had made. I went into my mom's old room upstairs, the room that was once Grandma and Grandpa's, the one she hadn't used for almost a year since moving downstairs. It had been converted to the nursery, and the alcove ceiling was painted a clean white, a blank slate for Lily. I walked into Jean's room and noticed everything had been tossed around in their haste to get to the hospital. Then there was my own room, and I recognized that the room hadn't changed, but I had. I opened my desk drawer and found my flower collections. I turned the page to a ring of pressed daisies and tried to think about the girl I was then. The next page was an assortment of blue flowers collected last spring. Violets, phlox, and bluebells. I had not yet known Cali, or Al, or my dad. The collection I had been working on in July, the pinks and the oranges, had abruptly stopped, and I struggled to piece together the chain of events that led me to this moment now.

I put the collections away and looked at my belongings scattered about the room. I felt an odd detachment from everything. I began cleaning off my shelves, removing the children's books, the stuffed animals, the reminders of a past I could no longer hold onto. I cleaned the shelves nearly bare except for a couple of bigger books and the little golden toad figurine Aunt Jean gave me when she first arrived. I suddenly wanted to fill the room with new things and new memories. I wanted this space to reflect who I was becoming. I needed my own blank slate.

When I went back downstairs, I crawled onto the couch and flipped on the TV. The newscasters had announced that George W. Bush had won the presidency. I watched as John Kerry gave his concession speech. I thought about the people in the waiting room at the hospital and how happy they must be. *Surely some good will come out of this,* I thought. Then, I thought of Jerrod at the checkout lane at Buehler's. He was probably thrilled too; maybe this wasn't such a good thing. When the speeches were over, I flipped through the channels and came across old reruns of *Law and Order*. I never much cared for adult shows like this, but I didn't want to be placated by cartoons. I wanted the gritty, dark scenes, the mystery and intrigue. I got about halfway through an episode about a man who was accused of killing his wife before I fell asleep.

When I finally woke up, it was four in the afternoon, and I heard my mom rustling. I went into her room and found her struggling to lift herself out of bed. "Here, let me help," I said, putting out my arms to brace her like I had done hundreds of times before. She took my arms and lifted herself up and over into the chair. It was this familiar act of care, this allowance of vulnerability, that assured me that although my mom was putting on a brave face, she still needed us. She wasn't giving up just yet.

"Thank you, Bug," she said. "What a night."

"Right. Lily is so beautiful."

"She really is. Reminds me of when you were a baby."

"Really?"

"Oh yeah, you know you were also so tiny. You didn't weigh much more than her, and your little hand gripped my finger just like Lily gripped yours this morning. That was the moment I knew I didn't just have a daughter; I had a best friend."

"I felt that," I said. "I don't ever want to leave Lily. I want to show her everything I know."

"You're going to be a wonderful cousin, almost like a sister."

"Almost like a best friend."

"That's right." She leaned back into her chair and winced.

"Are you in pain?"

"Eh, only the good kind. The kind that results from pushing through an immense amount of excitement and stress. I can handle this kind of pain."

We spent the rest of the evening watching more *Law and Order* and eating frozen meals. It had been so long since it was just the two of us, and it was nice to hang out like the old days even if that meant a half-nuked pan of Stouffer's meatloaf for dinner. Around midnight we both went to our separate rooms and slept the whole night through. This time I did have one dream.

Al, Jean, Lily, and I were all sitting on a blanket having a picnic, and everything was white—our clothes, the sky, even the ground, were covered in little white flowers, and it looked like snow was falling all around us. We weren't smiling or talking, we just sat quietly together. It was as if we were spiraling through the universe like that. Then the middle of our picnic blanket cracked open, and the Earth split into four quarters, each of us on our own piece. But, instead of becoming frightened and scrambling to get back to each other, we all just drifted off, each going our separate ways. As I watched them drift away, I felt a deep sadness, as if they were saying goodbye to only me, off to form their own universe. When I woke, the dream was still misty in my mind, and though I couldn't piece it back together all the way, I was left with a feeling of loss. I tried not to let it bother me though, because just a moment later the front door opened. The three of them had come home, back to me.

"This is your new home," Jean said to baby Lily, who was in her carrier being held by Al.

"And you remember Sadie," Al said, exposing her little face. She immediately reached out her hand when she saw me, and I went right up to her and placed my finger inside for her to hold.

"Where's Anna?" Jean asked. "I want to show her the birth certificate with the little footprints. They're so dainty."

"She's still in her room; she may not be up yet."

"Oh, I guess it is early. My internal clock is all messed up," she said, laughing. She walked away toward my mom's room, leaving Al and me with Lily.

"Can I hold her again?" I asked.

"Sí." Al unbuckled her and handed her to me. Everything was right again. The remaining uneasiness from my dream fell away, and I whispered to Lily, "You're my new best friend."

The entirety of that special day was spent in the living room with Lily. We took turns passing her around, talking about Lily's birth, and watching her breastfeed. As I watched Lily suckle, I couldn't help but think how beautiful it all was. Jean was glowing, and she was already proving to be a wonderful mother. She kept me close to her and showed me how to change the little diapers, how to burp her, and so on. Al made us lunch, and my mom told us stories about when I was a baby, and how I would lay on Grandpa Louie's belly for hours at a time. I wished I could remember him, but something told me he remembered me, wherever he was. She talked about Grandma Sam too, and for the first time the pain in her eyes had faded. Jean's too. It was as if Lily's arrival healed everything. Perhaps it was the continuity, the knowing that life keeps going, which released their pain. I was sure that I felt some release too. The release of my childhood, of Cali, of my father's absence. For the first time, I thought about my half-brother, Henry, the boy growing up in Bexley that I should probably go meet. But for now, it was enough to enjoy the love that filled the house.

NOVEMBER WAS SPENT watching Lily grow. In just a short number of weeks, she had gained two whole pounds, and her head was sprouting dark chocolate curls. Her eyes were bright green, and we truly did look like sisters when comparing the baby photos. Jean was often found pumping milk at odd hours of the day, and Al tried his best to be home as much as possible despite the ever-increasing amount of work he was contracting. My mom held steady, continuing to have seizures and sleeping a lot, but she had not gotten any worse. I didn't miss any school after Lily was born, but I certainly wanted to. It was so hard to be away from her and my mom, and I felt guilty leaving Jean to care for both of them.

Thanksgiving was fast approaching, and I had concocted a whole idea about it. I was scared to admit that ever since my mom fell this past summer and her condition worsened, I suspected she was just going to hang on through the holidays. I was having routine nightmares that this theory would come true and, by admitting it, I might will it into existence. I didn't dare tell anyone. It was fine when I woke up in a panic in the middle of the night because Al or Jean was usually up feeding Lily. They must have assumed her wailing had woken me, and I let them believe it. They'd tell me to go back to sleep, but often I was so startled by my nightmares that I'd offer to put Lily back to bed, and they'd hand her over in their half-asleep states.

Lily was the only living thing that I told anything to, and in those dark hours I'd recite my dreams to her. I'd tell her how I would see Cali standing in my room, watching me sleep. She was always just standing there, and it wasn't scary so much as unnerving. I'd tell Lily, "Cali is in my room again," and she'd look up at me with her little dark eyes as if to say, *It's okay, I'm here with you.* I don't know why Cali haunted me the way she did. Perhaps I felt guilty about our abrupt good-bye. Perhaps I yearned for her friendship. I thought often about tracking her down somehow. Knocking on the doors of every house in the area until I found hers. I thought I could post a stakeout by the elementary school and wait for her to leave. But the thought of such a lengthy investigation felt like too much. Besides, she lied about everything she ever told me, from whose class she was in to her own name. I remembered the early days of knowing her, questioning if she was real. Thinking, *How does this girl know these woods better than I do?* Sometimes, I'd still convince myself it was all just a fantasy. But that didn't make me feel better. Regardless of how I felt about our friendship, it was like clockwork; I'd toss in my bed, having nightmare after nightmare about losing my mom, then I'd wake up and see a flash of Cali before my mind collected itself.

As Thanksgiving grew closer, the pit in my stomach grew wider. Like a sinkhole into the depths of the earth, the edges continued to give way. I knew I was hurting myself by not talking about the ideas in my head, but I was ashamed and terrified to give them life. So, I let them stew. There were only two ways it could go, and both would give me relief. Either my mom would indeed pass away soon, and I could begin to move on; or she wouldn't, and she'd keep hanging on, as would I, no matter how difficult it was. Half of me felt terrible for thinking this way, and the other half told me this was all part of the process. The next two months would give me the confirmation I needed.

THANKSGIVING BEGAN on a cold autumn day. My body was rigid from the worst night of sleep yet, or lack thereof. I had dreamed about my mom screaming that she didn't want to die, and when Lily's wailing woke me up, the two blended in my mind. When I tried to fall back asleep, I kept returning to the same dream and waking up over and over again. At one point I even threw my pillow across the room to try to shatter the illusion of Cali, who was standing there watching my nightmares unfold, barefoot and sullen-eyed, but all I did was knock over my lamp. I told myself that I just needed to make it through today and everything would be okay.

I went downstairs to check on my mom, and she too was rigid. I had to feel her forehead to assure myself she hadn't passed from this world in the middle of the night, something I was doing a lot lately as she slept more and more. But when my hand rested on her face her eyes fluttered open.

"Good morning," I said to her softly. "Happy Thanksgiving."

"Happy Thanksgiving, Bug."

"Cold out there."

"Cold in here." Despite several blankets over her, she was shivering. "My body feels frigid."

"Mine too. But Al will be putting the turkey in the oven soon, and that'll warm us all up!"

"That's right. I think I'll stay here a little while longer though. See if I can't work up some body heat. Do you think you could bring me my typewriter?"

"Sure thing." I went to retrieve the machine from the other room and handed it to her in bed. "What have you been working on all this time?"

"It's a secret," she said, putting her finger to her lips. "You'll find out soon enough!"

With that, I shut her door and went up to the nursery. Jean was feeding Lily when I walked in.

"Hey, Say. How'd you sleep?"

"Fine," I lied.

Jean's face twisted as if she expected me to say more. "I know you're lying."

"No, I'm not."

"I heard you screaming, Sadie. And did you throw something? I heard a crash."

"I was just having a bad dream."

"Well, do you want to tell me about it?"

"Not really. It was silly."

"Doesn't sound silly. You've been waking up a lot in the middle of the night, and while Al and I appreciate your help,

I don't think you're doing it out of kindness. We suspect you've been waking up because you're having lots of bad dreams, and it's keeping you from sleeping."

I didn't say anything and walked across the room to straighten up the changing table, turning my back to her.

"I'll take it that I'm right. Call it a mother's intuition."

I scoffed. "I have bad dreams sometimes. But so does everyone."

"Well, bad dreams often signal something happening in the conscious world. I notice you don't talk about Emmi anymore. What happened?"

"I don't want to talk about it." I felt myself tensing up, growing defensive.

"Well, is it your mom?"

"Can we just drop it?"

"Sadie, believe it or not, I know exactly how you're feeling. I've had bad dreams most of my life. The doctors told me I have insomnia. They've even given me medication for it. But you know what? It all stopped when I came back home. I have never slept better in my life since returning to Juniper, and it made me realize I was just running away from what was scaring me."

"I'm not running away from anything. I'm not like you."

I didn't have to look at Jean to know my words crushed her.

"Trust me, Sadie. You don't have to physically run from things to be running. You can run from your own thoughts, but they'll always find you in your dreams. Now, it's Thanksgiving, and this is supposed to be a happy day. I'm not going to make you tell me what's going on, but I want you to know that whatever you're feeling, I'm probably feeling too, and I think we could help each other if we talked about it. I'm here for you, and I love you."

I didn't say anything, but I turned around to look at her.

"Lily loves you too." She bounced Lily on her lap. "We are thankful for you."

"I'm thankful for both of you too." I felt my muscles release. "I'm sorry. Can we just get on with the day? Someone needs to kick Al out of the shower so we can get the turkey started."

We moved through the motions of the day, cooking turkey, sweet potatoes, mashed potatoes, cornbread, cranberry sauce, green beans, and apple pie. Jean kept her eye on me, and I knew it was to comfort me. I knew I should confide in her about the thoughts I was having, that she was probably thinking the same things I was. But she also wasn't throwing pillows across the room. Aside from my mom dying, Jean had a lot of good things going for her. A healthy baby, Al, and the return to her home. I didn't want to burden her with my fears, and I knew I wasn't going to be able to tell her everything. Maybe I could release a bit of the steam by letting her in though, just a little.

When we finally sat down to eat, we realized we had made an abundance of food. My mom laughed at the sight of it. "This is more food than Sadie and I used to eat in an entire year."

"Well, that's just plain sad, Anna," Jean said. "Don't say that."

"I'm kidding of course. I just can't believe we cooked all of this for four people."

"Hey, I'm basically still eating for two."

"And I'm going to bring leftovers for my crew tomorrow," Al said. "Most of them don't celebrate Thanksgiving, so it'll be new to them."

"Let's go around and say what we're thankful for!" my mom said. "I'll go first. I'm thankful Jean and Al have moved in and that they brought Lily with them."

"I'm grateful for Lily too," I said.

"Me too," said Al.

"I'm grateful for two types of potatoes," Jean said, and we all laughed.

The rest of the dinner went fairly smoothly, with only some mild squawking from Lily. I was hyper-focused on my mom, watching for a seizure, though still trying to have a good time. I could tell Aunt Jean was trying to distract me because she kept asking questions about school, Emmi, Mr. Foster, and whether or not I was interested in any boys. "Fat chance," I told her. "Boys are gross if you ask me."

"Well, I take offense to that," said Al, smiling.

"You're the only boy I'll ever love, Al," I said to him sarcastically.

"Fine by me," he replied. "Less for me to worry about."

"You can like whoever you want, Sadie," my mom said.

"Will you guys stop?" I demanded. "I don't like anyone."

"All right, stop picking on her," Jean said.

When dinner was done, and the pie was served, things quieted down. We picked at our plates, unable to take another bite. My mom looked concerned. "I want you all to know how grateful I am for you," she said, holding back tears. "In a lot of ways, this has been both the worst year and the best year of my life."

"You don't have to say it, Mom. We know."

"Well, I want to. I want each of you to know what it has meant to me to have you so close during this whole thing. I haven't felt alone in this. The support and love you've shown me have been my only source of strength. I know you're all going to be okay."

Al held his hands over his eyes. "I love you, Anna. I love each of you, and I've not felt like I've had family for a long time. But here, this house, this town, my beautiful wife, my baby girl, my sweet Sadie, I have everything I need. You've all made me feel like I belong."

He got up to hug my mom, and they held each other tight. "You're a good one," she said to him. "You'll protect all of them."

Aunt Jean was crying now too, which made Lily cry. The only one not getting emotional was me. I felt broken inside, unable to muster even a simple phrase to say how happy I was too. A few weeks ago, I was so happy. So grateful. But now at this moment, I felt as cold as ice. I knew I had to get my thoughts off my chest, but I didn't know how to articulate them. So, instead, I stayed silent. Jean hugged me, wrapping me in her warmth and love, but I couldn't return it.

That night when we all went to bed, I stayed up. I couldn't stop my thoughts from racing. We had made it through the day, and it was a blessing, but a deep sense of dread had set in. I knew it was probably our last Thanksgiving, but ironically, it was also our first one in so many ways. My mom and I very rarely did anything for Thanksgiving, and now that we finally had enough money and family to conjure up a real holiday meal, all I could do was mourn it all. I thought about when I was younger, about six years old, and I came home with a class project to show my mom. She was still working at the library in those days, and when I showed her the turkey made out of the shape of my hand, she said she would hang it on the front door of the library for everyone to see. And she did. It stayed there for two years because the only one who would have taken it down was my mom, and she refused. She said it had built a reputation as the smartest turkey there was, and it had a life of its own now. I loved the library, running through all the tall shelves of books. My mom would play hide-n-seek with me there after hours, and we always had the best hiding spots. My favorite was in the kids' section under the giant fake tree in the center of the room. I loved looking up the trunk to see the light shining through its limbs. She'd always pretend she couldn't find me even though she knew exactly where I was.

I began to cry in the comfort of my room where my tears wouldn't upset anyone. I missed those moments in the library. I missed seeing my mom walk. I missed when she held me after I got a scratch. She'd put a bandage on me and say, "Kiss it, all better," after planting one on it. I couldn't fathom how I was going to move through the rest of my life without her. I hoped she would remember me wherever she was going next. I hoped I had enough love for Al, Jean, and Lily to keep me going. But I knew nothing was going to fill that void, possibly ever, and the impending sense of doom it brought made me never want to sleep again.

17

IT WAS NOW EARLY DECEMBER and the last of the leaves had fallen, leaving all but the pines bare and skeletal. I looked out at the bridge over Leaky Creek and could see deep into the woods. They seemed exposed, and it made me uncomfortable. I thought about Cali out there in the cold, and I once again was filled with guilt for leaving our friendship the way I did. Going to school became extremely difficult. I had now missed nine days, but Mr. Foster didn't address it until one day when I ended up with a D+ on a paper about what I wanted to be when I grew up. I haphazardly wrote about being a veterinarian, pulling from childhood dreams without applying any real context. Mr. Foster's single comment said, "See me after class," and I sat through the rest of the morning rehearsing what I would tell him.

When the lunch bell rang and all the students flooded out, I stayed seated at my desk, unsure of whether to get up and approach him or not.

"Sadie, I wanted to ask you how things are going at home," he said from across the room.

I responded with a shrug.

"Is your mom still holding up okay?"

"I guess."

"What about the baby and your aunt, are they doing well?"

"Everything is fine."

"Okay, it's just that I know you're a bright kid, but you aren't responding to the prompts you're given. Your test scores have been in the normal range, until this one, but I know you can do a whole lot better. Do you have time to do your homework at night?"

"Yes… I just don't feel like it."

"Well, Sadie, I understand that. And the winter break will be a good time of rest for you. But until then you have to try a little harder. Otherwise, I'll have to call your mom, and you know I don't want to do that."

"Please don't. She's got enough to deal with."

"I know she does, but she wouldn't want you to be falling behind like this."

"It's just temporary. I haven't been sleeping well, and I'm tired."

"Well, you know the school counselor is always here for you if you need to talk."

"I'm good for now, Mr. Foster. But thank you."

"Okay." He was contemplating what to say next. "Just hang in there, okay kid?"

THE NEXT DAY was a Saturday, and I was eager to do nothing. I didn't let on that anything was happening at school. Al and Jean continued to let me take care of Lily in the night. No one was asking me about my homework. They also stopped asking about

Emmi. It was as if she never existed, and that's exactly how I felt about it.

I watched reruns of *Seinfeld, Will and Grace,* and *George Lopez,* flipping through the channels every time there was a commercial break. Everything was quiet, and even Lily was managing to let everyone rest. Then I heard it, the thing I never wanted to hear, my mom's scream. It was like an animal crying out, gasping for air.

"Mom!" I shouted, running to her in the study. She had fallen out of her chair and was convulsing on the ground. The pages of her latest project scattered around her. She grabbed me and began speaking gibberish. I tried to make out what she was saying.

"I have to finish!" she shouted. "I have to finish the story!"

I tried to calm her down. I pet her head, I held her shoulders, but nothing was working. Aunt Jean came running downstairs and ran to my mom to help me hold her steady. We watched her lose all consciousness, slipping away from the room, leaving her body on the oak floor, her typewriter mid-page. After what felt much longer than a few minutes, she stopped moving, and her breathing slowed down to the point that we thought she had stopped taking in air altogether.

"We have to get her to the ER!" I said, instinctively knowing this wasn't just another seizure.

"Al is out on a job!" Jean said frantically. "Lily's car seat is in his truck!"

"None of that matters," I said, pointing to my mom, nearly lifeless in front of us. "We have to call the ambulance."

"Okay," Jean said and got up to go to the landline.

"It's going to be okay, Mom. We've got you."

She was completely unconscious. Her feet bare. I thought if we were going to the hospital, she probably needed socks. I took my own off and started to put them on her. The hospital was always cold. After slipping the second sock on I glimpsed one of the pages next to her foot. I couldn't help but read it, even though it felt like a betrayal of her privacy.

It was a scene about two girls, screaming at the sky. Stirring the birds from the trees. Wailing until their throats were raw. It jogged my memory of the time Cali and I did the same thing after her mom disappeared. My mom grunted and I began gathering the pages, trying to restore their order.

"The ambulance is coming, Mom. Just hang on a little while longer."

The bright lights of the ambulance swirled through our house as it pulled into our driveway, and two medics came out with a stretcher. I pointed them to the back of the house, and they strapped her in. I hopped in the ambulance with them, and Jean stayed behind to pack up Lily and call Al.

The next twenty minutes were a blur. The medics were shouting off numbers at each other and trying to get my mom to regain consciousness.

"Anna," they said repeatedly. "Anna, stay with us."

I looked at her body in disbelief. I held her hand and noticed her fingernails were blue. She was so still, and the loud sirens wailed as we rushed toward the hospital. When we reached the entrance, they didn't tell me what to do, and I just followed them in, all the while trying to keep a hold of her cold hand. The room they took us to seemed sterile, devoid of more than just dirt and disease.

A young woman in green scrubs and curly dark hair twisted into a large bun on top of her head walked through the metallic doors. She did not see me standing there.

The medics rattled off more numbers to her, and she relayed orders to her team. About ten different people were surrounding my mom, and I stood in the corner staring in terror. Soon, a nurse was pushing me out of the room.

"You can't stay in here," she said, and I let her push me out into the hall. "The waiting room is through those doors. Do you have anyone with you?"

I continued staring at my mom, or at least what I could see of her in between the nurses who were hooking her up to a bunch of machines. I was stuck in place, like roots were coming up out of the floor and curling around me, restricting my body, consuming me, dragging me down below.

"Do you have anyone with you?" the nurse repeated.

"No. I'm alone."

"Tell the woman at the desk that you need to use the phone. She'll help you. You have to go now."

"I want to stay." Suddenly the blood rushed back into my face. "Please!"

"You can't be here," the nurse said. "We'll come out and update you very soon. I have to get back in there, okay?"

"Please save her!"

"We will do everything we can." She put her mask over her mouth and rushed back toward my mom.

I ran into the waiting room and told the woman at the desk I needed to make a call. But when I dialed the house, no one picked up. Jean and Al must have already been on their way. I took a seat and felt the roots creeping up around me again. Another twenty minutes passed, and finally they arrived.

"Sadie!" Jean shouted, running up to me. "What's going on?"

I broke down in tears and buried my head in her chest. "I don't know, they didn't tell me anything and pushed me out of the room."

We waited for a little over an hour before a doctor came out and spotted us. Jean and I ran up to her, and Al followed carrying Lily.

"You're the family for Anna Watkins?" the doctor asked.

"I'm her daughter," I said. "What happened?"

The doctor looked down at me from her charts and her whole demeanor changed. She softened and began to speak slowly. "Your mom is alive, but she had a very big seizure, which caused her to stroke, cutting off oxygen to her brain. We don't know how long it lasted, so the extent of the damage is unknown. I see from her charts that she has bladder cancer. Do you know what medications she's taking?"

Aunt Jean's face went stark white, and suddenly Al was trying to nudge me back toward our seats. He wanted to shield me.

"No, stop protecting me," I said to him firmly. "What did you say, Doctor?"

"Well, we're running some tests now to help us determine what to do next, but for now she is stable," the doctor said, looking back down at her charts. "We'll keep you posted and let you know when you can go back to see her."

"Thank you, Doctor," Jean said.

We sat back down in our seats. I was fuming and Aunt Jean was being extremely cautious.

"Sadie—" she said, reaching out to me.

"How could you keep this from me?" I snapped.

"It was your mom's wish. She said one disease was enough. She didn't want you to worry."

I left the ER waiting room, walked down some halls, and found a private seating area near a vending machine. They didn't come after me, thank God, and I allowed myself to cry. I let the tears flow at first, and then I began to sob. I cried harder than I ever had in that lonely corner of the hospital. I held myself tight, wishing for it all to end. I felt myself struggling to breathe between the waves that were crashing into me. Swell, hit, recede. Swell, hit, recede. When the waves finally slowed, my thoughts returned. *My mom has cancer.* Bladder cancer, caused by the medication. The medication was too risky, but my mom chose to do it anyway. The doctors must have confirmed it after her last panel with all those scary results. I didn't know how they hid it from me. I didn't know why I hadn't noticed the vast shift in her decline. I was drifting, sinking, barely staying afloat. But how could I not have seen it?

After I collected myself somewhat, I walked back to the waiting area where Jean and Al were. I sat as far away from them as I could. I didn't make eye contact, but I knew they could see me. Their guilt permeated the entire room. Four hours later, the doctor came back out, and I walked up to her immediately. She told us that Mom had been moved to the ICU, and we could go over and visit her. We walked to the other side of the hospital, not talking, a thousand miles of impenetrable distance between us as we traveled through hallway after hallway, following the signs to her room. We found a small vacant waiting area and got situated. Another nurse came over and told us she could allow one visitor back at a time, so I went first, not even looking at them for approval.

My mom was hooked up to a bunch of monitors, and there was oxygen running to her nose and an IV in her arm. She was propped up with pillows and looked to be asleep.

"Mom?" I whispered softly. She did not respond. "How could you keep this from me? We don't keep anything from each other."

But I realized what I said wasn't true. I had kept a lot from her over the past several months. I struggled to confide in her about what I was experiencing with school, with my nightmares of Cali, with my falling out with Emmi, and even deeper, with her and the progression of her disease. It made sense that she too was keeping things from me, but I felt deceived all the same.

I sat with her for about an hour, and she never woke up, never even flinched. I went out to the waiting area, passing the invisible baton to Jean, who went in to see her next.

"How did she look?" Al asked.

"Not good." I was terse.

"I'm so sorry," Al said. "I'm sorry I didn't let you know. I know you're old enough to hear it. I don't know why I hesitated."

I didn't care much for Al's blubbering. I simply leaned in for a hug. He squeezed me tight, and all my rage dissolved.

Jean walked back out after some time. "She didn't wake up," she said, defeated.

We waited for a while, and Al went to get us some snacks from the vending machine. I decided to go back in after about an hour.

"Mom?" I said again, thinking maybe if I spoke more, she might wake up. "We're all here. Me, Jean, Al, Lily. We're waiting for you to wake up. Will you please wake up? We need to know if you're okay."

I waited another five minutes then said, "Don't die, Mom. I'm not ready."

Just then her eyes fluttered open, and she looked around the room, unable to focus.

"Mom, I'm here. It's me, Sadie."

Her deep eyes searched the ceiling, dancing for a moment until she closed them again. The sun was beginning to set, and the room was growing dark. Al's vending machine snacks had not held me over, and my hunger forced me to leave the room. When I got back to the waiting area, Jean and Lily were gone.

"She's feeding Lily," Al said. "How's she doing?"

"She opened her eyes, but she couldn't focus on anything."

"Did she speak?"

"No. She fell back asleep."

Then I saw my mom's doctor, Dr. Fratello. Finally, a familiar face.

"Hi, Sadie," he said. "We've been running tests, and I'll tell you right now because I know you need some answers, the results aren't good."

I wanted to collapse onto the floor, but Al held me steady.

"I'm coming!" Jean ran up to us with Lily. "What did I miss?"

"Hi, Jean," Dr. Fratello said, letting her catch her breath. "The scans show the damage to her brain has worsened since the last time we checked. There is significant inflammation, and it may be impacting her ability to see and speak. It may also be what's caused this stroke."

"Is that why she couldn't look at me?" I said, worrying she might be blind. I couldn't imagine anything worse than that.

"Possibly," he said. "Her immune system is very weak, and she's up against a whole lot right now. Her cancer has spread rapidly."

"Will she make it through the night?" Jean asked.

"She is stable," Dr. Fratello said. "There's no reason to assume she won't. But I think it'd be wise if you started to prepare for the worst."

18

A FEW DAYS HAD PASSED inside the hospital. More tests were run, and my mom continued to float in and out of consciousness. Then on the fourth day, she finally woke up. Although she wasn't making eye contact, I could tell she was present.

"Mom, what do you need?"

She began to make raspy sounds in her throat. I put a cup of water to her lips, and she took a sip. "Sadie."

"Hey, I'm here."

"What happened?"

"You've been in the hospital. You had a stroke, and the doctors are taking care of you."

"I don't remember."

"That's okay," I told her gently. "Want me to go get Jean and Al?"

"No, not yet."

"Mom, can you see?"

"Yes. Why?"

"The doctor said you had inflammation in your brain, and I thought you might be blind."

"Oh," she said. "Well, I can see right now. Not super clear, but I can see. Did I miss Thanksgiving?"

"No, Thanksgiving was a couple of weeks ago, remember?"

"No," she said, drifting off. Then Jean and Al came in.

"Anna! You're awake!" Jean said. The hopefulness in her voice annoyed me. "And you can see!"

"Hey, sis," she said weakly.

"We have to get the doctor! Al, tell the nurse."

Al left the room quickly and came back in with a nurse.

"Good morning, Ms. Watkins," the nurse said. "My name is Jasmine, Jasmine Robinson, I've been one of your nurses the past few days. It's so good to see you awake and talking."

"Thank you," my mom said. "Is Dr. Fratello in?"

"He will be this afternoon. I'll call him and let him know you're up and alert."

Nurse Jasmine jotted down her vitals and left the room.

We all watched the small TV suspended from the ceiling in the corner of the room. Emeril was whipping up some kind of mushroom dish. I thought of Helen and my sadness deepened further. Then Dr. Fratello finally arrived.

"There she is," he said, using a small light to check her eyes. "So, you can see me?"

"You look handsome as ever," my mom said, joking.

"Ahh, in good spirits," he replied. "And how's everything else feeling?"

"I feel heavy, like my body weighs a ton."

"Anna, I'm sorry to tell you things have gotten worse. Do you want me to talk to you in private?" he asked, glancing around at us.

"Maybe that'd be best."

"No, Mom. Please, let me stay. I need to hear it."

"Sadie, your mom wants some privacy," Jean said. "Let's go."

I was growing very sick of the small waiting room and couldn't stand another minute in there. But it was only about thirty minutes before the nurse told us we could go back in. When we returned, my mom was lying all the way down in the hospital bed.

"They're going to keep an eye on me overnight, but if all goes well, I'll be released tomorrow. I'm very tired, and I need to go back to sleep. You should all go home too. I'll be fine."

"Are you sure?" Al asked.

"Yes. I love you all. We'll talk more tomorrow."

Going back to the house without my mom was strange. We had been coming back to shower, sleep, and change at odd hours. But now that we had a full night without worrying about what would happen when we woke up, it was as if we didn't know how to act.

"I'm not tired," I said. But the truth was I was exhausted. I hadn't slept for more than a couple of hours for the past three nights and had spent so much of my waking hours on high alert that I was running on a sort of euphoria. I had missed twelve total days of school, but I didn't care. I couldn't fathom sitting in a classroom while my mom was floating between life and death. No, I had to be with her. I had to protect her. If I had to repeat sixth grade, so be it. Getting held back couldn't make me any weirder than I already was.

"I'm going to go see if I can get Lily down," Jean said.

"I'm going to rest for a bit," Al said.

I was left in the dark living room and didn't feel like watching more TV. Then, it occurred to me that there was one person who I might want to keep updated about the situation: Gabe. I hadn't spoken to my father since our reunion that summer, and although I thought about him often, I never toyed with the idea of calling him. I pulled out our address book, a thick leather-bound journal that had scratched-out names and addresses on almost every page. Gabe Daniels was under the tab marked with a "D." It struck me then that we didn't have the same last name. Was he even on my birth certificate? How bizarre, I thought. It's like they knew it wasn't going to work out long before it fell apart. I knew how that felt.

I saw the phone number in my mom's handwriting in bright red ink and started dialing. The line on the end rang three times, then there was some shuffling and an exhausted "Hello." It was a woman's voice.

"Hi, this is Sadie," I said awkwardly. I could hear a child screaming in the background. "I'm calling to speak to Gabe."

There was more screaming and more shuffling, then the woman said, "Okay, hang on."

A moment later, Gabe picked up. "Sadie?"

"Dad. It's me."

"Oh my God, Sadie," he said. "Is everything okay?"

"Yes, well..." I struggled to answer such a simple question. Nothing was okay.

"Is your mom okay?"

"She's in the hospital."

"What happened?"

"She had a seizure, and it caused a stroke," I said. "But it's worse than that."

"How so?"

"She has cancer," I said. "Bladder cancer. She tried this risky medication."

"Oh no," he said, stretching out the sound. "Is she going to pull through?"

"For now." My voice was catching on itself. "But in case she doesn't, I thought you should know."

"Thank you for letting me know, Sadie," he said quietly. "It's so good to hear your voice. Do you think I should visit?"

"I don't know. They said she might be released tomorrow. I don't know what will happen after that."

"Well, if you need me, you just call. Doesn't matter what time it is."

"Okay," I said, unsure of what to say next.

"I love you so much," he said. "If you need to talk, I'm here."

"No, I'm good," I said quickly. "I've got Jean here...and Al."

Gabe was silent for a moment, and the screaming in the background finally stopped. "I'm so glad," he said. "Everything is going to be okay."

I was holding back tears at this point. How could he know that? "Thanks, Dad. Goodnight."

"Goodnight, Sadie Bug."

"Hey Dad," I said quickly before he hung up. "Why don't we have the same last name?"

"Oh," he said, laughing gently. "It's kind of funny actually. I loved your grandpa, Louie. He often told me I was like his son. He was honestly the closest thing I had to a father, even though my own father is still alive today. He was always distant and cold, but Louie was not. Louie came to all my football games and bought me and Anna hot dogs after. He treated me like his own. Do you know how proud he was of that house? He talked a lot about the family line, and you could tell it broke his heart, not that he had two daughters, but that his son was no longer with us. Oh lord," he trailed off. "Do you know about your mom's brother? He passed away when he was an infant. Oh, I hope I'm not the first one telling you."

"I know a little bit about him," I said. "It's okay."

"Thank goodness. Well, when your mom found out she was pregnant, Grandpa Louie had a tough time with it. He knew this was the moment the Watkins name would die. But your mom scoffed at that. Neither of us were much for tradition. She said, 'I bet Gabe wouldn't care one bit if our baby was a Watkins, would you, Gabe?' and I said your grandpa was the kindest man I'd ever met, still is, and we weren't married so technically you could have ended up with either of our names. When it got right down to it, it was me who made the decision, and we wrote 'Watkins' on the birth certificate and never looked back. It was so natural for both of us. I've never regretted it. It made your grandpa so happy, and it was my way of thanking him for being there for me. I still miss him every day."

"I'm sorry."

"For what, Sadie?"

"That you lost him. That must have been so hard."

"It was for both your mom and me," he said softly. "But he left me with so many lessons, and now I am a better father because of him, or at least, I want to be."

"You are a great dad," I said. "I'm sure."

"You know, I'd really love to have you visit us," he said. "Whenever you're ready."

"I'll think about it, I promise."

After we hung up, I felt the tree roots twisting around me again. I still was not ready to meet his wife and his son, but it was his story about Grandpa Louie that convinced me it might not be so bad, if I could just let go of the hurt he caused. My dad clearly loved me, but bridging the gap of nearly ten years seemed impossible. Perhaps it wasn't too late to start now, though. I allowed myself to think about the possibility for some time. If I could get out of this house, get away from the history, the pain, maybe I could heal from everything that had happened and was still yet to happen. I fell asleep on the couch and dreamt about it—no nightmares, no Cali looming in the corner. It was just peaceful rest, and when I woke the following morning, I had a small seed of hope that I had thought might be lost. Not hope for my mom's survival, but hope about my life without her.

LATER THAT MORNING, we went back to the hospital. My mom was up and disconnected from the monitors. She had her clothes on, and she had color in her face, but still looked very sick.

"Time to go home," she said.

We buckled her up in her wheelchair and we left the unit, but not before nurse Jasmine stopped us in the hall. "Ms. Watkins," she said. "I don't know if you remember me, but I wanted to thank you before you left."

"Of course, I remember you, Jasmine," my mom said. "You've taken wonderful care of me."

"No..." she said, embarrassed. "That's not what I mean. When I was little my grandpa took me to the library often. The one in Juniper. That's where I grew up... With him."

"Who's your grandpa?" she asked.

"Philip Robinson. Most people call him Pip. He owns the diner off Violet."

"Your grandpa is Pip?" I asked. "No way!"

"Yes, way," she said smiling. "And he basically raised me. My dad wasn't in the picture, and my mom... Well, she struggled a lot. So, I lived with him on and off."

"I do remember seeing a sweet little girl at the diner sometimes," my mom said. "I guess that was you!"

"Yep, that was me. But, Ms. Watkins, on one of the days my grandpa took me to the library, you were there, and I told him I needed to ask you a question. I ran up and asked you if a Black girl could be a librarian."

"You did?" my mom said, wide-eyed. "What did I say?"

"You told me that I could be whatever I wanted to be. You told me I was smart and capable, and I shouldn't let anyone stop me, especially because of the color of my skin."

My mom smiled sweetly, unsure of what to say next.

"Well, I didn't become a librarian. But I did become a nurse. I always remembered the way you treated me. No one had ever said anything so kind to me. I was one of the only Black girls at school, and the teachers and other students knew about my mom and her problems. It felt like they expected me to be just like her. It felt like that was the only way to go in my life, and I didn't have a whole lot of examples otherwise. But you did more than share your kindness, Ms. Watkins. You gave me a stack of books and an even bigger list of books to check out when I had finished those. You gave me Maya Angelou and Toni Morrison. You gave me examples of Black women who were successful, and those books helped me get where I am today. That's partly because of you. You opened that door for me."

My mom sat for a moment, taking it all in. "Jasmine, you had everything you needed to succeed inside of you all along. I was just there to help you find a book. You did the work, and you are successful today because of that work. Truly, you are a tremendously talented nurse. I am happy to have received your care."

"And I yours," she said. "Thank you."

They hugged briefly, and we left the hospital. My mom was beaming with pride, and I suspect it meant a lot to her to know that in her life, albeit a short one, she had made a difference. And of all people, it was Pip's granddaughter. The man who ran the diner, who was best friends with Grandpa Louie, who made funny little jokes, who always remembered our favorite orders. Juniper wasn't the most accepting place. I knew that firsthand. But love persisted in such small, seemingly insignificant ways.

WHEN WE FINALLY got my mom home and comfortable in bed, she told us all to sit down. "Dr. Fratello and I discussed my options yesterday, and I've made some decisions that I want you all to listen to, okay?"

We nodded in unison.

"I can't remember the past three weeks. I barely remember Lily being born, and that scares me. Dr. Fratello told me memory loss is common in my situation, and with the state of my brain, I could begin to have more lapses in memory. So, I want to say this all now before I forget."

I could see that what she was about to say was going to upset her. But she took a moment to collect herself. "My care is going to get increasingly difficult, and so I've decided I'd like to get a home hospice nurse. This nurse will come around several times a day to monitor everything and help me perform my most basic tasks. She'll also make sure I'm comfortable throughout the rest of this process. I'm not going back to the hospital."

"What does that mean?" Jean asked.

"I've signed the papers, and I will not receive further medical treatment. No more tests. No more strange medications that don't do anything or just make it worse. When the end comes, I wish to go peacefully here at home. Do you understand?" she asked, looking at me.

"Mhm," I mumbled, trying to be strong.

"Now I don't know how long it will be. But my guess is it will be soon, especially now that I have discontinued my treatment. So, I'd like it if we spent the time we have left holding each other close."

"We can do that," I said. "Whatever you want, Mom."

"Okay, well, the hospice nurse will be here first thing in the morning. For now, I'm pretty tired, and I'd like to rest. But I'd like it if we all were together this evening when I wake up."

We left her room and shut the door, all of us staring at each other in disbelief, unsure of what to do next.

"So, she wants to die," Aunt Jean said. "I don't believe it."

"Jean, this is her choice," Al said. "One we can't make for her."

"But she has to keep fighting." Jean began to talk quickly. "There must be more treatment options. This can't be the end."

"She just said she is done trying different treatments," he said. "We have to honor that."

"She's just losing hope. She's depressed. But there's still so much to explore! She's giving up too soon. We should get answers, if not for her then for Sadie."

"I don't need answers, Aunt Jean," I chimed in. "I just want her to be comfortable like she said."

Jean exhaled, looking defeated. Without another word, she stormed off, cutting off the conversation.

Al and I were alone together now, and I didn't know what to say. I had so much energy still and needed to move. It was an unusually warm December day, and I thought we should take advantage of it. "Maybe we could play some soccer?" I asked him.

"Are you sure?" he asked. "You don't want to talk?"

"Not really," I said.

The two of us kicked the ball around the yard, which was wet and muddy. I was getting pretty good at this point and began to feel some confidence with the ball.

"You're a natural," Al said after some time.

"Hardly," I said. "I just have a good teacher."

"Well, I enjoy teaching you."

"I called my dad last night."

Al looked sincere. "That was a good idea, Sadie. Did you tell him what was going on?"

"Yeah," I said. "He's a bit much though."

Al laughed. "Why do you say that?"

"Because it was more apologies, more over-showering with love. I feel like I have to take care of him, and I can't."

"I'm sure he doesn't mean to be like that. He just holds a lot of remorse."

"Well, he shouldn't. My mom and I have been fine without him. And he has his own life now."

"Do you ever think about visiting him? I'd be happy to take you down there."

"I guess I'm thinking about it more now, but I have to see this through with Mom."

"Sí. You're a brave kid, Sadie. A very brave kid."

I didn't know how to reply, and instead kicked the ball hard in his direction. He swerved quickly out of the way and looked back at me. "Sorry," I said. "I'm not brave. I'm just doing what I have to do. She needs me, and I'm going to be there."

"Well, is there any way I can be there for you? Jean told me you're having bad dreams."

"Just sometimes."

"I had bad dreams when my mom was dying. The most horrible dreams, actually."

"Like what?"

"A lot of the time she was just lost or trapped, and I couldn't save her. Sometimes I'd even see her in my room."

"Like in real life?"

"No. But it felt like she was watching over me, and it didn't go away for a long time."

"It's kind of the same for me. Except instead of my mom, it's Cali. My friend from the woods."

Al looked confused. "I thought you said she was imaginary?"

Now I was embarrassed. At this point the magic, what was left of my imagination, was gone, and all that was left was guilt. Cali *was* real, and I had left her when she needed me most. I did to her exactly what Gabe did to my mom, what Jean did to my mom and to my grandpa, what Grandma Samantha did to all of us. I was no better than any of them for leaving Cali, the closest thing I had ever had to a best friend.

"What's bothering you?"

"I just wish I could do some things over."

"We all do, Sadie," he said. "It's a part of life."

A COUPLE OF WEEKS PASSED, and Christmas was a few days away. The hospice nurse, Rose, was around routinely, even though my mom spent almost every minute asleep. I barely noticed her presence, and for that I was grateful. Al's work had slowed down for the season, and he was spending more time at home, which I was also grateful for. Though my nightmares hadn't stopped, they had seemed to ease somewhat since our conversation. If anything, my body was just used to waking up in the middle of the night, so I continued to help care for Lily. I looked forward to our early morning snuggles. She was so warm and cooed whenever I whispered to her. The news was repeatedly warning of a big cold front moving through and to expect heavy snowfall. We were hunkering down, and Jean was making sure we had food, flashlights, and all the necessities should the storm bury us. I thought she was being dramatic, but the news was signaling that it was going to be bad.

"Why did you get so many fruit snacks?" I asked her as she was shoving the boxes in the cabinets.

"It was all they had. That and some Velveeta. The stores were swept clean."

"Well, it is almost Christmas."

"That's true too," she said.

Rose came out of my mom's room without saying a word. She looked concerned.

"Hi, Rose," Jean said. "How's she doing?"

"I am worried," Rose said, folding her hands inside her uniform, "about the storm."

"We are too," Jean said. "It's supposed to hit tonight."

"I should get home," she said. "I'll do my best to make it out in the morning."

"Well, listen, Rose, don't trouble yourself too much," Jean said. "We can take her off your hands for a few days. It's Christmas—spend it with your family. I know her medication schedule, and she's asleep most of the time anyway."

Rose nodded and left the room. There was something she wasn't saying. She packed her things up, took a quick soft glance at me, and left the house promptly, touching my shoulder on her way out.

"She's odd," I said.

"Sadie, that's not nice. She's just being respectful of the situation."

"Okay, but she could at least say goodbye."

"Her goal is to be as discreet as possible."

I scoffed, and we continued to keep busy around the kitchen.

THE DAYS GREW COLDER, and the snow began to come down heavily. Reports continued about power outages farther west in Illinois and Indiana. On Christmas Eve, Rose called and said she was unable to make it out of the house. A thick layer of ice coated everything, and although she was doing her best to keep her car unburied by the snow, the doors had frozen shut.

"It's okay, Rose," Jean said. Her voice was going lower, and I couldn't hear the rest of the conversation.

Jean handled much of my mom's care that day and, like Rose, she also seemed to not be saying something. Every time I went to check on my mom, she was asleep. Then, after dark, I tried to check on her one more time. Her eyes were open, and her breathing was labored. It had this rattle-like sound, like she was drowning within herself. But she didn't appear to be struggling.

"Merry Christmas Eve," I whispered to her. "Are you in any pain?"

"No," she said weakly. "I'm on the good stuff."

"Good." I patted her arm. So thin. She had lost a significant amount of weight over the past couple of months and was eating very little. Her vision was spotty at best, and I could tell she was having trouble focusing. "Can you see?"

"It's the funniest thing," she said. "I can see my dad."

My heart sank. This was the moment Mr. Foster had talked about. The visions set in, ready to carry her to the next life. Was this it? I contemplated going to get Aunt Jean and Al but thought it best not to cause a scene. "What's he look like?" I asked her calmly.

"He's wearing his favorite pajama pants, and he's so young. He looks so happy. He's saying, 'Merry Christmas.'"

She was smiling and looked so at peace. It was hard not to cry. I wished I could see him too. "Is Grandma Sam there?"

She took a moment to respond, then said, "Yes, she's here. She looks exactly how I remember her. She's telling me it's safe over there and not to worry."

"That sounds so nice, Mom," I was trying not to choke on my words. "Do you want to go with them now?"

"Not yet," she whispered. "But soon."

"That's okay, Mom. You can go when you're ready."

She looked almost relieved when I said this, and she drifted off to sleep.

THE NEXT MORNING, I woke up without a nightmare and immediately went downstairs to see my mom. I walked right past the presents by the fireplace and found her up in bed. She was propped up and awake when I walked in, which filled me with joy.

"You're here!" I said, hugging her tightly.

"Merry Christmas, Bug," she said, kissing my head. "How's the storm?"

"Oh, it's wicked!" I told her. "The snow is like two feet deep, and it's freezing cold."

"A white Christmas. My favorite."

"No one is awake yet. Do you want some tea?"

"I'd love a cup of tea. And would you wheel me in front of the tree? I want to watch."

I could practically lift her into her chair on my own at this point and only needed a little toe lift from her. There was hardly anything to her.

"Merry Christmas, Say," Jean said, holding Lily in her arms as she entered the living room. "Ready for presents?"

I shrugged. I had barely given any thought to Christmas. I normally had an intense excitement for presents. Though it was never much, it was the one time of year we had some abundance in our lives. My mom always made sure I had a small stack of presents to open. The usual: shoes, socks and underwear, a sweater, and always something fun. One year I got a giant art set that folded out into three compartments, with oil pastels, markers, colored pencils, and watercolors organized in neat trays. Now, I looked at our tree before us in the same living room—the same, but entirely different. There were now more presents than I'd ever seen, and my mom looked dwarfed by them. What a paradox, to see this room flourishing and her in such anguish. This all felt like too much. I just wanted to turn off the lights and let the cold take us.

Then the power went out.

Jean ran around flicking the light switches, "Oh no. Oh no. The news said this would happen."

"It's okay," Al said. "We can start a fire. Here, we've got wood. We'll keep it warm."

After a few minutes of fiddling with the starter, Al got the fire roaring. The immediate rush of heat was nice. "Time for presents," he said enthusiastically.

For the next hour, we exchanged our gifts. Al gave Jean a small pendant necklace, and Jean gave him a toolbox with a bunch of tiny drawers. Lily got a teddy bear the same size as her, and I got a lot more than I knew what to do with. Al gave me a pretty felted journal and sparkly gel pens. And we gave my mom a soft blanket and placed it on her lap. She brushed her hands over it and smiled. Part of me hoped she was battling the disease, that the cancer would leave, that everything would go back to how it was just a couple of months ago. But then, I thought, that wasn't much better. I tried to erase the ideas running through my mind and focus on the moment, on Lily's laughter, on my mom's serene expression, on all of us being here together. But I hit a wall of despair that I just couldn't climb. After presents, I went up to my room, saying I wanted to try on my new clothes, not caring if anyone believed me or not. I just needed space.

When I closed my bedroom door, I felt a wave of sadness billowing up, like I might burst into tears. It took an internal force to block, something I might once have called bravery or strength, but now realized wasn't any of those things. It was anger. I was furious that I had to watch my mom wither away. She had lost everything so quickly. In the spring, we were driving home from another routine appointment, and now, not even a year later, she was completely immobilized. My mind continued to travel backward. Two years ago, we were having tea in our garden on our little baby-blue wrought-iron patio set. Four years ago, she was chasing me around at the library. The further back I went, the healthier my mom became. If I could have just stayed there, everything would have been fine. The thought that time would keep moving me forward made me want to vomit. I curled up in bed and must have fallen asleep, because a couple of hours later, Aunt Jean knocked on my door.

"Sadie," she said. "Do you want to play with Lily? I need to clean up the mess downstairs. Besides, it's freezing up here."

"Is she awake?"

"Lily? Yes, and she's babbling my ear off."

"No, Mom?"

"Oh, no, sweetie. We put her back in bed when you went upstairs. She didn't protest."

I couldn't handle the look Aunt Jean was giving me. "I'll play with Lily."

Downstairs, Lily was giggling, her gummy smile huge and contagious. I couldn't help but make her laugh, the little chirps giving me the smallest amount of joy to combat the terrible feelings I had inside. Outside, the snow was coming down fiercely, and one of the framed pictures of the three of us fell off the wall. Aunt Jean looked at me. We both knew the wives' tale: *A picture falling foretold a death*. Like the universe needed to send us more reminders. She picked up the shards of glass and tossed them in the trash.

That evening, I went into my mom's room and roused her. She fluttered her eyes open. "Are you excited for Christmas?" she asked, seeming to have forgotten that it happened earlier that day.

"It is Christmas, Mom."

"Oh," she said, seeming undisturbed. "That's so nice."

She tried to lift her head but couldn't. I pulled her up and set pillows behind her, so she was sitting up slightly. She seemed to be regaining some lucidity.

"I have something to tell you, Bug," she said. "It's now or never."

"What?" I asked, my eyes growing wide.

"I've been keeping it a secret. I wanted to be sure."

She drifted off a bit, struggling to maintain control.

"Do you remember when we found that skull in the woods?" she asked. "What was that thing?"

I was taken aback. I looked at her, perplexed. In all my time spent in the woods with her, I didn't recall finding anything. Maybe she meant when I found the doe skull that day with Cali and brought it home to her. She was disgusted by it, but it was still in my room. I realized that keeping the skull in the house against her wishes was the very first thing I had kept from her. I could so easily trace the memories of my mistakes now.

"Do you still have it?" she asked.

"I've kept it under my bed," I said, trying to keep her on this train of thought. "Sorry for keeping it from you."

Her eyes looked like they were watching a movie. "I always wanted to go to California," she said. "To see the palm trees and the city lights."

Now she must have been talking nonsense. I had never heard her talk about California before. Not once. She must have been recalling what I told her about Cali this summer. But I couldn't trace back to that memory.

"No, Mom, you never wanted to go there."

She seemed to snap into focus. "Sadie," she said, her eyes now on mine. "Don't you remember me?"

She was freaking me out at this point. So small in her bed. Hair a mess. Eyes huge. In this state, she looked like a child.

A child I knew.

"Cali?" I said, barely above a whisper.

"It was me," my mom answered. Her voice sounded distant, strange, like a song reverberating from a far-off record player. "It was me and you playing in the woods that summer."

"I don't understand," I said. I couldn't comprehend what she was telling me, if she was actually telling me anything at all.

"We screamed at the birds."

I thought back to the page of her writing that I read before the ambulance came. "Mom, you're not making any sense." I let go of her hand, which I realized I had been holding much too tight, and sat back in the chair beside her bed, unsure of what to say.

"We found a waterfall." Her expression was far off.

Was she recalling my story? Did I tell her I thought Cali was imaginary? I couldn't remember.

She snapped back into it. "It's in there," she said, pointing a finger at the drawer of her nightstand.

I opened the drawer and dug around. There were pill bottles dated from years past, a couple of coins, nothing out of the ordinary. Then I reached my hand deep into the back of the drawer, and it landed on something soft and white. The lucky rabbit's foot. Small, dingy, and looking almost the same as the day Cali first gave it to me, but with a little more age. I rubbed the soft familiar fur between my fingers. I hadn't seen it in months, since I gave it back to Cali.

"Cali," I said, looking up at my mom. "Mom?"

My mom smiled, still dazed. "I told you. It was me."

"I don't understand," I said, holding the rabbit's foot. "Your name is not Cali. You're my mom. You're Anna Watkins."

"You're the spitting image of my recollection," she said. "All this time passed. I wondered if I'd never see you again. I wondered if I was right about it all. I couldn't be sure, of course. But I remember watching you run toward my house, every time we played hide-n-seek. You always ran toward my house. I think, deep down, I knew that something wasn't right. But I was so young. I was just a little girl. I couldn't make sense of it."

I took a moment to collect my thoughts, hardly able to piece together what she was saying.

"It felt like everything stopped when my mom died, and it stopped for a long time, all the way up until you were born. I remember holding you in my arms. This time you were *my* Sadie, my daughter, my life force."

I held my mom's hand and let her go on.

"You were the best friend I ever had. I know now why you

never came back to the woods after that summer. But you've come back for me now. You've come to take me away."

I decided I didn't need to understand. I let myself feel everything at that moment and began crying. Her dark eyes, just the same as mine, the same as my best friend's, welled with tears.

"You're always with me when I need you most," she said, her fingers shifting slightly in my hand. "I'm ready to go now. Will you take me back? To the forest?"

"Mom, I'm scared."

She was silent for a while and drifted off again.

"I know nothing makes sense right now," she whispered with her eyes closed. "I felt the same way when I lost my mom. But, Bug, it's not going to be the same story for you. It's time for a new beginning. You have Jean and Al. You have Lily. You have Gabe if you'll let him in. You have a whole future ahead of you, and I know you will do incredible things. You're magic. You're true magic."

I held her hands, trying not to shake. "I'm not ready to say goodbye," I whispered.

"You loved me enough to say goodbye before," she said. "Time to do it again."

"I love you, Mom."

"I love you too." And she fell asleep.

As I lay next to her, I watched her breathe in and out. In and out. After a while, Aunt Jean came in and laid with us. She held me like my mom held me. Running her fingers through my hair. At some point, I must have dozed off, and when I woke up, I noticed Jean was also asleep. The sun had barely crested over the horizon, and a sliver of gray light cast through the room. I looked at my mom. She was still. Pale as the moon. Wisps of red hair around her. A crescent smile across her face. Even in death, she was beautiful. I held her ice-cold hand and looked about the room, as if expecting to see her, to see Cali in the corner, but it was silent. There were no ghosts, no magic. It was peaceful.

After a little while, Jean woke up. She stared at her sister, taking it all in.

"She's so beautiful," Jean said. "I didn't know it'd be so beautiful."

"She's at peace," I said. "You can tell."

"You certainly can," she said. I watched tears stream down her freckled cheeks. "I love you, Anna. I love you so much."

Outside, the world was cast in ice. The great cathedral of trees across Leaky Creek was strewn in white, and a thick layer of crystal coated every surface of our gleaming castle. The world had frozen over, and time was sealing this moment, this bond, between the three of us. Three women, each containing a universe, each in their own state of transition, each holding an infinite number of possibilities for what could come next.

19

LILY WAS CRYING, but I lay in my bed, unmoving, unnerved. I couldn't get myself up. I didn't want to. It had been six nights since my mom slipped from this world, and I cocooned myself in my room, hollowing out a nest of blankets and pillows. Lily missed me. I'm sure Jean and Al did too. But, despite their best efforts, I couldn't leave. I drifted in and out of the room to grab food, to use the bathroom, to change, to brush my teeth. Automatic motions. Mostly though, I just lay in my bed. I didn't even cry, I couldn't. The lights had come back on at some point, though I never used them. I was content to sit in the dark, in the cold. I thought about my mom, trying to reconcile our last conversation. I ran over her words in my mind. *You're always with me when I need you most.*

I tried to put the pieces together, but the more I dwelled on it, the more I convinced myself that my mom's last conversation with me was just the ramblings and madness of a dying, diseased mind. Yes, that was easier. Some kind of telepathy maybe, the interweaving thoughts of the mother-daughter connection. Anything was easier to believe than the idea that my mother was somehow simultaneously playing with me in the woods as a little girl named Cali and also dying in her bed. No matter how hard I tried to push it out of my mind though, to rationalize all the evidence away, the rabbit's foot, the doe's skull, I always came back to the gut-punch of her telling me she was ready. *You loved me enough to say goodbye before. Time to do it again.* If I hadn't said goodbye to Cali that day, could I have kept my mom alive? No. None of it made sense.

As I lay waiting for Lily's cries to subside, I thought about the doe skull under my bed. I thought about the initials carved into the fallen oak. I thought about my conversation with Aunt Jean, about my grandma's suicide. All of the evidence splayed out in the recesses of my mind. I closed my eyes and tried to conjure up an image of Cali, willing her return. I wanted to prove to myself she wasn't real. If she could just appear in the corner of my room, I'd know it was all in my head. Then a soft knock started at my door. I retreated into my covers.

"Sadie, it's me," I heard Aunt Jean say on the other side. "Someone wants to see you."

I poked my head out to see that she was holding Lily.

"Can we come in?"

I didn't respond. She came over and sat at the foot of my bed, balancing Lily on her lap.

"It's midnight."

"So?" I muttered.

"It's the New Year. Hello, 2005."

Again, I remained silent.

"I know how much you miss her. Trust me. I'm missing her too."

"It's not the same for you."

"No, it's not." We sat silently for a while. Lily made bubble noises; her dark eyes sparkled in the moonlit room. "I hope she's somewhere happy."

"I know she is," I said. "I just wish I was there with her."

"Me too." Jean was stifling her cry. "With all of them. My mom, my dad, my sister. I can't believe she's gone."

"It's my fault," I said. "I let her go."

"I think, maybe, she let herself go," she said. "Just like my mom. If it's anyone's fault, it's mine. For not being here sooner, for not being enough. I've never been enough."

"You're enough, Aunt Jean," I said, reaching for Lily. "You're enough for both of us."

I gave her a moment to collect herself. I could tell she was struggling with the loss of my mom just as much as I was. It wasn't fair that I had been keeping her at arm's length. I decided to let her in.

"Did Mom ever mention a friend in the woods?" I asked her. "A girl just a little older than her? It would have been the same summer that Grandma passed away."

Jean composed herself and seemed to be thinking hard about my question. "That summer was very dark," she said. "I don't remember much of anything after my mom died. Your grandpa was barely holding it together. Things at home started falling apart. The kitchen was empty. The garden overgrown. The mailbox stuffed to the brim. The three-year age gap between Anna and I felt like light years. I couldn't look at her without getting angry at my mom for leaving us. When I finally started to come out of my grief, I slipped right into her role. I started doing the grocery shopping. Cooking. Cleaning. Doing the laundry. I was barely thirteen when I was balancing the checkbook with my dad. And he was not nice to me. I know you loved your Grandpa Louie, but he said hurtful things. He had so many rules. I know now that he was just grieving too. But the way he'd look at Anna and the way he came to see me were two very different things. He treated her with warmth and love and shielded her from the worst of what was happening at home. I didn't resent Anna for that, but it only made us drift further apart. We used to play in the woods together all the time growing up. It was our castle. We'd sit by the creek and catch tadpoles. We'd play hide-n-seek. But a string of events made it impossible for me to ever return to those woods. I'm sorry—" She cut herself off. "What was your question again?"

"Never mind," I said. "I am so sorry, Aunt Jean."

Aunt Jean hugged me tightly. "I miss her so much."

"Me too," I said. "Me too."

ANOTHER WEEK PASSED, and still the house remained dark. Classes had begun and I knew it was time for me to return to school, but I couldn't fathom how I'd be able to sit in a classroom. I went downstairs and flicked on a light. Everything seemed to be stuck in time. The Christmas tree was still there, tinsel shining in all its glory. The journal and gel pens Al gave me lay under the tree. I walked into my mom's room for the first time since she passed, and the bed was made. Her wheelchair was positioned in the corner. The pill bottles had been discarded. And there, resting on the pillow, was the small white rabbit's foot. I picked it up and held it in my hand. Maybe it could bring me back to her, I thought, and slipped it into my pocket. Our lucky talisman.

I heard Al in the kitchen. "Hey," I said, startling him.

"Oh, Sadie," he said. "You scared me."

"Sorry," I said, giving him a hug.

"How are you doing?"

"I'm okay," I said. "But I don't want to go to school."

"I know," he said, brushing my head. "I know."

"Do you think I can skip a couple more weeks?"

"I think you need to try to go back. You need to see things happening outside of this house."

"But what will the other kids say?"

"They'll probably be sad for you," he said. "They care about you."

"Yeah, right."

"Hey, do you ever go out to the woods in the winter?"

"Never."

"Maybe there's something waiting for you out there."

I thought about it for a moment, then decided to humor him. I bundled myself up and put on my snow boots, a bit small since the last time I had to wear them. The creek was frozen over, and the forest was still crystalline. The air smelled clean, and it was mostly silent among the giants.

My boots left deep prints in the snow, and my breath formed clouds around me. I struggled to make out my usual path toward the clearing, but when I found it, it was bare and undisturbed. Everything was asleep, hibernating, and for a moment I thought about how nice it would be if I too could crawl back into bed.

A big gust of wind rolled through, and a dusting of snow twinkled down. "What are you trying to tell me?" I whispered to the woods.

I sat for a moment, waiting for a response, anything, to show me that this was not all there was. Surely, life couldn't be this cold. After some time, I began to wander back to the house, dismayed and heartbroken. Never again would I walk these woods with my mom. Never again would I walk them as the person I was before everything changed. And yet, beneath this blanket of snow was the same landscape that had harbored my memories, my love for the natural world. Acorns had fallen from their mother oaks and were coated in the earth. They needed this cold, this period of quiet. Without it, they wouldn't be able to recognize the sun's return. They would feel the ground heating up and they would know it was time to break from their shells, it was time to grow.

WHITE OAK ACORN

Quercus alba

20

I GOT UP THE NEXT MORNING and put on my warmest clothes. I brushed my hair. But I did not look in the mirror. Whatever I was going to see in myself wasn't going to be very convincing. I was not ready to return to school.

Al drove me, and I saw a giant banner hanging on the front doors of the building that read *Happy New Year* with a giant *2005* scrolled across the bottom. The students were forming their groups, filing in. I looked at Al as if to say, *Do I have to?*

"Go on," he said. "Call me if you need to."

I made my way into the building and immediately heard the chatter of the students around me. Their eyes were on me as I walked toward Mr. Foster's classroom. All of them must have found out somehow. When I got in, I promptly took my seat, not saying a word to Mr. Foster or anyone else.

"Good morning, class," he said, making eye contact with me. The other kids turned and looked at me too. Emmi was the last to turn around. "Let's get into today's lesson."

The morning went by painstakingly. Mr. Foster was giving a lesson on gravity, and I did my best to sink into it, learning about the mystical forces that kept us tied to this planet. It was hard to keep my mind from wandering. When the lunch bell finally rang, Emmi swooped me up before I could even leave the classroom.

"Everyone is really sorry about your mom," she said.

"Yeah," I said, unsure of what to say.

"We made you this." She handed me a big card with a panda on it. "I made sure as many kids signed it as I could."

I opened it up to see scrawled messages. *I'm sorry for your loss. Stay strong. My family is praying for you.* The sentiments made me cringe. These kids didn't care about me, they never did. They only wanted to piggyback off my despair. Just then, Jacob Williams came up to us and said, "Hey Sadie, I'm really sorry about what happened."

"Thanks," I said, folding the card up and slipping it into my textbook. Jacob stood there awkwardly, smiling at Emmi, and then gave me a slanted frown and walked away. The last thing I wanted to do was enter the cafeteria and have all the kids staring at me. "I'm not feeling well," I said to Emmi.

"Do you want me to take you to the nurse?"

I nodded, accepting this small act of kindness from her, and together we dodged the double doors to the cafeteria and booked it straight to the main office. I called Al and told him to come get me.

"Are you sure?" he said. "You don't want to try to stick it out?"

"No, I really don't."

Within fifteen minutes, Al was in front of the school in the truck. I was thankful he didn't make me wait and suffer the rush of students leaving lunch. I hopped in the truck and didn't say a word. Al took us on a drive, not going anywhere in particular. When we reached an intersection, we noticed a funeral procession coming up behind us.

"Stop the truck," I said. "Mom said you always pull over for these things."

Al did as I said and pulled over; all the other cars on the road followed suit. We waited for the procession to pass. The hearse went by first, followed by a stretch limo. Two boys were staring out the window. We locked eyes, and I thought of Helen, the patient in the hospital, the one who lost everything. Those could be her boys, I thought. That could be her. Helen's words rang in my head, *What can you do?*

While we waited for the cars to pass, Al was respectfully silent. When we finally got back on the road, he asked me what happened at school.

I handed him the panda card from Emmi and my other classmates.

He flipped it open and squinted to read the tiny, inscribed wishes. "Who's Lacey?"

I rolled my eyes.

"Well, she wants you to sit with her at lunch. Anytime."

"I'm sure she does." I was sarcastic. "I wish I never had to go back to that school."

"*Niña*, you're going to have to try to finish out the year. School is important."

When we got back to the house, Jean was burping Lily, who was fussing about it. The living room was full of tension, the kind that brought tears or worse. I realized this house was almost more miserable than the school. Apparently, I didn't want to be anywhere. I dropped my backpack by the door and walked up the stairs.

I laid in bed the rest of the day, watching the snow fall onto the road outside my window. Everything was lifeless. Around three o'clock the school buses started rolling by. I thought about the kids on those buses going home, eating dinner, fighting with their siblings, watching TV. How normal it all sounded. I turned back into my covers and tried to force myself to sleep. Then, there was a knock at the door downstairs. I heard Jean answer it but couldn't get a read on who it was. A gray Honda was parked in the driveway, one I didn't recognize. Then Jean came upstairs and cracked open my door.

"Sadie, it's Emmi," she said. "She brought you your homework. I think she wants to see you."

I looked at Jean, then at my room. It was a mess. It was an embarrassing pit of sadness. I couldn't let Emmi see it. But it was too late. Emmi had come up the stairs and was peeking out from behind Aunt Jean. She came right in and hugged me.

"I'm so sorry you had to leave today," she said.

I melted in her embrace and began to cry, really cry, for the first time in weeks. Jean closed the door, and the two of us sat down on my bed. "I'm sorry my room is a mess."

"You should see mine," she laughed. "I'm sorry about our sleepover. My mom, she..."

"You don't have to explain."

"She's an addict," Emmi said. "She uses. She tries hard to stay clean, but then she goes on these benders and... Well, you saw what happened. She cleaned up again over break, and this time she says it's for good. But she always says that. I need you to know she always says that. It doesn't mean anything."

"I'm sorry, Emmi," I said, not fully understanding what she meant.

"As awful as she can be though, she's still my mom. I still love her. Then I look at you and see what you've gone through, and I can't imagine it. I'm sorry I wasn't there for you. I'm an awful friend, really, I'm not even a friend at all."

"I shouldn't have left you that night," I said. "You needed me too."

We looked at each other then, all our secrets out, deciding how to move forward.

"Thank you for coming over, Emmi," I said, wiping the tears from my eyes. "It means so much to me."

"We didn't have homework today. Mr. Foster let us off easy. I just wanted to see you."

We laughed together. Then she took note of something across the room. It was the journal and pens from Al. He must have moved them up here. It was his and Jean's gentle way of putting the house back together. Everything just kept moving forward. She walked over and ran her hand across the cover. "This is beautiful."

"Thanks, my... Al got it for me."

"Is that your aunt's boyfriend?"

"More like her husband. They're getting married soon."

"That sounds exciting."

"I guess, I haven't thought about it."

"There's a lot to look forward to, you know."

I perked up, running my fingers through my hair, trying to look halfway decent. "I just don't know what to do with myself now that she's gone."

"What do you think she'd want you to do?"

I thought about it for a moment. "I think she'd want me to live my life. To go to school. To make friends. To have a normal family."

"No one's family is normal. Especially mine."

I thought about Emmi for a moment. Her mom's tendency to be absent. To come home at odd hours in the night only to sleep off two or three days before drifting back out. I wondered if maybe she really did understand.

"I think the worst part is that I just don't feel like a kid anymore," I said. "I feel like a different person. I don't want to do anything I wanted to do a year ago. All the kids at school seem so much...younger."

"I feel that way too, but I think everyone is kind of where we're at right now. We're all growing up. We're all figuring out who we are."

I sighed and sat there thinking about it for a moment. "I think I will go to school tomorrow."

Emmi's eyes lit up. "Really?"

I nodded. "I think I'm ready."

"I'm so glad. I don't know what to do when you're not there."

Emmi's mom was still waiting outside. I could see Aunt Jean freezing out there talking to her through the car window. We said goodbye, and that was it. She was off, back out into Juniper. To her apartment, to her brother, to her life where things were just as messed up as things were for me here. I opened my journal, and I wrote the date at the top.

January 10, 2005

I don't remember the last time I felt time. It's been moving in and out of my reach for months. If I slip the clock back, I can go to a time when my mom was healthy. I can see her tending to our garden, stocking books on the shelves at the library, chasing after me through the forest. She's tall and bright. And when she hugs me, I feel safe, like nothing could hurt me if she was there next to me. I miss her so much. It's a pain like I've never felt. I've lost what makes me whole. How is that supposed to change?

If I zoom forward, I can see far far far. I can see myself in all different places, just like Aunt Jean. I can see myself by the ocean, the waves crashing at my feet. I can see myself in the mountains, so high up I can reach out and touch the clouds. I can see myself grown. But how am I supposed to get there?

All I want is to feel time again. I want it to move without it feeling like I'm hurtling through space. I want it to move without it feeling like I'm being dragged by my hair one inch at a time. I want it to be safe to feel time. Beating like a heart. A heart that is without its mother. A heart that isn't all the way whole, but that can love all the same.

It felt good to see my thoughts on paper. Once the words stuck to it, they couldn't get back in my brain. I began to write every day, sometimes multiple times a day, just to get all the thoughts out of my head. I wrote about my mom, about my last conversation with her. I wrote about Aunt Jean, Al, and Lily. I wrote about my father and one day going to Bexley. I wrote about Cali and the toads. I wrote everything down, and every time I closed the journal, I felt a little less heavy. The journal entries soon turned into stories, each bringing me closer to my mom and her beautiful capacity for storytelling. Then, after an oral presentation in class about what we'd do if we had a million dollars, I realized I had a knack for it too, and so did the other kids at school. They started giving me ideas, and I'd come up with a story for them on the spot, enthralling them with my words. Soon my stories were bringing me closer to them, and I slowly came out of the shell I had worked so hard to encapsulate myself in.

By the time spring rolled around again, Emmi and I were inseparable. There were many days her mom would pick us up and take us to her new apartment. It was much bigger and had an island in the kitchen. They even got a dog. Emmi's mom would cook incredible meals with melted butter, cheese, and spices. We'd watch TV and play board games until her mom said it was time to drive me back home. On other days Emmi would come home on the bus with me, and Al would make us quesadillas. We'd play with Lily, and we'd talk for hours. Jean would sometimes come into my room and paint our nails or teach us how to put on makeup. Emmi loved Aunt Jean and always talked to her about her travels.

The house continued to come back together. It took us a long time to take the tree down. Something about it being up comforted us. I told Aunt Jean if we took it down, we might forget about those last precious moments opening presents by the fire. We agreed we'd take it down one piece at a time. So, every day, we wrapped one more ornament, removed some tinsel. When the star finally came off the top, we knew that was it. Al returned to work, and Jean stayed home to manage the house. Like the tree, the piles of hospital bills dwindled. I'd sometimes hear Jean and Al talking in hushed tones about how much they still owed on my mom's treatment. It seemed wrong that there was anything outstanding given that the doctors couldn't save her.

My mom's ashes remained on the mantel. We never did have a funeral, mostly because of the money. My mom wouldn't have wanted a big fuss anyway. Lily began to crawl and started to put everything in her mouth. She babbled nonsense all day long, and there were times when I felt like I could understand her. I never missed another day of school that spring. Mr. Foster didn't need to have any more conversations with me about my grades, and I managed to pass all my tests. By all measures, I was doing well. I didn't have any more nightmares, and when I did feel sad, I wrote in my journal. I also picked up reading again, and it gave me solace to go to the library whenever I needed more books. Still, even as the leaves began to produce buds and the grass grew greener, I couldn't bring myself to go into the forest. I didn't know if I'd ever be able to again. Like Jean, the magic might have been lost on me after losing my mom. Or maybe it was something else. But I wasn't about to find out.

IT WAS A PERFECT MAY DAY the morning of Al and Jean's wedding. We set up an arbor in the backyard and picked a bushel of pink tulips for Jean's bouquet. We invited some Juniper faces, like Pip, who brought his granddaughter Jasmine, the nurse who cared for my mom during her last hospital visit. Emmi and her family were there too. And my dad and his family. Meeting Julia and my little brother Henry wasn't quite as difficult as I had anticipated. Julia was a kind woman—her eyes told me as much—and Henry looked oddly like me, even though he was only two. The morning went beautifully, with simple vows and soft cheers all around. When the ceremony was over, we had cake and talked about how Jean and Al met. After everyone went inside, I remained out by the arbor, taking it all in. Then, my dad approached me with a cup of tea.

"Do you like tea?" he asked, handing me the warm cup.

I was reluctant to drink it, but I didn't want to appear rude. I pulled the cup to my lips and drew in a sip. It was bitter but comforting. There was no longer that dirt taste. In fact, it reminded me of my mom.

"I've been wanting to give you this," he said, holding a large folder in his hands. "But I wasn't sure when the right time would be."

I looked at him curiously. "What is it?"

"Well, Sadie Bug..." He paused hesitantly. It felt good to hear my nickname again, the one that only he and my mom had used. "It's a book."

"A book?" I was puzzled.

"Your mom wrote it," he said. "She mailed it to me after Thanksgiving. There was a note attached that said to give it to you after she was gone."

I suddenly felt hot and set down the cup. "Why would she give it to *you*?"

"For safekeeping, I suppose." He looked embarrassed. "And Sadie, I don't know if she wanted me to, but I did read it."

I didn't know if I should be hurt. If she sent it to him, she obviously didn't mind if he read it. She may have even wanted him to read it.

"What's it about?"

"It's about two girls, Cali and Sadie, and their adventures in the woods. The detail is magnificent. The characters she depicts are so vivid. I mean, I know it's based on you. But what she captured here feels so real. I think we should try to get it published in her honor. After all, she did want to be a writer. I think that may be why she gave it to me. She knows I have connections in Columbus. But first, I think you should read it. "Here," he said, handing the folder to me. "It really is for you, Sadie."

Inside was a complete manuscript. Not too dense, but thick enough that I knew this was it. This was the project that got my mom out of bed in those final days. This was what she had worked on during those long hours in the study. Her life's work.

"I knew she was working on something, but she never told me what it was," I said. "I've scoured the study so many times since she passed and never found anything."

"Sometimes we keep things secret until just the right time. Sometimes we're just not ready." He patted my head. "I'm going to head out now, Sadie Bug. I'll come back and visit you soon. Call me, okay?"

I hugged him and said goodbye. After he walked away, I sat with the manuscript in my hands, feeling the weight of it. I wanted to devour it in that instant, but I also knew I needed privacy. The house was still buzzing inside with the excitement of the wedding. That left only one option. I held the manuscript close to my body and headed for the bridge over Leaky Creek. The mother oaks swished in the spring breeze, greeting me as I entered their domain. As I made my way to the clearing, I felt as though I was stepping back in time. Spring beauties, violets, and bluebells speckled my path. Birds chirped, and before I knew it, I was completely embraced by the forest.

When I reached my spot by the creek, I pulled the manuscript out of the folder and rested it on my lap. I took a moment to collect myself, not wanting to spill tears all over the pages. I noticed how every square inch of the woods was bursting with new life. I heard a snap behind me, and just as I turned, a figure swished through the trees. I swore I caught a glimpse of red hair, and the hairs on my neck stood straight up.

"Mom?" I whispered.

After a moment, I turned back and looked at the fallen tree over the creek. Our initials were still there, notched into the side, worn and barely visible. *C+S.*

EPILOGUE

I WAS DRIVING UP THE INTERSTATE, counting the mile markers until I was home. Like most kids from the Midwest, I had to leave. There's this sense of feeling trapped when you grow up here, and if you're not careful you'll lose sight of the cage. But the older I get, the more I realize the cage isn't Ohio, it's something else, something even less tangible than these imaginary borders. Something deep within, like an instinct.

I pulled into the old Watkins house. It's different now—updated, modern, loved. Al and Jean have done wonders over the years to keep the place from collapsing. Lily, who's now eight years old, burst through the front door and rushed into my embrace. She told me in her high-pitched voice, just a little too loudly, about the recent flooding; she's worried the creek is going to overflow and engulf the house. Al and Jean waved at me from the porch, waiting for their hugs. I held them both tightly, telling them how much I missed them, but not quite ready to go back inside. Al said he'd get my things from the car and Jean told me to follow Lily out back.

"She's been dying to go to the castle with you," she said, giving me a knowing wink.

I took Lily's little hand as we walked toward the bridge. "You know, Lily, the bridge is going to hold," I said. "It always has, ever since Grandpa Louie stuck it there."

"Are you sure?" she asked, looking up at me.

"Positive."

We walked down the pine-laden path with its mosses and ferns. I've walked this trail a thousand times. And a thousand times more I've contemplated the events of that year, the year I lost my mom. It's difficult to come here, even though I'd moved hundreds of miles away, even though it had been eight years since we lost her. Even though I'd had a year to find myself somewhere else.

After graduation, Aunt Jean and Al drove me out to San Diego where I studied biology. I was doing well in school, but just recently, as my freshman year in college was ending, I got word that my father wasn't doing well and decided to stay with him in Bexley for the summer before I entered my sophomore year.

Gabe and I ended up reconnecting after my mom's death. We bonded over my mother's story, which I've held onto all this time. I never could tell him what it was really about; that the relationship between the two girls in the forest was real. Even now, at twenty years old, I still have trouble believing it myself. But maybe that's the point. Maybe not everything has to be explained for it to be believed. Nonetheless, our relationship never quite reached a point where we could revisit old wounds.

Throughout my high school years, we stayed in touch, and I did eventually visit him and Henry. But now I've learned he is suffering from an acute form of Hodgkin's lymphoma. Why both of my parents, my grandfather, Helen, and so many others who called Juniper home had succumbed to cancer and disease was still beyond my reach. I wondered if there was some kind of environmental connection. Was our land poisoned? Was the water safe? Was the air toxic? Or were these all just one-off occurrences? A matter of coincidence. That's why I chose biology. I wanted to know more.

Jean and Al were set to stay in the house forever, despite its constant desire to fall to ruin. Al's business remained steady, and Jean became a yoga instructor, which suited her perfectly. She was currently on a raw diet and trying to convince all of us that whole foods were the key to longevity. Some things have changed significantly. I guess that's why they say you can never go home. Pip's went out of business. He passed away in 2008, and Jasmine felt that without Pip, there could be no diner. Juniper had grown from a measly cornfield into a sprawling town of nearly thirty thousand folks. The crops were replaced with cookie-cutter neighborhoods, the once quaint and quiet place I called home encroached on by developers. With more people came more traffic. More street lights. More everything. Still, the forest remained, and I hoped we could preserve it for as long as possible.

Lily let go of my hand and began collecting flowers. Seeing her in that moment, curious and full of wonder, I felt myself transform. All the heartache and trauma of that dark time in my life washed away. My imagination flipped back on, and just for a moment I could be that brave child again. The one who screamed at the sky. The one who created whole worlds.

"I miss you, Sadie," Lily said. Her richly dark hair breezed across her eyes as she stared up at me. "I'm happy you're home."

"Lily, this will always be my home," I said, looking down at her. "Our home."

Lily's expression shifted, so swiftly, like any young child's would. She let reality pass over her, and I caught a glimmer in her eye that told me maybe she too lived with the pain from the history we all shared. But I sincerely hoped she didn't. I hoped she was too young to understand. I hoped her imagination thrived for just a little while longer. I hoped she could wait to grow up, to take her time. Then her eyes lit up and she said, "What's California like?"

I smiled and brushed the hair out of her deep eyes. "The trees look like they have feathers on them."

"Palm trees!" she said excitedly.

"Yes, that's right," I said. "And I have this special place I like to go where I can look out over the city and see a million twinkling lights."

"Can I visit you?"

"That's up to your mom and dad. But hopefully one day you can! We'll go to the beach and the Golden Gate Bridge!"

"I can't wait," she said. I watched her bare feet as she ran up the trail. So small and so free. She had her own special place in the clearing now. Sure, it was the same place that was once mine. The same place that was once my mom's and Aunt Jean's. Perhaps it was even the same place that belonged to my grandmother before them. For generations, women had been coming to this spot by the creek to find peace, and sometimes, the forest gave it.

ACKNOWLEDGMENTS

ALTHOUGH THIS STORY is largely a work of fiction, I could not have written it if it were not for the many intimate and magical moments spent with the characters of my own life.

To my first and best friend, my mother, Tess. You have been the guiding force of my life, reminding me who I am whenever I feel lost. You have protected my personhood and embraced all of my ideas with the kind of love and respect that only a mother could. You've shown me what it means to be a mother, and I hope that one day I will be as integral to my children as you are to me.

To my sister, Lexie, for showing me what strength looks like. You are the brightest light in my life, and when I'm with you, I never think about the what-ifs or the scary things. You show me that even when things are hard, there is so much to be grateful for.

To Kaitlin, with whom I share the memories of my later childhood. We lived out the last days of our imagination together, and sometimes, I think, you and I could still see all of those impossible things we saw if we just put our heads together. You inspired the most beautiful moments between Cali and Sadie in this story.

To Mat, for sitting with me on the porch all those summer nights when I first started dreaming up this book. And for listening to me read those first few chapters, and helping me make sense of how to tell the story that was in my heart.

To my girls, Diana, Jordan, Kassity, Kelly, Olivia, and Bailey, I hope you know just how much I value our friendship and what it has meant to me to walk alongside such a powerful group of women in this life.

To my father, Gary, for always giving me a safe place to grow and bloom into the writer I am today.

To my grandmother, Donna, for raising me among the trees and the birds. And my grandmother, Sue, for showing me how to embody my art in everything that I do.

And of course, a massive thank you to my team at Boyle & Dalton. Emily Hitchcock, Clair Fink, and Heather Shaw, you have all been an absolute necessity in this very long journey to seeing my first book published. You've given me the confidence I need to bring my writing to its final form.

Lastly, a final thank you to you, reader. Publishing is a terrifying prospect because once the book is in your hands, it's no longer mine. For so long this has been just a story between myself and I. Now I can only hope that it has brought you just as much magic as it has to me.

ABOUT THE AUTHOR

CASSANDRA J. KELLY holds degrees in journalism and environmental science from Ohio University. She continues to call Ohio home and loves spending time in nature with her Australian Shepherds, Bonnie and Eva. *The Clearing* is her debut novel. Learn more about her and her most recent work at cassandrajkelly.com.